TIM
TIDE

TIME'S TIDE

ADRIAN HARVEY

Urbane
PUBLICATIONS

urbanepublications.com

First published in Great Britain in 2019
by Urbane Publications Ltd
Suite 3, Brown Europe House, 33/34 Gleaming Wood Drive,
Chatham, Kent ME5 8RZ
Copyright © Adrian Harvey, 2019

A CIP catalogue record for this book is available
from the British Library.
ISBN 978-1-912666-23-2
MOBI 978-1-912666-24-9

Design and Typeset by Michelle Morgan
Cover by The Invisible Man

Printed and bound by 4edge Limited, UK

URBANE
urbanepublications.com

'Space plays a role in all our behaviour. We live in it, move through it, explore it, defend it. We find it easy enough to point to bits of it: the room, the mantle of the heavens, the gap between two fingers, the place left behind when the piano finally gets moved.'

The Hippocampus as a Cognitive Map,
O'Keefe and Nadel, 1978

For Bryan Robert Harvey

1958

There was only the slap, slap, slap of the sea, cold and slow, the stutter of water on board, the sound of muscle straining against the weight of the moon. There was no wind, not even a murmur, nothing to ruffle the surface. The oar strokes were as a cat's paw on a still pool. Even here, on the deep water of the fjord's mouth, the surface moved carefully, holding its breath, slick as an old window pane. Caught unawares: the sea had not been expecting them.

On other days, the sea would crash into the hull, tower over the gunwales, threaten to suck the boat below; it would howl and rage, but today even the man's breathing, pulling in time with each twist of the oar lock, was muffled only by the low sky. Einar had not spoken for an hour, intent upon his labour, upon his resolution, his mouth lost beneath his whiskers. The woman too had buried her voice. Even Glæta, standing behind the boy in the belly of the boat, had settled into stillness, staring off to where the green trim of the shore edged the grey flatness of the sea.

The boy trailed his fingers in the water, an unobtrusive disruption to the calm, a little rebellion against his abduction. His father had announced his intention the night before, with the fish still steaming in the dish. They were to cross to Hesteyri in the morning, for the sake of Glæta. She had given no milk at all since the day they had left, six years before, and Einar had come at last to the conclusion that the cow missed the grass of home, the air and light that brushed it into lushness. So they would return. For the sake of Glæta.

The boy had lain awake all through the milky night trying to recall Hesteyri, before the people had abandoned it to the wind and the snow. He had been just eight years old then, and the memories of his first home swirled through his drowsing, a blur of green and grey and violent white; warm summer days and bitter winter nights; friends; his brother. His brother had been dead by the time the village had raised their hands to consent to the leaving. Every hand but that of his father. That was what his mother had said, half in pride, half in sadness. The thought of his mother's sadness more than any other denied the boy his rest.

The sky's grey had lightened by shades, drowning any hope of sleep, and he had risen at three thirty, no longer able to contain his restlessness. He had left the sleeping house and walked up above the village, beyond the Hólskirkja, and up the valley, skirting the steep flank of the mountain Ernir. Where the stream kinked around a vast rock, he had rested, watching the char flash in the water below. He had pulled his cap down over his ears and smoked one of his forbidden cigarettes, listened to the water chuckling over the smooth stones, and thought about Hesteyri, unsure where irritation ended and fear began.

Only another hundred metres and they would be there. *Tófa* cut a line through the slow sea, surging on towards the abandoned shore. The boy turned, to look back along the boat, past Glæta and his father's broad back, to where his mother sat in the stern, her hand resting on the tiller, easy on the languid sea. A glimpse of her greying hair fell from under a red head scarf. Her eyes darted and glinted, searching beyond the boat. Her feet were already among the supple grasses and anarchic flowers of the meadows above Hesteyri. The ghost of Hesteyri.

'Almost there now, Eiríkur. How far, would you say?'

His father's voice cracked the slow rhythm of the day; Glæta stirred, her hooves shifting uneasily on the uncertain boards.

'Fifty, maybe sixty metres. I can see the bed.'

Eiríkur did not wonder long how his father had known the nearness of the shore without a glance over his shoulder. Maybe it was an intuition, or simply the changing sound of the oars breaking shallower water. It was the same each day when they returned from the sea, the catch stowed where Glæta stood now. When he was at the oars, Eiríkur had to twist and squirm to see what lay behind him and yet his father had no need, simply allowed the boat and the waves to guide him to where his will led. It was a skill that, in time, would pass to him, he was sure. How could it be otherwise?

Einar slowed his stroke, allowed the drag of the shore to pull the boat towards the lethargic surf. The green rocks below grew paler, clearer, as the shelf of the sea bed climbed upwards to meet them. On the shore, Eiríkur could see the shabby village houses that remained, those that had not been dismantled and carried across to Bolungarvík, to Hnífsdalur, to Súðavík, to all the places along the coast to which the people of Hesteyri had scattered. The church still stood under its red roof, the cross still proud over the gable end of the bell tower, but the white walls were tinged with green and grey. The boy felt the sounds of the past rush over him and into him.

Then there was solid sound, a clattering and scuffing, the water gurgling about the violent rocking of the boat, and Glæta's strangled lowing; then the crash of cow into water, the spray and splash of her awkward dive, her bovine cries as she pulled and struggled towards the shore, rising up from the surf and onto the little beach, to the turf beyond. Above the clattering water and animal moans, his mother's laugh was joined by that of his father, and then of Eiríkur himself, before the boy followed the cow into the cold water, trailing the boat's painter behind him.

The fire crackled within its ring of stones, consuming drift wood gathered from the shore. While the coffee brewed and his clothes steamed, Eiríkur chewed on a piece of dried fish. His mother's quiet singing drifted behind him from where she sorted through the tarpaulins and blankets, the pots and pans. A way up the slope, his father stood with the cow as she grazed, tying her halter to a clutch of creeping birch. Eiríkur wondered where his father feared the cow might run.

'Get out of those wet things and wrap this around you.'

His mother held out a grey and blue blanket, which Eiríkur took with gratitude. The day had got no warmer, despite the absence of wind. As he pulled off his jumper and undershirt, Jóna reached to the fire and placed her hand on the coffee pot for an instant.

'Einar! There's coffee if you're finished with that cow.'

She reached across for an enamel cup and poured thick blackness into it before offering it to Eiríkur. By the time her husband had reached the encampment, she had set out a cup for him too and, as he drank, she poured the remainder into her own mug.

'What do you think? Helgi Gunnarsson's place?'

Einar pointed to a blue-board house, the windows and door obscured by heavy storm shutters. It stood just above the church, near to where the track led off up beside the stream. They had transported their own house across to Bolungarvík in the late summer of 1952, when Einar had accepted that they would leave Hesteyri for good; others, like his friend Helgi, had left their house as well as their home. While the weather in July was benign even on this forsaken peninsula, the nights would still be cold and the foxes would make short work of any unguarded food: they would need to impose themselves on another's unwitting hospitality.

Helgi Gunnarsson seemed as good a host as any other. He had moved south with his wife and son, to the city, tired of fishing and the vicious winds of the West Fjords. If he ever knew that Einar had used his house, he would most likely be untroubled by the imposition; he might even be grateful for any care and attention that his property might receive.

Einar had sat on the steps of Helgi Gunnarsson's house after the vote that had sealed Hesteyri's fate. Helgi had talked excitedly through the night about his plans for a life with electricity and plumbing, while Einar had quietly bargained with the ghost of his eldest son for forgiveness for his abandonment. As the bottle of Brennivín had been drained, both men had found their own accommodation with their departure from the place where each had been born, where each had buried their own fathers next to their grandfathers. Einar looked now at the blue boards of the house and wondered if Ólafur's ghost still lingered in the timbers.

The morning was bright and the slant sun offered up a welcome warmth. Jóna scanned the landscape contentedly. The fjord was even more beautiful than she remembered it and, on a morning like this, it was hard to recall the dark, deep days of winter, the ice and wind and hunger; the months when inaction and confinement, the empty waiting between scant meals, had gnawed through the soul as much as the stomach. Such memories were lost in the fuzzy brightness, however, and it was with unexpected hope that she carried the empty pail down to where Glæta strained at her mooring.

Without looking up from her grazing, the cow allowed Jóna to take an udder in each hand and gently squeeze and pull towards the waiting pail. Fresh, thick milk streamed down rattling against the galvanised steel. Jóna was silent for a long moment, simply staring at the white liquid still swirling in the pail. Tentatively, she tried again and again Glæta gave milk, content to let Jóna stop and start several times until, giggling, she had collected a hand's width in her bucket.

Standing, Jóna ran a hand gently along the cow's flank, then moved to look her directly in the eyes, cooing to her, pushing her forehead into Glæta's muzzle. Then she was away, running pell-mell up the slope to the blue-board house, shouting for her husband, her son, shouting for joy. The soft turf carried her effortlessly upwards, the very earth cosseting her in her gladness, and she reached the steps before either Eiríkur or Einar had pulled on their boots. In girlish elation, she stood before them, swinging the pail coquettishly in front of her skirts.

'My God. Is that, is that milk?'

Einar was dumbstruck, but slowly his own joy rose and he strode down to his wife in the one boot he had managed, the woollen sock of his left foot sucking up the dew. Unperturbed he looked into the pail that Jóna held up for him and inhaled its sweet warmth. He had known that the cow would give milk once she had returned to her birthplace but had not expected the air and the grass to work its magic so soon. His arm around the waist of his wife, Einar threw back his head and laughed until they both shook. Eiríkur watched on, happy as much with his parents' closeness as with the prospect of something other than fish to eat.

<hr>

With summer slowly slipping by, Eiríkur ranged ever more widely over Hornstrandir, exploring the deserted peninsula like a cat establishing its territory. The fish snagged easily onto Einar's lines and Glæta continued to produce milk; the land gave up crowberries, thyme and angelica without complaint and the boy had more energy than his duties demanded; certainly, much more than his father's winding reminiscences could absorb. The names invoked no faces, the events played out as beyond a mist; stories of brutal storms scouring the shore, of vast whales dragged up and dismembered, of teeming shoals of herring hauled up from the sea. The story that Eiríkur wanted, despite himself, his father would not tell: his older brother remained in a state of immaculate confinement, ever present in his absence. The tang of guilt hung in the fog of silence, and Eiríkur could not escape the conviction that it belonged to him.

He had been just six years old when Ólafur had died and his memories of the death were blurred. He knew only that his brother had been taken in the darkness of winter, by malevolence and spite. He recalled much more clearly the sadness that had fallen over his parents in the months that followed, that had then been carried on his father's oars across the ice fjord to Bolungarvík. And he remembered the careful protection that his parents had wrapped around him, then and since. His memory of Ólafur living was as vague as that of his passing, distorted by the myths and silence that surrounded him, and he did not know if the joyful, boisterous, golden child had once been made of flesh, or had simply grown into the space he had left behind.

Eiríkur's exploration of the valleys and passes above Hesteyri continued and, one day in early August, he found himself beside the half-finished almost-road that rose from the ghost village. Built by the men of Hesteyri after the herring had gone, when there was no work, it had been paid for by the new government, eager to find a reason for Icelanders to remain on Hornstrandir. But the road had never been finished and was simply a rough stone track. It petered out in the stone fields at the pass, just above a pool, headwater to a flight of waterfalls that staggered down to the broad beck that gathered behind the doctor's house. It was from here that Eiríkur set off through the rock field under Kagrafell and snaked up the mountain's flank. Soon he was among the snow and ice that clung to the uplands, a memento of the winter's harshness. Melt water, cupped in icy depressions, shone aquamarine in the low sun; the winter's snow crunched under his boots. On the summit crag the snow gave way to verglas, coating the rocks with slick treachery. There, hanging above the fjord, Eiríkur could look down on the whole bay, the scattered remnants of the village and the decrepit whaling station.

A breeze raked over the crag and Eiríkur felt the chill nudge into his bones, a reminder that summer would not last forever, would soon in fact be gone. His father had yet to say when he would relent, would allow them to return home, but it would surely be before the gloom started its gathering. A shiver ran through him and he dug his hands into his pockets. His right thumb felt the course rasp of the match box, the glossy suppleness of his cigarette packet. He did not need to look to know that only two remained, and the idea of smoking one of them filled his imagination. He searched the summit plateau for a route down, so that he could be out of this wind, in a sheltered spot that would allow for the precious indulgence to be enjoyed fully and at leisure. Below, a tarn nestled in a hollow, backed by steep slopes to the west, south and east; the smoothness of the pool suggested that no wind found its way to its shore. He picked his way down towards its shelter.

The water's margins were scattered with small boulders and Eiríkur selected one near to the brink, where the tarn's water cascaded over in a thin jet, down into a steep ghyll cut into the mountainside. Taking his seat, he slid one of the battered cigarettes out of its packet and examined it. It was a little bent towards the tip, its paper no longer crisp, and he carefully straightened it, running his gnawed fingers along its length repeatedly. When it was as straight as it could be made, Eiríkur placed one end between his lips and fumbled with a match until it burst into a brief and fizzing frenzy. He sucked greedily on the cigarette until he could hear the crackling of the paper's consumption, and then he inhaled. Only once he had released this first gulp, did he look up to take in the view.

The mountain niche opened to the north, looking across the peninsula, to where the shore lay exposed to the winds that blew down from the Arctic, over the Greenland Sea. He could trace the crenulations of a hundred bays and inlets, ridges and valleys, each cut against the deep blue of the sea. Looming over the broad bay of Aðalvík, like a fat finger pointing to the north, was the mass of Straumnesfjall. He searched its broad back until the little scratch of colour, a flag, indicated where the soldiers had made their base. They had been sent there three years after Eiríkur and all of Hesteyri had left the peninsula, in order to listen for the planes and missiles that would surely scream down from the north, to bring death to the Atlantic shores and the cities of the Midwest. On occasion, he had seen the Americans in Ísafjörður, smiling and relaxed, enjoying the comforts of the town. But he had also heard the rumours: how sometimes, in the depths of winter, these young men, ripped from their homes in the distant plains and drained by the wind, the darkness and the cold, would walk out from their barracks, out of the compound, to the edge of the steep cliffs and step off into oblivion. It was not their winter, its misery had not been learned from the womb, and annihilation was preferable to the endless night they had found at the edge of the world.

The last of his cigarette scorched his lips, burned his fingertips, and he cursed as he shook the stub into the void, where the wind caught it and carried it off. He watched the space it left, the great, green, falling space of the mountains, and decided that it was early still, that neither his mother nor his father had need of him for a while longer. There was time yet. The boy picked a path that shadowed the ghyll as it cut its way northwards.

He left the stone fields behind him after an hour or so, and he was glad to see the tufts of grass and sedges, the clumps of Moss Campion bulging from the grey gravel, that signalled the return of easier going. The roar of a waterfall announced the point where the flat ground dropped away to the coast and as he neared its edge, the expanse of the valley opened before him.

Descending from the ridge, Eiríkur scuffed his boots on the loose earth and rock that fringed the course of the waterfall down to where the meadow was thick with orchids. In another hour he was at the mouth of the stream, now some twenty metres wider, on a beach under the sand-caked bow of Mannfjall. The waves broke in from the open ocean, rolling and ripping across the margin of land and sea. The wind swallowed all sound but that of the water's crash and suck.

Despite the force of the wind, the sun shook free of its cloudy shawl and warmed Eiríkur's face, cast its glow across the sand. Above the elemental roar, Eiríkur almost heard the laughter of another time upon this stretch of shore, of solid sunshine and of his brother. There had been no wind that day, only a gentle breeze tugging at his loose shirt, brushing Ólafur's hair, against the grain, into his wide eyes. And the surf had been kinder as they ran barefoot through its tingling pull, chasing each other, Eiríkur squealing as his brother caught him; collapsing breathless, giggling on the soft dry sand; the feeling of wonder as Ólafur explained the meanings of the clouds; the touch of Ólafur's hand in his as he led him back up the beach, towards the warmth of his mother's embrace.

His brother must have been ten years old then. Ólafur would be dead before the end of the year, lost in the darkness. But the rediscovery of that last summer, the only summer he would ever know with his brother, brought back the giddiness of childhood. Kicking off his boots, and tugging away his woollen socks, Eiríkur ran laughing to the fringe of the freezing surf. The surging waters snaked around his ankles, the sand sucked gently at his feet, and Eiríkur threw wide his arms to embrace the wind.

It was late when he reached Hesteyri again. Light still of course, but the food would be done, the things washed. Where the almost-road crested the last ridge, Eiríkur paused. He felt inside his pocket for his cigarette packet and weighed for a moment the pleasure of smoking the last of them against the disappointment of being without the prospect of smoking. He satisfied himself with the satin touch of the crumpled box, resolving to find his father and smoke his cigarette beside him, while the old man smoked his pipe and they talked as men. With this determination, Eiríkur strode on, down towards Helgi Gunnarsson's blue-board house.

Before he reached it, behind the church, he saw the kneeling figure of his father among the graves. The twisted growth that snarled about the other rusted crosses and headstones had been stripped back from one, and the plot had a startled mien. Einar still held his knife, loose in his left hand. Eiríkur watched for a little while, at a distance, hardly daring to breathe. They had been in Hesteyri for almost six weeks, but the grave had remained untended through all those days. Only now had his father found the time, or the courage. Slowly, Eiríkur approached, tamping the sedge noisily underfoot, hoping to alert his father to the presence of another in good time.

'You've been gone a long while, Eiríkur. Your mother was worried.'

Einar did not look up, but instead left his gaze on the little headstone. Over his shoulder, Eiríkur read the names of his grandfather and his brother, along with some others that he did not know: five names in all. The ground around the plot had been cleared meticulously, and a clutch of yellow poppies lay across at the centre of it.

'Today is your brother's birthday. I thought I should, well, tidy things for him. Seeing as it's his birthday. You missed your dinner.'

Only now did Einar turn to look at Eiríkur. The trace of tears clung to his eyes in a pink rawness, but he smiled warmly at his boy. His right hand searched though his pockets, finally reappearing with a large piece of dried fish.

'You must be famished.'

Eiríkur accepted the fish gratefully. While he chewed, he extended his other hand to help his father to his feet.

'I went to the north shore today. To the beach in Aðalvík. I'd been there before. Not since I was very young. I remember playing there. With Ólafur. I remembered him clearly. More clearly than I think I ever have. Perhaps he came to play with me again. For his birthday.'

Eiríkur punctuated his words with swallows of fish, eager both to eat and to share these thoughts with his father. Einar watched as he spoke, his face flickering between joy and sorrow. His arm encircled the boy's shoulders and he led him down towards the shore, where the gentle waters of the fjord slopped against boulders rubbed smooth by generations of storms. As they passed, Jóna watched from the steps, silent, curious.

'Your brother was a fine lad. Much like you. But he never had the cares you've had. Never lost his brother, nor lived with parents that had lost their son. What do you remember of him? What would you like me to tell you?'

Einar emptied the ash from his pipe, tapped its bowl into his palm three times, then pushed in a fresh wad of tobacco. Before he had retrieved his own matches, Eiríkur brought a light in his cupped hands to the pipe and watched while his father sucked down the flame. Einar looked on with amused fascination, which grew deeper as Eiríkur pulled a bent cigarette from a battered carton and lit it. The boy drew clumsily on the smoke, but while it provoked a gagging cough, it was clear that this was not Eiríkur's first cigarette.

'You've become a man under my very nose, Eiríkur. If I still sometimes treat you like a boy, I am sorry.'

The low sun dipped behind the hills and the bay darkened into a grimy dusk. It was past midnight now, but neither father nor son wanted to leave for their beds, even if the birds had settled into silence. Eiríkur had never asked, at least not out loud, about his brother's death, and neither his father nor his mother had ever spoken of it. Eiríkur remembered only that his brother had fallen ill and been sent to bed. He had not seen him again, alive or dead; the fever had taken him in the depths of winter and his burial, under the snow and ice, had been conducted without ornament. Eiríkur had been too young to venture out into the wind to witness the interment. The frozen ground had swallowed Ólafur along with his brother's memories of him, memories that only now had begun to find their way back into the light.

2008

The blunt voices downstairs barely bubbled up through the carpet, but he sat listening for a moment or two in any case, deathly still so as not to dampen them further. The late spring sun cut into the bedroom, bringing with it the sound of songbirds chattering in the garden. A car's engine rumbled to a halt somewhere in the Close. He thought he heard an aeroplane scraping across the sky.

The now dead phone still lay in his hand and Árni roused himself sufficiently to return it to its cradle. The sound of the duvet rustling beneath him, the bed grumbling at the shifting weight, the dull plasticity of the point where the handset met its base: all these erased the slow breathing of the world outside, made his immediate surroundings solid once more. He was wholly in Cambridge once again.

His wife was laughing now, enjoying an unheard joke made by one of the children, or perhaps by Chloe. The girl had been babysitting for them for years now, since Ben was small, and he wondered whether it was his wife's affection that kept her employed, even though their youngest was already at school. Freyja was almost the same age now as Chloe was when she had first sat for them, and she would be quite capable of looking after her little brother. Árni had had neither sitter nor sibling to watch over him, and when his mother was busy he had learned to fend for himself. His grandmother had led him to school on his first day, but he had then been left to find his own way, gradually picking up friends to accompany him. The memory of his grandmother, and of the care of his mother, chastened him, reminded him that he had not been so self-reliant, so independent, after all. In any case, as he had just said to his father, things were different here.

He smoothed his trousers to the knee and stood up. The dressing table mirror showed a man he only barely recognised. Older, of course, with lines crowding about his eyes, but it was the trace of defeat that ghosted those eyes that troubled him most. Even on his birthday last year, there had been a bright-eyed optimism, despite the flecks of grey, the slackening jaw line. But this was the last year of his thirties and that truth had arrived with renewed malevolence during the phone conversation that had just ended. His father's evident decline was as a premonition, a marker to his own mortality. Árni twisted a knot into his tie as if wrapping his own noose.

Below, there was the sound of a television igniting, music and squeaking voices that set his teeth on edge even at this distance. Then came footsteps on the stairs, the creaking boards of the landing and the tightening of the door knob.

'Are you almost ready, sweetheart?'

Charlotte was already retying the tie, brushing something from his lapel, smiling. All of it irritated him, confirmed that this evening would give him no pleasure, would be a thing to endure. They were his friends of course, people he liked, at least in theory. And the restaurant was perhaps his favourite place to eat in Cambridge. But there was something about the eagerness of his wife's smile, the quaver in his father's voice, and the sense of time passing that sucked all the anticipation from the party. He watched her study him.

'What's up? Everything OK with Eric?'

He had never liked the way that she did not even try to pronounce his father's name correctly, anglicising its subtlety into two blunt syllables. She had encouraged the children to use it too, rather than grandpa or, even better, *afi*. They saw very little of him, so they had never had the opportunity to develop the flavour of the word. But still, the word 'Eric' on the lips of his children seemed presumptuous, disrespectful, too removed from their origins.

'He's OK, I think. Well, no, not really. He sounds... vague. I think he is finding it hard without mum.'

Árni was still finding it hard without Hrefna, and he had not lived in the same country as his mother for seventeen years. Simply the knowledge of her abstract absence was enough to cast a shadow across his days when stirred unbidden into being, like a half-remembered song. He could only imagine the extent of his father's loneliness.

'Well, it's only been a couple of years. Of course he'll still being grieving for her. Did you thank him for the card?'

Despite the distance, Árni had always received a card and present from his parents at each birthday since he had left home for university, even when he had traded Reykjavík for Cambridge. It had usually been a book: there were not that many shops in Ísafjörður, the nearest town of any size to the village from which he had bolted. But now, with his mother gone, there was just the card, the heartfelt greeting written in a shaking hand. It was the same design as the year before. Árni wondered if his father ever made it out of Bolungarvík these days.

'Yeah, of course. He didn't remember sending it, to be honest. And... well, he forgot a couple of times why I was calling at all.'

Charlotte's frown passed in an instant, but even fleeting affirmation cut him to the stomach. It wasn't just his overreaction; Charlotte thought it too, if only as one of many possibilities. The stroke of her palm on his cheek steadied him and he felt renewed gratitude for her presence. Unlike his father, he was not alone.

In the years after leaving home, Árni had eaten anything but fish. As a doctoral student in the strange new country, his diet had comprised chicken curries, lamb kebabs, and anything with fresh vegetables. Precious little that was edible grew in the West Fjords, where the summers were short and chill and the winters devastating to everything but grass and stunted shrubs. In the brief daylight months, you could find little berries and his mother had shown him those that were good to eat, but even they had been tart and acidic. When they had had a little money, there was lamb, but his father was a fisherman, rowing out each day in the long boat to harvest whatever the North Atlantic had to offer. There was seldom money to spare for meat, but there was always fish.

With age, came a remembrance of the tastes of his childhood. By the time his mother died, he had already adopted a normal British attitude to things from the sea: a slightly whimsical variant on proper food, a healthy alternative, nice every now and then. But with her death came the memories of the life he had had before and of the food that had sustained it. As a kind of alimentary remembrance, he began to seek it out whenever they ate in restaurants. He brought herring home in various states and tried to introduce his unwilling children to the pleasures of fish without batter. It was inevitable that he would want to celebrate his 39th birthday at the best fish restaurant in the city.

The restaurant was on the edge of the Midsummer Common, hanging over the river Cam, and was reached by way of an iron footbridge. A crossing of water, even here, so far from the sea. Charlotte folded her arm through his as they walked over the sluggish stream, and Árni felt the softness of her lips pressed against his cheek, the gentle pressure of her fingertips stroking away the trace of red they had left. It would be alright; whatever it was that troubled him, it would be alright. Árni wanted to protest, to scream that it would not be alright, but she had not verbalised the reassurance, only implied it with her touch. It would be madness to declaim his own imaginings. That was the behaviour of lonely old men who already had nothing else to lose, who were already lost, already forsaken. Árni was not yet forsaken, despite his fears.

In the meadow, a cluster of cattle, rust brown, browsed the grass beyond the path. They reminded him of his neighbour's cows when he has growing up and he paused to consider them, to wonder if they still stood in the field above his father's house. The slow deliberateness of the beasts brought to mind another fragment of the past. His grandmother had told him a story about a time when the whole family, Eiríkur included, had rowed off back to Hornstrandir one summer with their cow, who wouldn't milk at home. She had twisted his hair gently around her fingers as she told him how the cow had been so excited at her return to the land of her birth that she had leapt into the sea and, within hours, had begun to give milk, for first time in years. The idea had struck him as magical as a boy, but now, having completed two science degrees, the biological impossibility of the story was simply laughable. He shook his head and sighed; the squeeze of Charlotte's hand, her careful, questioning frown, pulled him back and he laughed so as to banish the thoughts. Without a word, he turned and guided his wife into the restaurant with a soft hand on her back.

The upstairs dining room burst with polite greetings as they entered, the murmur of good wishes and congratulation. Wine glasses chinked and hands were clasped; cheeks were kissed and crisply wrapped gifts were thrust into Árni's hands. Charlotte left him to the embrace of his friends and faded to the back wall, to greet her brother and his wife. For a moment, she watched Árni, hopeful that the swell of affection would overwhelm the darker things that had gripped her husband for the past weeks. There were smiles of course, and laughter; excitement greeted each gift, each congratulatory word. He accepted the glass of wine with light abandon. And yet, Charlotte could not unsee the shadow that had hung over her husband all day. She wished only that it would leave, that its intrusion into her life, their home, would end.

'How's the old sod coping?'

His wife slapped the back of Christopher's hand in rebuke, startling both he and his sister. Charlotte was used to forgiving her brother for his abrasiveness, but Jacqui had known him only for five years. She still enjoyed the virtue of expecting better of him. Charlotte studied her sister-in-law's face, her hurt exasperation, then turned back to her brother.

'He's fine. Had a lovely day, I think. If nothing else, he enjoyed not being in work.'

The word caught at the back of her throat and she stumbled over others in search of an apology. It was less than a month since Christopher had had to carry his belongings from his desk in a cardboard box and file out onto the London street with many of his former colleagues, men and women like him, whose careers had been punctuated by global events. Pictures like this, from London and New York, had flickered across the evening news for months, so when their mother had rung to let her know that Christopher had been made redundant, she felt that she had witnessed the event itself; the abrupt, numbing ending of plans and hopes for hundreds, but also for her brother.

She had called, and wept, and asked questions, tried to reassure him that it would all work out, and all the while he had sounded calm, blasé, reconciled. When the call had ended, she'd tried to talk to Árni about it, but he had shrugged with the same equanimity. His father had lost what few savings he had months before, he had said, and the storm of the crisis had already wreaked a trail of disruption across the whole of Iceland. She had pushed him for some sympathy at least for her family, but he had shrugged again, said that he was sure Christopher would be fine, and that it was only a job, not something important.

There had been a time when these words would have been impossible for her husband. For most of their life together, Árni had been at his happiest when he was at work. He had carried the joy of working from his studies into his post-doctoral research and into his first proper job with the Department; even when he had left the University for the job with a pharmaceutical company, his love for his research had endured, had sustained him, at least for a time. She had envied his professional advance all through the early years of the children's lives, when she had left to one side her publishing career, putting her own public life on hold. But since she had returned to work, Árni had been less absorbed, less completed by his role in the world. Even as she again blossomed into the light, he withdrew, resentful, unwilling to define his dissatisfactions.

Charlotte had assumed that his mother's death had precipitated the change, compounded by concerns about his distant father. That at least she could comprehend and excuse. But the suspicion that he was simply sulking about getting older, nearing forty, would not quite leave her, and she realised that she too had her expectations. She looked at Jacqui and smiled her apology.

She felt Árni's hand in the small of her back and realised that the rest of the guests had begun to take their seats. She watched him shake Christopher's hand, brush Jacqui's cheek with an almost-kiss, then let herself be guided by that hand again to an empty chair in the centre of one side of the long dining table. While the young waitress took orders, she looked along the faces of her husband's friends, nodding a greeting to any that caught her eye. Almost all were like them: people who had come to the city on account of the university, as students or as staff, and who had yet to make the decision to leave: only her brother lived elsewhere, heading to London for work soon after his own graduation.

Only one of the party had actually been born in Cambridge. A joiner, rather than an academic; a maker of furniture who had left school when he could to learn his trade. Sam had been Árni's next door neighbour when he had first arrived in the city. Charlotte had been unsure at the time if his befriending him had been a gesture or a genuine affinity, but as she had got to know him, she had realised that her taciturn scientist was not inclined towards such gestures or any artifice. Charlotte's own predisposition for signs and signals had been exposed by the enduring friendship.

It struck her that everyone else was connected to Árni through past or current work, even the other Icelander at the table. There were a number of her husband's compatriots in Cambridge, almost all, like Árni, working around the University and the biotech industries that were rapidly expanding in the city. But only one was close enough to have been invited to the party, a pretty blond woman, whose voice trilled in a way that entranced virtually every Englishman that she encountered. Charlotte watched her and wondered if Árni might have ended up with someone like her, perhaps even with her, had he not come to England.

Árni's hand was on her bare forearm, his skin warm and soft. His eyes twitched upwards, to where the waitress waited, pencil point poised upon her pad. She did not know how long the girl had been hanging there, unsure as to how best attract the attention of her faraway customer, and she fumbled over the items listed on the menu, before settling on the trout. Árni's hand still rested on her arm but his eyes and attention had drifted to the other side of the table, where conversation had turned to news of a former colleague. She did not recognise the name and instead watched the golden hairs on the back of his hand shimmer in the candle light. Only when she felt his hand stiffen fractionally did she chase the words once more, seeking to catch their shape as they danced on the choppy air.

'He's got the Novus job? The Associate Directorship? My god. I thought about going for that but guessed it was out of my league. He can't be much more than thirty, can he?'

The hand was gone, and Árni was gnawing gently on the skin around his third fingernail. She rested her own hand lightly on his shoulder. It seemed so small, so pale against the dense dark wool of his jacket. She thought of asking if he could pass the wine, anything to slacken the tension in his back. There had been a time when others spoke of Árni in this way, flushed and frustrated by his rapid rise.

'I wouldn't worry about it. I hear their share price is taking a hammering, what with everything going on. They're highly invested in the States. Might not turn out to be such a golden ticket after all.'

One of Árni's colleagues, a soft faced man in his early fifties, smiled his reassurance from across the table. Charlotte recognised him only in the abstract: there was a man, an acquaintance, a friend, who occasionally popped up at social events, his worn features apologetic, grateful, but she could not say for certain that this was the same man. She did not know his name, but she was grateful for his intercession, for the loosening of her husband's shoulders, the ghost of a chuckle that she welcomed despite its maliciousness. Released, Charlotte scanned the rest of the guests.

Her brother tight in flirtatious conversation with his wife; Sam shaping unseen structures with voluptuous hand movements for the pretty Icelander, her eyes glittering as they followed each gesture; everyone talking, smiling, eating. This would not be so bad an evening.

The garden's fresh warmth breezed into the house, carried on the evening's bright sunshine. The light danced through the shadows of laden trees, chasing over the soft pale fabrics and supple wooden surfaces of the living room. Visitors assumed that the aesthetic had been carried into the home by Árni, an echo of his Nordic origins. But the coolness of the rooms flowed from Charlotte's rejection of the patterned clutter of her own upbringing. Her childhood had been played out in pastels and pelmets, framed by festoons and dado rails. The house reflected her choices rather than his.

Árni looked about him as if seeing the room for the first time. He forced himself to catalogue the origins of each object, its arrival and provenance, bringing into consciousness the history of himself, his life with Charlotte, the growing distance from his own origins. Standing, he straightened the cushions on the sofa and looked at the clock on the mantelpiece. It was almost seven. He caught sight of himself in the mirror hanging over the fireplace. He was still wearing his work clothes, which were much like all his other clothes. The only marker of homeliness was the tail of his shirt that had found its way loose of his trousers' waistband.

'Hey, you two! It's time to call afi. Come in here so that I can put us on speaker phone.'

From the kitchen, he heard the thud and clank of a pot being returned to the stove top, and the scraping of a chair on tiles. Freyja was the first to emerge, glad of the chance to leave her homework on the kitchen table, even if it was to talk to the funny man who could not speak English properly. Her mother followed, a wisp of golden hair falling across her eyes. Behind her, Ben trotted clutching a stick of carrot in his fist.

As every year, Árni told the story of why his father was called Eiríkur, after the Viking that had come to Hornstrandir from Norway a thousand years ago; why they had their last names as a result; how their afi had been born on the day that Iceland declared its independence, and how every year, as a boy himself, Árni had thought that the festivities and celebrations were being held in honour of his father rather than his nation. At this, Árni would raise his mug of tea in a toast to the country of his birth, while his wife and children suppressed their giggles.

For the first twenty years of his life, this day had been spent with his father. Under endless light, Eiríkur had talked to Árni about the past and the future, about the strip of land across the fjord where he had been born, land which even this near to midsummer was still gilded by snow. Even when he was old enough to understand that the parties of his neighbours were not for his father, he chose to elide the country and the man. And now he had left both. For almost two decades he had celebrated the day at a distance, from the shadows, and when night eventually fell in the east of England, he thought about his father, sitting outside the little clapboard house, drinking Brennivín alone in the midnight sun. The sadness this thought evoked tasted of guilt rather than longing, the sense of a duty unfulfilled rather than a pleasure denied.

'Halló? Hver er þessi?'

The dialling tone ended, collapsing into the sound of clattering plastic and laboured breathing, then a gruff voice, fractured by sixty years of cigarette smoke, broke into the hiss.

'It's me, dad. We just wanted to wish you a happy birthday.'

'Hello Árni, it's your father. Are you well?'

'Yes, we're all well. I have the children here. They want to wish you a happy birthday too.'

Freyja led her brother in a stuttering rendition of '*Til hamingju með afmælið*' while her mother stroked her hair in encouragement. Árni wondered if he should have made a greater effort to raise them bilingually, if what had become his decision to root them more securely in the soil of England had been based on simple laziness. Charlotte, of course, had not encouraged him, although she had never argued against it. Perhaps if he had, there would have been greater reason to visit; perhaps his father would have met his grandson more than twice, once as a baby and then when Árni had taken his family to Bolungarvík to bury his mother.

'That's beautiful. You both speak Icelandic very well. Let me get your grandmother, she will love to hear you speaking Icelandic. Where she has got to? She was just here…'

Árni snatched the phone from the base and switched off the speaker phone. He stared stonily at Charlotte and, with a twitch of his head, urged her to take the bemused children through to the kitchen.

'Dad, we've been through this. Mum died. Two years ago. She had a stroke.'

He heard his father's heart break for the hundredth time. The effort to keep his voice level, calm, to squeeze out the urge to snap, the welling tears, was Herculean. Harder still was resisting the questions that teemed around him about his father's recent memory lapses.

'I know she's dead, Árni. I am not an imbecile. But you don't understand. Your mother is often here with me. Not as she was perhaps, but we talk all the same.'

He did not have the heart to take this one comfort from a lonely old man. It was comfort that he himself should rightly have given. Maybe not all the time: even if he were willing to make that sacrifice, he could not reasonably expect Charlotte and the children to tear up their lives and exile themselves to the darkness and the ice. But he could visit more often, could call more often, could be a better son. The least he could do was to allow his father his phantasm. He turned the conversation to news of his life, of the children's progress at school, and questions about neighbours and the weather.

They spoke for about fifteen minutes further and, by the time he rang off, the conversation had revived its more usual and mundane rhythms. Charlotte called him to the kitchen, where plates and glasses and cutlery and a meal that was not fish awaited him.

'Maybe I could get him a laptop for Christmas. Then we could Skype him. Keep in touch a bit more. He could see the kids, feel a bit more connected.'

Charlotte looked up from her plate, barely able to contain a snort of laughter, her grin twisting eventually across her mouth.

'Your dad? With a computer? Do they even have the internet up there?'

Árni was surprised that this slight offended him. He had chosen to leave at least in part to escape the isolation of his home shore, trapped as it was outside of the normal rhythms of human progress. He had no idea how good the broadband was in Bolungarvík, but he knew that mobile coverage was better there than it was here just five miles beyond the city, even on the flat land of the fens.

'Yeah, of course. I'm going to get him hooked up. Get him a laptop. Next time I'm over, that's what I'll do.'

The blood rose bloomed into the soft whiteness of the tissue. He was startled by the brightness of the red and by the speed and solidity with which it established itself, filling it entirely before the first of the pain arrived. The dull, aching hotness of riven skin came eventually, and he forced out its sting in the hiss of an angry expletive.

The force of the word carried to the kitchen and Charlotte was already in the doorway before her question of concern had been formed. She looked at the half-constructed cabinet, the discarded screwdriver beside the kneeling Árni, and the glut of blood nestled in his cupped palm. A drip clung to the corner of a bloody tissue, and she watched as it separated and fell towards the chaos of cardboard, polythene and carpet.

'Oh my god, are you OK?'

He had no idea how she had crossed the room so swiftly; her arm across his back, her hand on his neck, was a surprise. When she took his injured hand in her own, lifted it to inspect the damage, her touch was so tender that he was flushed with the sensation of being a child once more. Unremembered memories of his mother's gentleness sent helplessness spiralling through him. The quivering giddiness might well have been the effects of blood loss or shock, but the rational part of his mind was lost within the comfort of abdication.

He inhaled sharply when she pulled back the sodden tissue, revealed the inch-long snag of skin and flesh and gore. He wondered what a palm reader would make of this unkempt branch to his life line, then only at the slow pumping, the rising dome of viscosity. His stomach clenched and he swore once again. Suppressed waves of pain jangled up his arm. His eyes became hot, damp.

'Freyja, darling? Will you pop upstairs and fetch the first aid kit for mummy? Quickly, please. Daddy needs a plaster.'

From the kitchen, the sound of his daughter, her chair sliding on the tiles, the scrape opening further the searing sharpness in his hand. He heard her padding feet, heard their resentment at having been disturbed, and he turned his back against the empty door frame, so that she should not see his wound, his eyes, when she appeared within it. She would not simply do as she had been asked, but would ask questions, with sullen curiosity, until Charlotte provided satisfactory answers that made the journey upstairs worthwhile, or at least non-negotiable.

'Freyja. Please. I need the first aid kit. Quickly.'

Árni tried to picture his daughter's face behind him, hoped that it would contain concern rather than petulance. He waited for the complaint, the question, the challenge, but it did not come: only the rapid thump of feet on stair carpet. He looked up from his wound to see his wife's face, but whatever urgency had spurred his daughter had evaporated into a gentle smile. Beatific.

The tumbling of feet, then the warmth of Freyja's breath on his neck, announced the arrival of the first aid kit. He lifted his hand a little, so that his daughter could get a better look at his mortality; in the edge of sight he could see her face screw up in disgust, and he twisted his head to smile, to kiss her cheek, before Charlotte's single word sent her back to the kitchen, to resume whatever had been distracting her before the crisis. It was a Saturday, so it was unlikely to be homework. Drawing perhaps. He was sure that she liked to draw.

Charlotte was already busy with cleaning the wound and he watched her delicate movements, so slight that he barely felt their effects on his broken skin. Cleansed, the wound did not look so bad. Deep and ragged, but capable of being contained by untrained but careful hands. He felt the skin prickle around his left temple, where the scar was, and he thought of another wound, in another time and place. He had been five years old, playing on his own on the beached carcass of *Tófa*, his grandfather's boat. Testing himself against himself, as there was no one else, he was jumping from thwart to thwart, imagining the chasm contained swirling lava, or razor-sharp ice, or a fearsome faxaskrímsli in a boiling sea.

His grandfather heard his yelp. He had fallen, catching the side of his head on the oar lock. A glancing blow, the pain was nonetheless sharp enough that Árni's yelp had soon become a scream. But it was the blood that still clung in his memory. So much blood. When he thought about the accident as an adult, it was the sea of blood that remained: the red lines running down his wrist, the slick impenetrability of its gloss on his palm. And his grandfather.

Einar had reached him before the second scream had rasped its way fully from his throat. There had been calm words, and a gentleness that seemed irreconcilable with the gnarled and callused hands, weathered on a thousand seas. But the softness of the smile and his eyes, remained most strongly of all. As Einar had cleaned and dressed the wound with wadding taken from a leather pouch, deep within the old man's coat, his warmth had soothed away the boyish sobs.

'*There. All done. Feel OK?*'

Charlotte smiled a grown-up smile, practiced on children with scuffed knees over the years. Árni looked at the bandage's neat tucks, the pin clamped snugly, unobtrusive. No blood seeped into the fresh whiteness. The padding damped down the pain that undoubtedly lingered within its nest.

'*Not bad. You could be a nurse. Don't suppose you'll have been able to save me another scar, though.*'

Her hand ran over his temple, lifting his hair back onto itself before her lips brushed the pale line across his skin.

'Afraid not. I'm no more skilled with a bandage than your mother was. But I think it's sexy anyway, if that helps.'

She chuckled, and Árni felt a pang unfelt for several months. With his uninjured hand, he ran a finger the length of the scar, tracing its unseen route exactly. He wanted to touch her hair, her cheek, but instead shifted across the carpet to lean against the wall, clear of the scatter of coated MDF planks.

'Not my mother. My grandfather. He was down by the shore with me when I fell. It's my only clear memory of him as a man. Those huge hands. Knuckles like barrels. And yet he had the touch of a surgeon.'

She came over then, sat next to him, her straight back twisted against the wall so that she could rest her head on his shoulder, run her hand down his arm until it rested in its crook. In the silence of a few minutes, the sound of their breathing and the scrape and scratch of a pencil from the kitchen tussled on the firm air of the living room. She inhaled deeply, sucking in her husband's neutral scent, holding it like tobacco smoke, intoxicating.

'He carried me back up the hill to the house. When my mother saw me, she smothered me in kisses and fuss. But my dad. My dad just stood there, looking from me to afi, something like terror on his face. Didn't talk to me directly, asked afi what had gone on, how I was. Seemed afraid to touch me, almost like he thought I'd break. And this was before grandad died. He got so much worse after that.'

Another silence. Charlotte shifted as minutely as she could, unfurling the twisting of her spine a little before coming to rest again against his shoulder. Her fingers found the back of his hand and she traced shapes into his skin, fingertip strokes across corrugations of bone and vein. His hands were like her father's had been when she was a girl: neither coarse nor hard, but thick all the same; not smooth, but full of strange rises and creases, ridges like armour on the knuckles. She could only imagine how the hands of a man scoured by the sea would look.

'He wouldn't let me near tools. When I was growing up. Anything with a blade, or an edge. Meant I never had to clean the fish of course, but it's probably why I'm so, uh, useless at this kind of thing.' Árni nodded at the strewn elements of the unmade cabinet, jumbled on the floor. 'Sam thinks it's hilarious. I used to go into his workshop, pick up a screwdriver or something and just hold it. Forbidden fruit. He thought I was mad.'

He was overstating things. Burnishing a small truth in his life into something defining. Making his father sound neurotic, even then. It was a misrepresentation. When a log came ashore in the winter, he had been tasked with chopping as much wood as any of the other boys in Bolungarvík.

'He didn't wrap me in cotton wool or anything. There was just some sort of fear he had around me. As if he thought that if he got too close, I would come to harm. Understandable. Superstitious, but understandable. He wouldn't let me work with him out on the water once I turned 12. We could still fish for fun, on fine days. But not work. Instead, he sent me to tend to a neighbour's flock, up on the fells. That was tough enough, dangerous sometimes. But, to him, at least it wasn't the sea.'

His father still owned Tófa, still used it. On his visits home, Árni would only need to see the hull to feel the past lap against him. The harder days, when money was tight. The back-breaking work of his defiant, distant father. The village life that bled inevitably into the sea, the life from which he was exiled, out on the hills, with only Siggi Baldursson's sheep for company. But mostly, the boat carried the two clear memories of his grandfather that he still retained.

1975

With the addition of new wood, the fire crackled in the range, slowly waking to the dark morning. It would be a while yet before the flames gave any real warmth, and Hrefna pulled her cardigan about her. She turned to face the room, standing so that the remnants of last night's heat might creep through to her skin. Outside, the sky suggested a hint of grey, but the yellow light of the lamps in the neighbours' windows drowned the day's incipient promise, glowering across the snow. It would be two hours yet before the sun rose above the mountain, and even then the drizzle would ensure that this windless day would never give much light. She longed for summer, for the light and warmth of limitless days, the return of the flowers in the meadows above Bolungarvík.

The coffee pot spat and fizzed on the stove. Hrefna shouted for her husband and wondered why her mother-in-law had not yet stirred. Jóna was often first to the kitchen, especially since Árni had arrived. Now that he was bigger, he required less of her, but Jóna still helped about the house as much as she could. Although she knew she should rouse her son, she decided to leave him be. He would start at the school later in the year, and his chances to sleep on, undisturbed, would then be over. Hrefna poured a small cup of coffee for herself and took a bite of bread, watching the fine rain and sleet swirl outside the window.

'Has the rain not lifted yet?'

Behind her, Jóna was straightening plates and spoons at the table. Hrefna did not respond at first, instead watching the gloom coalesce for some moments more, enjoying the last drops of the day's quietness. The squat bank of cloud that obscured the stars and the lightening east was just a formless billowing of unseen droplets, the progenitors of the sleety streaks stumbling towards the earth, and yet she studied it as if it were a book containing secret truths, knowledge of the past and of the future. But those truths remained opaque, and she returned to the bright kitchen.

'It'll last all day. There's precious little wind and no break in the clouds. Spring can't come soon enough.'

Jóna chuckled. Each year that she had lived, spring had come too late and winter too soon. At least here, although it was only 20 kilometres further south, the winds did not cut as deep as they did in Hesteyri. There was electricity here and Ísafjörður, with its doctor and its supermarket, was only a short distance away. The ground could be covered in even the fiercest wind. Only in the deepest snow did Bolungarvík know any of the isolation that lasted an entire winter over there.

'You look tired. Are you feeling unwell?'

Jóna's eyes were ordinarily lively and bright, a defiance of her whitening hair, but today there was a ghosting about them, a dark listlessness, a sadness. Hrefna took the bowl of skyr from her mother-in-law's hands and pulled out a chair for her to sit. Jóna accepted it without complaint.

'Not unwell, just tired. I dreamed such dreams that I feel I hardly slept at all. The elves came to visit me, I think. They were trying to tell me something, but the rain kept falling, filling up the house until the water was above my waist, and I couldn't hear them anymore. The water was gushing so fiercely, so loud. I tried to shout for Einar, but he wasn't there. I was alone, and the water rose to my neck. I woke up so many times, and Einar was always there, snoring in the

bed beside me. But every time I felt asleep the elves returned, and the water, and Einar was gone.'

She took a gulp of coffee, her hand trembling a little on the cup. Hrefna placed her palm across Jóna's forehead and felt for an abnormal temperature, but there was none. With a frown, she sat down and cupped Jóna's hand between her own, as you would a bird.

'Dreams are funny things. I read that they often hide their meanings in strange signs. Whatever the elves meant to tell you, I'm sure it will become clear in its proper time. We have more important things to concern us right now. If those two don't get up soon, there'll be no fish left in the sea. Not with the English trying to claim them all for themselves.'

Both women laughed, but with no little bitterness. The so-called war was over, but it was well known in the West Fjords that English boats still stole into Icelandic waters, plundering fish. Einar did not work with one of the ocean-going crews, preferring to fish as he had always done, from the open wooden boat that his father had built seventy years before; it had been fitted with an outboard motor now, but Einar still kept to the coastal shallows. Nevertheless, the dispute had depleted the shoals upon which the family relied.

Hrefna poured the remainder of the coffee into their two cups and set about making a fresh pot. As she did so, she turned on the radio, filling the kitchen with breezy music. She swayed in time with the loping rhythm, her light voice trilling sounds that seemed to fit with the unfamiliar tune. Soon she would have to set out into the drizzle, down to the quayside and her shift at the processing plant. For now she wanted only to enjoy the warmth of the range and the gaiety of the music.

Under a sooty sky, *Tófa* barrelled in the swell. There was precious little wind, nothing more than a stiff breeze, but they had come out to the mouth of the ice fjord, where the boisterous northern ocean spilled into the shelter of the bay. It was further than they would ordinarily venture, but the day was calm and there was scant fishing further in. While Einar laid out the lines behind, Eiríkur pulled at the oars. The drizzle gathered at his father's beard, running off in little rivulets onto the worn oilskin. Eiríkur looked at the flat low sky. There was no prospect of a break in the weather: the rain would remain, but at least now, in the relative warmth of the day, the sleet had abated. There was only wetness to contend with, above and below.

As he baited the hooks and dropped them into the sea, Einar whistled a snatch of half-remembered melody, just as he had on a thousand such voyages. The few gulls drifting above replied in kind or held their counsel, intent on the lines that trailed below the grey surface. Otherwise there were no animal sounds, just the conversation of wood and water: the blades of oars stirring the sea, or the slop of a wave over the gunwales. There would be time for talking when the work was done and they had only to wait for the fish to come to them. There was always time.

With each pull, Eiríkur would lift his head to watch the distant shore. He had worked this coast, alongside his father, since he had been twelve years old, and knew every inlet and shoal. When he had left school, he had joined his father each time he had set out, no longer simply at weekends and on the early summer mornings. When illness or injury meant that Einar was unable to hunt for fish to feed the family, then the son had taken up the task alone. Eiríkur had respected, if not understood, his father's attachment to

Tófa: most of the other men of Bolungarvík had taken larger boats, or joined the crews of those that had. Even so, he had been grateful when the outboard motor had arrived, its case manhandled off a ship from Reykjavík by five curious neighbours, and he had no longer had to pull the boat out onto the open water by hand.

Einar had asked once if he would not rather continue his studies, perhaps attend college to get some qualifications that would free him from a life on the water. But despite his father's encouragement, Eiríkur had barely considered the idea before embracing a life that lay alongside his father in the belly of *Tófa*. The hours he had spent in quiet communion with him since had confirmed that it had been the right decision. Their words may have been sparse, but they had been set on such a wide canvass that he had grown to know the man better than many sons. The constant company of one son seemed, in turn, to compensate for the absence of another.

'Do you remember that summer, over at Hesteyri? That was a summer: full bellies and none of the problems we have today. We could see to ourselves, with no bills. I often think of it. I wonder whether it might have been better. Over there. For you and the boy.'

Einar was gazing off to the north, to where Straumnes marked the end of the peninsula, lost in the low clouds that clung to the sea. Beyond, unseen, the northern ocean stretched off to the ice, and Eiríkur thought about the winter, about his mother, about Hrefna, and about his son. But he swallowed the thoughts, did not raise again his brother's ghost, to accuse his father.

'Of course I do. It was a fine summer. And do you remember Glæta? The way she leapt from Tófa into the sea, how she swam for the shore? And the milk she gave? It was the sweetest milk I have ever tasted. At the time, I thought you were mad. But I am grateful now, glad that you took me there, to see where I am from.'

Einar looked up from his pipe, into which he had carefully stuffed a wad of tobacco, and smiled beneath his beard, content at the easiness between them. He had not, after all, spoiled the boy, and neither had he been hard and aloof like his own father. He had loved the man dearly, but he could never have told him that he had thought him mad.

'Why don't you ship those oars, have a smoke, and maybe rest a little? The current will do our work for us with the fish.'

Happy to comply, Eiríkur pulled the oars into the boat and retrieved a cigarette from deep within his coat. Curling his back against the rain, he slipped loose of the rocking boat and let his mind wander over the waves, carried on the smoke's release, as far as Bolungarvík and his wife, the warmth of her skin, the softness of its touch. He thought about his boy, about how he had grown so fast, and he turned over the thought that maybe it was time to try to give him a brother, or a sister; once he was at school, maybe then Hrefna would have more time. Some in the village said he had waited too long already.

A little way off, over to his right, something broke water at the edge of his vision, a dark shape that flashed above the surface for a moment, then was gone. Eiríkur turned to face the now empty stretch of water, then back to his father. Einar was busy with a stick of dried fish, oblivious to all else.

'Have you heard of sightings in these reaches, dad?'

'Sightings?'

Einar looked up, perplexed. His eyebrows twisted into an awkward knot of weathered skin and coarse hair. He followed his son's gaze out across the choppy water, to the dark spaces between white cresting waves. But there was nothing to be seen.

'You know, skrímsli? Sea monsters?'

It was true that he had heard stories, like everyone, of monsters lurking along the coast, living on shore or in the deep, taking sheep or vessels depending on their mood. While he believed these stories to be true, he had never seen such a beast himself. Years before Eiríkur had been born, when he had been a youth himself, there had been stories of a *fjorulalli* roaming the beaches to the west of Hesteyri in the twilight, sometimes taking sheep and once even taking a man: his body was later found, drowned but otherwise uninjured, on the shore near the herring station. More recently, he had seen a fisherman, from Bíldudalur, talking on the television about being confronted on the water by a terrifying creature, shells rattling from its scaly back, with bulging, bulbous eyes and the snout of a pig. He accepted these things as true, but he believed they were rare enough to cause no real harm.

'No lad. It was probably a seal. They come up to whelp at this time of year.'

Eiríkur nodded absently. Deep within him he held the certain conviction that creatures beyond the realm of man were never far: *skrímsli* slipped under the dappled waves and elves slunk away, shadows in the edge of sight. Perhaps he had seen a seal, but it seemed as likely that it had been something more malevolent.

Tófa jolted Eiríkur back to himself. Larger waves surrounded them, their peaks breaking easily over the boat. The sea had taken them further out, beyond the headland, and the current was still more unruly here. Without needing his father's shouted instruction, Eiríkur scrambled for the oars, to release them so that he might row back to quieter seas. The first dropped easily into the water, secure in its lock, and Eiríkur turned his attention to the right. The next wave arrived unseen, at the moment of greatest vulnerability, and the oar scuttled out of the boat and into the sea. It floated tantalisingly close to the stern, bobbing just beyond the limits of Einar's outstretched arm. In an instant, Einar was kneeling over the stern, his foot hooked under the thwart for balance. His fingers brushed the oar's slick shaft and he leant further out to close his fingers around it.

The next wave was not a big wave, but it hit the starboard flank of *Tófa* full square. Even Eiríkur, safely in the centre of the boat, almost lost his place; Einar disappeared into the roiling sea. Eiríkur had recovered his wits and his balance by the time his father shattered the sea's surface some metres away, flailing and floundering between the peaks and troughs, drifting ever further with every rise and fall, already beyond the reach of the remaining oar. Against the steady buffeting of the angry swell, Eiríkur scrambled to the stern seat. He shouted reassurances to his father and pulled hard on the engine's ignition cord, a foot braced against the boards. The stuttering roar faded after only a few rotations; he looped the cord again about the starter, pulled and swore as once again the motor failed.

Twice more he tried to ignite the outboard and on the second there was not even a cough of life. Einar was now ten metres from *Tófa*, his head as often beneath the water as above it. His grey eyes looked back in panic and sadness, even while his hands thrashed vainly against the sucking of the sea.

The coil of rope at Eiríkur's feet snaked into his consciousness. He had removed his gloves to smoke his cigarette and had not replaced them, no longer knew where they might be; the rope's wet coarseness cut into his palms as he unfurled the line so that he might hurl it towards his father. The coil spun out, arcing over the sea, hanging on the breeze before falling a couple of metres short of Einar. With something like a sob, Eiríkur hauled the sodden line back to the boat, coiled it again and stood to his full height, better to launch the life line to Einar. Again it span, arcing, spray shaking from its length, and he watched it curve to where his father's head bobbed, precarious.

He did not see where it met the water: another wave swept over *Tófa* and tumbled Eiríkur into the cold immensity of the ocean. The shock blinded him, stalled his chest, and the heavy wetness stole power from his limbs. For a moment he hung suspended, motionless, cut off from life and light. Like his father, he would drown here and he found comfort in that shared ending. Slipping, content, down into the silence, Eiríkur was jolted into a frenetic clawing at the water by the thought of Árni, of the tragedy of two sons robbed of their father today. Somehow, Eiríkur pulled himself to the surface, up into the pale grey above, animal desire finding the means to kick and pull until his blind eyes found the day's thin light. His mouth burst open and sucked in the cold air, stuffed as much of it into his chest as would fit. The salt burned his eyes when he re-opened them, blurring the world into greyness. The slap and rush of the water deafened him, poured into his throat when he tried to shout. Slowly sight returned, but revealed only more greyness, an empty, rolling range of grey mountains rising and falling around him. All else was void.

When it came, the smack against the back of his head was as unfathomable as the sea around him. But slowly he recognised the call of *Tófa* and he flailed his arms until he had turned in the water, to face the familiar boards of her prow. The painter trailed in the water and with it he hauled himself, by supernatural force, out of the sea and into the boat. He lay slumped in the sloshing water until his breathing calmed, until the air became dependable. Then he sat stupefied in the belly of the boat. Both oars and the rope had disappeared. Einar had disappeared. Eiríkur was alone on the ocean and with every rise and fall of the water, he knew with greater certainty that he could never reach his father, that he could never now bring him home. A chill crept into his soul and he began to shake uncontrollably.

Árni stood on the quayside, watching for his father in the thickening gloom. He felt his grandmother's hand rest gently on the back of his head, and its warmth seeped through the thick wool of his cap. It was time for them to meet his mother at the gates of the fish processing plant. Eight hours cleaning and packing would soon be over. But Árni stood unmoving, transfixed by the empty horizon. Most of the boats had already returned and, between Árni and the sea, the harbour sparkled with cascades of silver fish from boats to baskets to crates.

'Come on now, Árni. Let's go see your mum. She'll have missed you all day and it would be nice for you to be there to greet her at the end of her work. We'll come back after, I promise. Your dad and granddad will be here by then, I'm sure.'

Again he felt her hand at the back of his head, firmer this time, and he allowed her to guide him away from the brink and back towards the houses of the village. The plant was a little further around the harbour, with the gate facing the land. Outside, by the road, women milled about the low concrete platforms that served as a market place, buying surplus herring and char and ling for their suppers. The bulk of what the plant processed, however, was packed onto the trucks parked on the square of tarmac beside the west wall. Between them, a narrow, arched gateway gave access to the plant for the women that worked there. Between shifts, the gateway was sealed with a set of steel doors. The white paint flaked from them with each winter, and each spring another thick coat was applied, creating a moonlike surface of ragged craters and depressions. Already, the fresh paint around the hinges was streaked with rust.

The doors were open now, and a steady file of women passed through the gateway. Most still wore their hair tied tightly into their scarves, pulled back so that their skin shone with a reddish gloss, chill from the icy air within. Árni watched the familiar faces, waiting for the one that was most familiar. Hrefna emerged eventually, hidden behind the taller women that preceded her. She had tied her scarf about her neck, and her short fair hair fell in loose waves. She waved to her son and, as soon as she could pass the others, trotted over to where he stood with Jóna. Her embrace was so complete that the boy's world became filled only with the smell of fish and the soft pressure of his mother's cheek. Eventually she released him and, returning to her full height, she looked quizzically at Jóna. In response, she merely shook her head, minutely, tight-lipped. A little gulp of air flared Hrefna's nostrils.

'What have you been up to today, then, my love?'

Árni recounted how he had practiced his counting and learned some letters from the book she had given him for his birthday; how he had listened to his grandmother tell him the story of their old cow that had refused to milk until she was taken over to the lush fields across the water. They walked slowly back to the quayside, passing the last of the fish laid out on the concrete slabs. The boy counted to ten for his mother, and asked why they no longer had a cow. Unsatisfied by her answer, Árni petitioned both mother and grandmother about the merits of getting a new cow, one that he could look after; soon he had begun to speculate over the name he would give it. And all the while, the women looked out to sea.

Jóna rocked the boy in her arms, as much for her comfort as for his. It was late and Árni should have been in his bed hours before. But no-one wanted to be alone, nor craved the empty canvass of sleep onto which terrors could be painted. Even Eiríkur, exhausted and beaten in the other room, wrapped in every blanket the house possessed, did not sleep. Instead he watched his wife stoke the sitting room fire while he sucked at steaming spoonfuls of fish stew. His eyes were wide, so that his mind, in darkness, did not take him back to the sea.

It had taken him thirteen attempts to start the outboard motor. His frozen, red-raw hands screamed with every pull of the cord, and the cold set into his sodden clothes, bored its way into his flesh, through to the bone. His conscious will had left him, sunk with his father in the endless greyness below, but the same animal force that had pushed him to the surface breathed life into the spark that burst the vapour that turned the crank that propelled *Tófa* into calmer waters, towards the shore and life.

Had it been a month before, he would have been dead by now, the cold of the air finishing the work of the sea. But the late spring afternoon was kind and, although his body still quaked now by the fire, he was able to bring *Tófa* into the harbour before darkness fell completely. His mother had been waiting for him at the quayside, had helped his wracked body out of the boat and onto the land, had wrapped him tightly in her shawl, had rubbed his hands and his face until the blood-fire surged. She had not asked the question that Eiríkur could not answer and instead they stood, clutching each the other, sobbing their relief and their despair into the empty air.

The doctor had been and gone, leaving clear instructions for Hrefna. The boy had stood in the doorway while his father had been examined. He had watched the doctor take the patient's temperature and pulse, had asked him simple questions to which even Árni knew the answers. When he had left, Eiríkur beckoned for his son; Árni hesitated only briefly before plunging himself, sobbing, into the blankets that cocooned his father, never resting until his face found the coarse certainty of Eiríkur's beard. He had stayed there until his mother had pulled him away, so that she might feed her husband a little fish. Jóna had taken Árni to the warmth of the kitchen range, to sing lullabies to her grandson and to allow her son and his wife to their quiet rejoicing at their safe reunion.

Clumps of grey-white cloud scudded across the blue sky. The rain had cleared while he had slept, pushed northwards by the blustering wind; the same wind tugged at his clothes and at the tuffets surrounding him. In the house, Eiríkur slept on, watched over by Jóna. With his mother at the processing plant, Árni had been left to himself and he had slipped out of the kitchen door and into the little field behind the house. He had found a partial hollow from which to watch the clouds race by.

He had no memory of falling asleep, or of finding his way to his bed, and he had woken easily, despite the bright and vivid dreams that had gripped the night. Below, he had heard hushed voices and the pieces of yesterday reassembled themselves. When he heard the sound of the door signal that his mother had left for the processing plant, he had panicked, not wanting anyone else to leave the safety of the house. She had not said goodbye to him, just as his grandfather had not the previous morning.

From beyond the fence, he could hear the lowing of his neighbour's cows. Mr Baldursson preferred to find his living on dry land and kept a few animals by the house as well as sheep on the fells. Not for the first time, Árni envied his neighbour. He wanted to go to the fence, to hold out handfuls of grass for the beasts, but he would not allow himself such pleasures. He set his face into a hard frown and stared out to the sea.

Under the bright morning sun, the water was a rich blue, spotted with a thousand white points and blotched with the shadows of clouds that ran across its surface. In the distance, he could see the thin green strip that framed the fjord to the north. Somewhere between here and there, his grandfather was lost, unable to find his way home. Nearer, in the harbour, the few boats that had not already set out for the day were stirring, bobbing under the weight of crew, of gear being loaded. He wondered how they could continue as if nothing had happened, as if no tragedy had occurred, no loss had been sustained, and he hated them for it. But most of all he hated the sea; hated it so that he would not have to admit his fear of it; hated it so that it might let his father be.

2001

While his father fumbled with his cigarette, Árni stared out at the sea. On a day like this, it was hard to believe the vindictiveness of the fjord, so placid and deep was its blue. But August had always been a misleading month, hiding its anger under a sunny smile; even the summer rain, when it came, was self-effacing. And the rain would surely come, making this hour of golden warmth, of vivid green and blue, all the more precious.

'He's a beautiful boy, son. You must be very pleased. Has the look of my father, I think.'

Eiríkur's lighter sparked into life, cupped by weathered hands. His first inhalation collapsed into a cluster of sporadic coughs, which three short thumps to the chest did little to chase away. He tried again, holding the smoke this time without interruption. His teeth were yellowing, but there was only a little white in his beard. Not yet sixty years old, but the life that had hardened him had also marked him. His hands were scarred, the nails coarse, and the skin about his eyes was like beaten leather. Another cough, and then a thin wheezing.

'You're still going out then.'

Árni nodded at the sea. It was not a question, simply an acceptance of an unwelcome truth. He would rather that his father no longer fished at all, let alone that he did so still from the open hull of *Tófa*, with her unreliable motor and heavy oars. He sent home a little money each month so that his father no longer needed to risk himself on the water, but he knew that it was not the need for money that took his father onto the fjord.

'Of course. Someone has to put fish in the pot, money in the kitty. It's what a man does: provide. I feel badly enough that your mother has to go out to work.'

Hrefna had a job in the new supermarket in the village, something which he knew she cherished beyond her wage. Even so, her earnings, fattened by the modest stipend that Árni provided, meant they would be able to keep body and soul together, without the dangers of the sea. His father could get a job as a foreman at the processing plant, if only for his pride's sake, but there was no telling him. He would fish for as long as he could, until illness or death prevented him.

The cows in the neighbouring field announced themselves, bringing a welcome smile to Árni's face. That Siggi Baldursson still kept livestock was inexplicably pleasing to him. The cows' gentle presence provided a continuity, a connection with this place that he did not associate with loss. He watched their brown flanks nudging across the turf beyond the fence, the relentless grinding of their jaws, the flicking of tongues and tails; their smells and sounds laced the morning air with drowsiness. Árni realised he was smiling and that his father was following his gaze.

'We had a cow, back when I was a boy. A beautiful beast. There is something extravagant about a cow.'

Eiríkur's words frayed into the burr of the day, leaving an indistinct space between the men, a jumble of sharing and hiding, of intimacy and exclusion. Árni looked again to Baldursson's field, tried to imagine his father, his grandfather, tending to a cow. The image was too absurd, and he shook it from his head.

'Glæta. She was called Glæta. Once, when I was a boy, we rowed her over there. Stayed the summer. The three of us. And Glæta, of course.'

Eiríkur sucked hard on what was left of the cigarette, twisting the stub into the damp turf as he exhaled. With the same movement, he plucked the packet from his shirt pocket and tapped first a lighter, then a fresh cigarette from the upturned carton. As he always did, he offered the packet to Árni and, as always, his son declined with a sigh and a brief shake of the head. Eiríkur watched through the blue haze of smoke.

There had been a time when the boy had hung on his coat tails, tight as a shadow. Now he seldom came home. He had barely returned to Bolungarvík since his departure for the city: a handful of Christmases, a few summer visits, to help with paperwork or to introduce a wife, a daughter, and now a son. But he never stayed more than a few days, blaming work. It had been his explanation for missing his grandmother's funeral too.

Eiríkur had never understood quite what it was that Árni did, but he had never been less than proud of him. His only concern was that he was shut away in a laboratory all day, instead of being outside in the air. He thought about the boy who had spent whole summers outside; whole weeks without a roof, fetching Baldursson's sheep down from the fells while Eiríkur was out on the water, hauling fish from the fjord alone. It had been his decision, of course, and Árni had protested at first. But soon the boy had settled into his life on land and he had turned his back on the sea on his own terms. His son had found his own path, one that did not allow for the father to follow.

*'I was thinking. Maybe we could both take **Tófa** out onto the fjord tomorrow, see if I still know how to handle oars. Maybe we could take one of the cows.'*

Árni nodded towards the fence with a laugh. Eiríkur looked at his hands. The hands were clumsy shovels wrapped in salt-bleached leather, arrived from who knew where. He barely felt the cigarette between his calloused fingers. He smoothed the left palm along his thigh, felt its weight, until it rested on his knee. He squeezed, felt the tendons snarl under the pressure.

'It was a fine summer. With the milk that Glæta gave, your grandmother made curd cheese, flavoured it with bilberries. Your grandmother doted on you, when you came along. But you know that.'

Eiríkur's left hand rummaged through the tight-sprung shrubs, hunting by instinct for bilberries, his eyes fixed on the horizon. Árni breathed two short breaths, unsure if it had been meant as a rebuke, or a simple observation. It stung him nonetheless.

'So, what do you say? Shall we take to the water tomorrow?'

Eiríkur looked from his son to the sky, slipping into his mouth a small glossy berry as he did so.

'The weather should be fair, at least. Why not? If your arms are still up to the task. This is not inside work, you know.'

He tipped a clutch of berries from his palm into his mouth and chewed. Árni imagined the tart juice across his tongue, felt a welling in his own mouth, and looked to the shrubs about his place on the turf. None revealed their fruit to him, nor even differentiated themselves, species from species, that he might focus his search. When he had been a child, he had known which plant would give bilberries, which wild strawberries, and which stone brambles. He had known which weeks of the year would yield the sweetest fruit. Even as an adolescent, when dreams of the city and another life had already been seeded within him, he had remained connected to these hills, this shore. It was startling now to understand how fast and how far that connection had attenuated.

He felt his father's eyes on him, felt their curiosity, as if he were being studied for some clue as to what he had become, for some trace of his lost son. Unable to meet his gaze, Árni looked along his leg, stretched across the turf, his eyes coming to rest on the neat bow of his shoe laces. He twitched his toes, felt the movement ripple up and down through sinew and muscle. Árni knew enough to understand that virtually every atom in his body had been replaced in the time since he had boarded the bus for Reykjavík more than a decade before; that this body, now absorbing the golden warmth of the day, was not the same body that had awkwardly embraced his father at the bus station; this throat was not the throat through which he had spoken his goodbyes to his mother; and these were not the eyes that had seen his grandmother for the last time, waving from the door, as he strode off, clutching his stiff new passport, into the world.

Something caught at the back of his throat and he looked over to his father in search of an anchor. Instead of the imagined curiosity, he saw his father's body stretched out, eyes closed, fringed by grass. Only the heavy rise and fall of his chest, the whisper of drowsy breath, signalled that he was still present. Árni smiled and, without a sound, said the thing he had never before been able to tell his father.

■

A clock ticked somewhere behind her, measuring the slow passage of the day from its unseen shelf. Charlotte had not noticed it when she had entered the room, and so instead could only imagine its shape, the sweep of dark wood around a dirty white face, the curling hands moving slowly, so slowly, in their endless race. She wondered how much time had passed since her husband and father-in-law had slipped out into the bright morning.

She wriggled slightly in her seat and felt the air dragging through her sinuses. Hrefna looked up at the sound and smiled sweetly. Neither woman had mastered much of the other's language, and so they had sat in well-meaning silence, their focus upon the children. It was not so different in Camberley, of course, where the afternoons spent with her own mother had long lost any other focus, and only the frequency of those meetings allowed for the transmission of particles of information about other matters.

Freyja played quietly on the sitting room rug, twisting the arms and legs of a plastic doll, seeking out the most pleasing arrangement; Ben slept in his grandmother's arms oblivious to her cooing. Hrefna knew sufficient English to ensure that her guest had enough to eat and drink, but there were only so many cups of the startling coffee that could be consumed by someone brought up elsewhere. Charlotte had handed over her baby to Hrefna's waiting arms so that she would not need to decline a third.

She listened to Hrefna's gently trilling voice without comprehension, unsure if the sounds had meaning as well as kindly intent. Ben slept on, untroubled by the attention. Charlotte wondered why she knew so little of her husband's language. She had a degree in English and Spanish, and had for years taken night classes to maintain her French and Italian. Yet this had not equipped her with the energy or aptitude to learn Icelandic. On both previous visits to Bolungarvík, she had left resolved to learn more, but that resolve had melted like snow by the time the plane had reached Heathrow and she had packed her good intentions away with the suitcases. She was a graduate, a linguist and an editor, and yet this fisherman's wife at the edge of the world had to scramble through her limited English in order that they might understand one another at all.

Ben wriggled, stretched, began to gurgle in a way that suggested some discomfort may soon lead to tears. Hrefna looked up, catching Charlotte's eye with a smile, a twinkle, a sprightly mischief, and once again she could discern the origins of her daughter's elfishness. While Hrefna rocked the baby, settling him in a few short movements, Charlotte felt an unusual warmth in this wordless communion and wrapped herself in its embrace, grateful that it erased her muteness, if only for a time. Once again, she vowed to learn Icelandic.

Freyja had given up her attempts to find a configuration of arms and legs that would allow the doll to stand unaided. Instead she practised her braiding on the tiny head, the coarse nylon hair resisting her clumsy fingers, until this too became unsatisfying and she clambered to her feet and up onto the settee beside her mother. Her return awoke in Charlotte a sudden desire to have her children with her, close by; she held out her arms to where Hrefna still cradled Ben, and asked as best she could for her baby.

Beyond the little sitting room, the scrape of wood on wood and the muffled thud of feet announced the men's return. Charlotte turned hopefully, too obviously, towards the door. Árni saw both women, mother and wife standing hunched, his son offered up by the one, the other frozen with arms outstretched. They held their pose for a moment, hung like a scene by a Dutch master, the angled sunlight accenting the confusion of relief and resentment on Charlotte's face, until the rasp of Eiríkur's voice snagged time awake once more.

Her husband's question spurred Hrefna into motion and she passed Ben into his mother's arms and smoothed her skirt before slipping from the sitting room and into the kitchen. The sound of running water and the clank of pans soon began to babble, as Árni and his father stood awkwardly in the centre of the room. Eiríkur looked from baby to son before asking, at far too great a length, if he might be allowed to hold his grandson.

'Have you told your father your news?'

They had settled into the sitting room, Eiríkur taking his wife's place, Árni beside his own on the little settee, daughter on his knee. The broken exchange of questions and statements about Ben had become stilted, circular. It had demanded too much of her, given too little. A change of topic, even if she would understand only the substance, not the words to be used, was needed. Árni's frown and curt shake of the head lasted only a moment, interrupted by his father's question, framed in cheerful expectancy.

With a sigh, Árni rehearsed the details of the new research project he had established within the university, thanks to a major grant from a pharmaceutical company, explaining as simply as he could the nature of the work he would be doing. He spoke mechanically, without animation, certain that his father would grasp neither its significance nor implications. Eiríkur's understanding of biology extended little beyond the rudiments of infection and the mechanics of procreation. Years before, Árni had tried to explain his research, but the fact that certain cells within the brains of rats lit up when the animals entered familiar places had seemed arcane, the experiments with tiny mazes frivolous. That he would now be working with human subjects seemed unlikely to unlock his father's understanding, so he simply explained that there was a possibility that this work might hold the key to understanding memory and its loss, might lead to a cure for the terrible diseases that robbed people of their past, and of their present.

Charlotte watched, surprised by the tone of her husband's voice in relating the familiar story. At home, with friends and colleagues, even with her own family, Árni had been illuminated by the opportunity of the new project, the confirmation that he was one of a very few people active in perhaps the most exciting work in his field. But here, with his own father, there was none of the breathless pace of delivery, the frenetic hands were still, as was his whole body, stiff within the angle of the settee. In Cambridge, he had had to fight the pride bursting in his chest, but there was no risk of self-regard in this flat delivery.

Across the room, Eiríkur received that news with nodding encouragement, a hesitant smile struggling to meet what he was sure should have been his son's happiness. Charlotte watched his eyes, looking for whatever it was that gave her husband reason to withhold his excitement. But there was nothing, just love and a reticent sadness. She felt an anger at Árni, that it was he denying his father the full measure of the happy satisfaction to which he was entitled. Árni's bloodlessness could only be read as a denial, an injustice.

'Have you told him the best bit? About the interview?'

It was not what Árni believed to be the best part, but she realised a feature interview in a national newspaper would both be readily graspable by Eiríkur and would unleash Árni's bashfulness, which always appeared as excitement. Sure enough, he began to colour up instantly, his eyes dropping, flickering over a restless smile. Eiríkur leaned even closer in his chair, repeating as a question the word he only half understood, eyes sparkling.

He had heard of *The Times*, of course, if not of its Sunday sibling, but the qualification did not diminish the impact. He called to the kitchen, an excited sentence that clattered pots and drew Hrefna back into the room. Her hands were still smoothing an apron embroidered with a curling floral motif as she listened to the account of her son's triumph. For several moments, Eiríkur and Hrefna exchanged son and grandson, embracing each in turn. Their daughter-in-law watched on, clutching Freyja as she squirmed to be set free to return to the carpet and the unfinished business of braiding her doll's hair.

It was good to be back on tarmac. The newly surfaced road began just before Ísafjörður town appeared, the bright buildings clustered on a spit of gravel that reached almost across the fjord itself; masts swayed in the harbour that sheltered behind it. The road snaked around the bay, past the airfield and then around the headland, leaving his childhood behind him, obscured by mountains. The tarmac too disappeared and he drove carefully again over gravel. It hissed and ticked, chinking the underside of the car, every sound drawing flinches and anxious frowns from Charlotte.

All the roads, the good ones at least, had been like this when he had taken the bus to Reykjavík for the first time, to begin the adventure that had led him to England and to Charlotte. In the city of course the streets had been paved, and by the time he reached Cambridge he was no more surprised by tarmac than any of his fellows. Gravel roads, gravel highways, were just one other oddity about his origins, one other thing that set him apart, that distinguished him. He was bilingual: able both to smile at Charlotte's discomfort and to empathise.

From the back seat, Freyja stared wide-eyed at the falling land and stretching sea while her baby brother slept. Árni watched her in the rearview mirror and tried to see this landscape through her eyes, to capture her wonder at the shapes and textures of their surroundings, to understand her fascination with the bleakness of these edge-lands. As a child he had felt an affinity with the ruggedness and solitude, but with adolescence the place had seemed ever more drab and desolate. He had needed to leave, to find light and life elsewhere. Escape still seemed to be the right impulse, even now.

The oncoming car and Charlotte's gasp made Árni realise that he had been drifting. He slowed to let the other pass more easily: the young man behind the wheel wore his disinterest like contempt. Árni watched the freckled paintwork recede in the mirror as he again picked up a little speed. They rounded the headland and the sunshine caught the white dome of the Dranga glacier across the bay, its crisp brilliance masking the dirty blue that lay beneath; flat-topped mountains slipped away to the sea, black rock patched with snow, beached orcas basking in the blue light.

'That's pretty.'

It struck him as odd that he could not tell whether Charlotte's tone signified sarcasm or admiration. In the eight years that they had been together, he had come to understand many of Charlotte's subtleties: when a smile said what it meant; when flowers would elicit genuine joy; when not to express an opinion about her brother's behaviour. The clear cut voice remained a mystery however. There was something placeless, bloodless, about her intonation that seemed designed to strip away any meaning beyond its surface. While his grasp of the language's idioms and absurdities was almost native, the word 'pretty' remained ambiguous, especially on Charlotte's tongue. It troubled him, of course, that he could not always be sure that his wife meant what she said, but he had now reconciled himself to a life of dissonance.

'They make a racket. When the ice shears off especially. A really hideous, booming, cracking sound. Terrifying. Best seen from a distance.'

The road swept down into the mouth of the next fjord, skirting the water's edge. Only a low stone wall separated them from the languid movements of sea and kelp. Some few houses gathered along the land side, blind spectators to their progress. Árni took another glimpse of the glacier in the mirror. One day, he'd take Ben up onto one; let him hear its monstrousness for himself. If there was any ice left by then, of course.

'What's that?'

Charlotte was pointing out into the bay. The flat water was studded with grey lumps, boulders. Moving boulders.

'Hey! Seals! Shall we stop? Give Freyja her first sight of seals?'

Árni was already pulling off the road, into a parking place next to the sea, the car's nose pointing out over the water. Another car was parked alongside, its passengers disgorged, pointing cameras excitedly towards the seals basking on the low rocks some fifty metres distant: the little white church, with red windows and a red roof, was ignored by everyone. Except Árni. While Charlotte unclipped the children from their respective harnesses, he gazed at the church, distracted. It was the church where his parents had been married. It was the church where his grandfather and grandmother had been married, albeit when it had been in a different place. He had been brought here often; while the church at Bolungarvík had served for regular worship, the family had always come to Súðavík for more meaningful occasions, such as his own christening.

When time allowed, his father would make a pilgrimage to this small and simple wooden building, to remember the family's origins and to show that the church still belonged to them and to the other people of Hesteyri, in defiance of the bishop that had permitted its removal and relocation. His father still railed against the thievery of the priests in Reykjavík who had smothered any hope of return with their gift of that which did not belong to them.

The day before, in the field above the house, his father had talked about the past, about the summer he had spent with his own father, in Hesteyri, in the place of his birth. He had been 14 years old, on the cusp of adulthood. Watching his father remembering his grandfather and the places they had shared had dragged his heart back again, anchored him briefly to this place, to the shore and the sea. Yet even then, drenched in the August sun and his father's quiet nostalgia, Árni had been unable to see the magic that danced before his father's eyes. He looked at the little church, with some hope that its clapboard walls would kindle in him some sense of a past he had left behind. The green slopes beyond slid to the bright sea across the fjord, but his heart barely stirred. Something was lacking in him, some missing piece. His wife found beauty here, these tourists too; his parents of course also saw in these bare hills more than empty turf and harsh stone, but Charlotte had been weaned among the demure hedgerows of Surrey. This landscape had no call on her affection, there was no duty owed, and yet she felt something for this bright vastness that to him was simply a flat featurelessness. It was not a new thought, but it struck him, there beside the little church, that maybe something was broken within him. It was not the land that was empty, but himself.

Behind him, the cooing of his wife and the stuttering excitement of his confused daughter carried on the clean air. He wanted to join them, to point out the way that seals lay on their sides, a flipper in the air as if they were waving to shore. But he could not find the will to pull his searching gaze from the church, its low tower and the red corrugated iron of its roof. He knew the story too well, how the church had been loaded, piece by piece onto boats and carried from the empty village and brought here, but Árni had never felt the slow burning anger at the theft, had never quite understood how this place linked him irrevocably to Hesteyri, to the past.

1952

Einar watched the sun grow fat and red above the far horizon. An evening breeze skidded over the placid sea and *Tófa* rocked gently in its wake. The spring air still held the chill of winter. With a sigh, Einar looked into the case containing too few fish. With a weary hand, he trailed the line into the water behind him and took up the oars, pulling steadily once more towards the channel, despite the gathering dusk.

Without Páll Heimisson, the task was harder. Einar needed to pause his rowing frequently, to shift to the back of the boat so that he could let out more line, then scuttle back across the thwarts to take up his place at the oars, cursing. Heimisson had left weeks before, as soon as the season allowed. Others too had left, as they had each year since the war, since the herring plant had closed. Only 40 souls or so remained in Hesteyri, a few more at Aðalvík, a single family at Sæból. Each winter was a harsh reminder and each spring another family began muttering, planning and packing. When Ólafur had died, two winters before, Jóna had implored him to take heed, to consider Eiríkur's future, to contemplate leaving. But how could he leave? With his son and his father in this ground, how could he live elsewhere?

When his grandfather had landed in Hesteyri, there had been more than twice the number of inhabitants that clung yet to the fragile turf. By the time that the whaling station closed, the population had grown still further, and the herring processing plant that replaced it brought ever more people. In summer there could be almost two hundred people in the village and Einar remembered how it bustled when he was a boy. His father was already fishing from *Tófa* by then and his mother and sister worked in the plant; they had money, and lamb for the feast days. They were all dead now, of course, but they had worked unbearably hard to find their footing on this narrow strip of land, and their bones were as much a part of it as the stern crags of Kagrafell.

The sea wore copper freckles to the west. Einar stowed the oars and hauled the line back into *Tófa*. A few of the hooks were empty, but from most a fat char writhed, pink belly twisting and thrashing to be free. He whistled as he worked; it was some tune he had heard years before, half-remembered, and he stumbled and extemporised and found once more the melody, working the notes in circles, weaving them like a charm. He worked cheerfully, thoughtlessly, and the sun was down by the time the case was full and the line carefully wound. He would have to work into the darkness for some weeks more, until the days lengthened. But he needed no light to guide him back to Hesteyri. He had spent a lifetime hanging over this seabed, unseen yet familiar. He knew from his father how the water would pull at any point, and so knew the point he was at by the way the water pulled. He would be safe ashore before the stars had set firmly in their mantle.

The sea glugged and gurgled between the rocks along the shoreline, spilling over itself, leaving shreds of discarded hawser and other detritus draped over the slick basalt, or forlorn on the thin grey sand. Sometimes there were bottles, but he had never found one containing a message. Once he had found a dead body here at the margin, washed from some unknown ship, a stranger finding land too late, and the dreadful excitement haunted Eiríkur still.

He bent to pick another piece of drift wood from where it lay and carried it to his trolley, stacking it with the others. Not quite full, but soon; his chores for the day would be done then and he would be able to seek out the other children, who would be playing football in the pasture above the village. There were barely enough of them for a single team, and so they simply chased whoever had the ball, hacking at their ankles until the ball had been won and the chase began again with new quarry.

The Pálsson brothers had been the best players in Hesteyri, and Bjarki had made sure that there had been some rules to their playing, had insisted on goals being marked out and teams being formed. But since they had left, along with three other children, the games had become purposeless, haphazard. Aimlessly, Eiríkur kicked through a clump of flowers, scattering their severed heads across the grassy slope. From the other end of the bay, the sound of wrenching and splintering boomed from the snout of the glacier, reminding him of his task like a factory siren. He skipped and skittered back towards the shore, scouring its fringe for timber scrubbed white by the workings of the ocean. Soon he had gathered eight more pieces and he looked at the stack with satisfaction.

As he made his way home, the laden trolley dragged heavily through the sward. Its little wheels had become clogged with grassy garlands and would no longer turn. Yet despite his burden, his heart fluttered with pride when he pictured his bounty stacked in the wood pile; the more so when he thought of the whole trunk he had found, beached like a petrified whale a little way up the shore. These trees often found their way to Hornstrandir, dropped like matchsticks by the winter storms. His father had told him that they came from the forests of Siberia, felled trunks that had escaped the loggers. This one was as fat as Father Guðjónsson. He would stay up to show his father when he returned that evening from the sea, and he would carry the axe for him, so that he could break it into logs for the winter's fire. As he dragged the trolley, he practiced his whistling, sounding enough of the notes to make something like a tune.

His whistling stopped abruptly. His father was there, standing alongside his mother, hanging fish on the frame in the drying shed beside the house. Eiríkur checked, but the sun was still high in the sky; it was his father that was early, rather than he who was late. Curiosity outdid his pleasure at seeing his father, who had been returning from the sea after Eiríkur was supposed to be asleep for weeks now. He paused briefly by the yellow gorse to consider the mystery before setting off as fast as his strength would allow, pulling the cart down the shallow slope towards the house.

'You must do as you see fit, Einar my love, of course. But please do think of Eiríkur when you speak tonight. I ask only that, no more.'

His mother's voice carried beyond the drying shed to the wood pile, where Eiríkur carefully, silently, stacked the timber he had gathered, keener to overhear than to be lauded for his work. Yet, despite his care, his father's reply was lost beneath the cry of a tern, hanging on the air above the shed, seeking a way into where the fish waited. The boy too turned to peer through the slatted walls to where his parents faced each other, no longer concerned with their work. But there were no clues to the meaning of things in either their faces or their movements and Eiríkur stared too long, and his wide bright eyes drew his mother's attention like a beacon.

'Eiríkur. Good, you're back. We're having supper early today because your father and I have to go to the church this evening. Now, go and wash your hands.'

The boy complied silently. There would still be time surely to show his father the tree trunk, to watch his axe bite into the silver flesh, feel its thud through the turf, to wonder at the strength of the man, at the strength that must surely come with time to him too. The business at the church would not take so long. It was not a Sunday, so the pastor would have no claim on his father's time. It would be a meeting about nothing of importance, soon dealt with and forgotten.

The snow-flecked ridge hung more heavily over the village than the season would suggest, but the people of Hesteyri barely raised their heads towards it as they coalesced around the little red-roofed church, pulled like iron filings to a magnet. The thin clanking of the bell spilled from the tower, measuring the progress of the 28 members of the congregation that remained. The pastor stood on the steps, his black cassock stark against the bright white of the clapboard wall, the door's blood red. He greeted each in turn with a slow smile, which most returned; others grinned and spoke with the effervescence of a tumbling beck, while still others could only find it in them to offer a curt nod of recognition. With such a nod, Einar guided Jóna into the church.

The burr of conversation within further unsettled Einar and he took his seat without lingering to exchange more than brief pleasantries with his neighbours. From his place, he surveyed the empty spaces that had multiplied in recent years. Páll Heimisson had sat just behind with his wife and sons, but no-one now took those seats. Einar studied his hands, the nicks and calluses, the reeded nails and clumsy knuckles. With those hands he had built a home for his family, pulled slick silver life out of the cold hard sea. This labour marked him, was the badge of his inheritance; an inheritance that would surely blur to dust with the passing of the evening.

The bell stopped its clanking and the murmurs of the world were shut out with the closing door. Boards complained under Father Guðjónsson's footsteps, their groans left exposed by the hush of the congregation. All eyes followed the black-backed pastor as he proceeded to the altar, expectant. They knew of course what was to transpire. Even before the meeting was called, its purpose had been the current beneath every conversation exchanged throughout that summer, pulling thoughts from their spoken course. A neighbour had asked after a sickly child, and both knew the real intent carried by the question. Would they stay?

'Friends. I want to thank you for your time, for gathering in this way. We have a difficult decision to make this evening. No-one carries this lightly, regardless of their inclination. So I ask only that we conduct ourselves as neighbours, as friends.'

The pastor had not taken his usual place in the pulpit to speak, but instead leant against the end of the empty first pew, where Sigurðsson had sat until the previous summer. His face was calm, open, his eyes imploring as they cast slowly across the assembly. A cough was stifled somewhere behind, and Einar waited.

'Before we come to a decision, I think that it would be right to air all views on the matter. It is not my place to direct you, and I have no view myself: I go where God calls me and if that is to serve this congregation here in Hesteyri, or in some other place, then so be it. The choice must be yours. So I invite you, if anyone wishes to speak, to say your piece. With courtesy, of course, and with care.'

A pew bowed and flexed, and Einar turned to see Haraldur Jónsson rise to his feet. They had fished together, played football as boys, had endured the same winters; and when Ólafur had died two years past, it had been Jónsson's wife Hildur that had watched over Jóna in her grief. But even before the words stumbled from his lips, Einar had already seen in his flickering eyes the depth of weary surrender that haunted him. He listened as Jónsson spoke of the hardships his family had endured these ten years: he had worked hard on the road that the government had paid for, but there was little enough purpose to it and too little money. There had been such hope after Independence, even with the herring gone and the plant closed, but that hope had petered out with the road in the snowfields under Kagrafell.

Jónsson stuttered to his conclusion. It was surely time to abandon Hesteyri to the wind and ice, to find warmth and work across the fjord, in Ísafjörður or Bolungarvík or Súðavík; to leave the fjords for good, to find an easier life in Hólmavík, or in the city itself; they had done enough, given enough, lost too much. Einar could feel Jónsson's eyes on his back as firmly as he felt Jóna's hand on his. Others rose, emboldened by Jónsson's testimony. Men and women took their turn to lay out their litanies of misery, to reassure themselves as much as their neighbours that there was no shame in surrender. The mother who had lost her first born in the snows of late spring, who feared for the child within her; the man over from Aðalvík whose brother and nephew he had watched sink beneath the fractured sea while they scraped the waters to feed their children; memories of endless winters, lived under a pall of ice and want, while the storms beat through the bay, pinning down the village, immobile.

'What are we that would let the wind drive us from our homes?'

Einar did not look about the church, but kept his eyes fixed on his hands, knotted and twisting. He knew his wife watched breathless, anxious both that he should speak and at what he might say. He knew also that all the others were watching, that the pastor too looked on, but he saw none of them.

'Two years since I buried my son. Two years. Two years before that, we met like this, and we agreed that those of us that chose to leave should do so, with the blessing of the community, with no blame. Do you not think that I have often lain awake thinking of what I might have done, how I might have saved him from the fever, the hunger? But my father too, buried next to my Ólafur – our Ólafur – is in the same ground. This ground. Our ground. We all have loved ones buried here. We have all suffered, all gone hungry, all worked our hands and hearts red-raw. If we leave Hesteyri, will that count for nothing?'

The catch in his voice was fleeting, submerged in a pause and a heavy breath. Behind him bodies shifted with unease, wool and leather sighing against wooden boards; a throat rasped, but no-one spoke for some little while. Einar looked up, turned so that he might see the others, and be seen by them. The faces that he had known his whole life, or that he had seen new-born, no longer seemed familiar. Hesteyri was already no more.

'Friends, I say this not to spoil your plans. We will vote and I will respect that vote. If you all leave Hesteyri, then we will leave too. But there must be a vote. We cannot abandon our lives without at least being clear that, together, we are making that decision.'

One or two mumbled their support, but none rose to their feet. Einar dropped to his seat and let Jóna stroke his cheek, squeeze his arm. The pastor was already standing, thanking those that had spoken, and inviting further contributions. None came. When the vote was called, every hand but one was raised for leaving. Jóna's eyes filled with apologies as she joined the others.

■

The lengthening night had already announced the coming of

winter: by ten it was too dark to find the axe in among the wood still stacked behind the house. Snow flurries already scuttled over the hills, filling the passes, the valleys, licking at the edges of the village, of the sea. There, in the darkness of a late August night, the water glimmered with cold luminescence, as if the summer's light had been scuttled in the bay. Einar watched these ghost shoals ebb and flow beyond the red glow of his pipe. Unseen, Eiríkur watched his father and was in turn watched by his mother from the kitchen window.

The night had made further work impossible for another day and so Einar had slipped down to the shore, to bathe in the air of these dying hours. Soon it would be gone: Hesteyri, the life he had known, the ever-present hand of his father on his shoulder. They had agreed that they should settle in Bolungarvík, a smaller town than Ísafjörður, a compromise between comfort and what was comfortable. On a clear day, from the flanks of Kistufell, you could make out the bulk of Ernir, the mountain that hung above Bolungarvík. Einar had found the thought of living within sight of the familiar mountain reassuring. They would farm and fish, and Eiríkur would be able to go to school. Jóna could work in the fish plant: there would be money; there would be electricity. But there would not be this. Einar grasped a fistful of mossy turf in the darkness, pulling it from the ground beside his boot.

'Forgive me if I am intruding. I saw your pipe from the beach. I was walking a little. Feeling the sand, listening to the hush of the sea, before... before the winter.'

Had Einar been able to make out the pastor's face in the starless gloom, he would have seen the embarrassment he could only hear. The air moved and the dark shape shifted until it was seated on the ground next to Einar. His face flashed in the match-light and then was gone once more, leaving only the red tip of a cigarette.

A moment passed before smoke whistled out through the pastor's gnarled teeth and into the still air.

'*You spoke well, Einar. At the meeting. Many of us were moved, truly moved. I came here recently, have no family ties with Hesteyri, but even I could feel the pull of the land in each man in the church. If there was work, not one of them would want to leave. It is only the winters and the lack.*'

He paused at this point, to draw again on the cigarette, to lose himself in his private thoughts, never specifying what it was that was lacked. He did not need to. Einar knew as keenly as anyone what was denied to men on this strip of land: warmth, comfort, and full bellies. Medicine too.

'*Was it selfishness, do you think? My stubbornness? That took Ólafur from me? If I had gone with the first of them, taken the bairns to the town, got regular work on one of the bigger boats, would God not have taken him? Would I not have been punished?*'

Another crackle from the pastor's cigarette, then an exhalation that was more a sigh of sadness than a simple release of smoke. Einar could hear him lick his lips as he searched for the right words.

'*Einar, God did not punish you, any more than he punished Níels Starrason, when his boy got lost on the fells, hunting ptarmigan three winters back. You remember? We were all hungry that year.*'

Death was indiscriminate, it was true. It visited the blameless just as easily as the guilty. But Einar could not let loose the certainty that had he been among the first to pack his things after the meeting four years earlier, then his son would still be alive. That was clear and the priest could not absolve him. Only in Eiríkur, in seeing him safely into adulthood, here, in Hesteyri, had there been the hope of absolution. If he had been able to show his wife, to show himself, that it had not been the staying itself that had damned Ólafur, only then could he have been forgiven.

The pastor sucked the last of the smoke out of his cigarette, then stubbed it carefully into the dampening turf. It was late: the moon's cloud-glow lightened the sky beyond the fells, casting uncertain silver shadows on the water. A chill ran through both men, and each shifted a little in their place.

'Make a life for your family, Einar. Jóna is a good woman and Eiríkur a fine boy. And you are one of the best of us. You all deserve to find happiness, a future as well as your past. Where will you go, do you think? To Ísafjörður?'

Einar felt the pastor's hand through his oilskin, resting on his shoulder. He did not shake free of the contact, allowed the pressure to seep warmth into him. He flared the last life into his pipe and the match-light caught the pair in their dark conspiracy.

With the beginning of September came the end of Hesteyri. Each day, another family loaded their belongings into their boats. Most had little and simply pulled a tarpaulin over a jumble of stools and buckets and rolled mattresses before they pushed off into the fjord, every eye looking back to the people left on the shore. Some few others had paid the skippers of bigger boats, over from Ísafjörður or Bolungarvík, to carry every stick and bowl, their livestock, even their dismantled houses, almost as if they wished to take every piece of Hesteyri that could be moved; their lives transposed.

Jóna did not know where Einar had found the money, but she was quietly pleased that he had. She liked her house and, while her fondness was not born of a need for some connection to Hesteyri, she only pretended to mind having to sleep in a tent for a couple of nights while her home was broken into panels and planks and stacks. When the last of the fish was dried and packed, the drying shed too was taken down and its timbers loaded onto the *Bjarnarnes*, along with everything else that they owned. Their remaining cow, Glæta, was the last to board, before Einar secured *Tófa* to the larger boat's stern.

The pastor watched on as the motor boat cut a straight line into the fjord, then returned to his task, checking again the storm-bracing on the shutters and the doors of the church. Winter would soon be here. The wind that rushed through the fjord, chasing all before it down from the high pass at Kjaransvíkurskarð, tugged at the fastenings on the windows, scratched at the corners of the red tin roof above him. It rifled through his pockets, shoved him like a bully, yet he could not hate the wind: it was his only company in the now empty village.

The church secure, he walked down towards the jetty, one eye on the sea, anxious for some sign of his salvation. For now, no boat could be seen in the bay, nor even in the channel. He checked his watch. Not yet late, not even nearly. And yet. A tremor passed through him, a fear of being abandoned here, alone, at the start of winter. The wind clattered into him, insistent, remorseless, bringing a sting of light rain.

In the lee of the Jónsson house, the pastor was able to keep a match alight long enough to bring a glow to the tip of his cigarette. He watched the wind snag at the tarpaulin that covered his belongings by the shore, then looked out to the sea once more. The rain was snow now, light enough, like a dusting of icing sugar on a plate of *kleinur*, but the chill sent his hand diving inside the heavy coat to retrieve a flask of schnapps and some dried fish. The boat would be there soon enough, but in the meantime he may as well be as comfortable as the place allowed.

1993

The day was damp. He had every right to expect it to be sunny, as the previous days had been; days through which he had bound himself to his desk, tabulating figures and struggling with the nuance of their English commentary. He had designated this day as his day off at the beginning of the week and he had believed that the fine weather would sustain itself to make up for the unfairness of typing while the sun shone. It was no more than his labours deserved. He had every right to it.

He should have known, of course. Back home, the seasons shifted in moments and his three years in Cambridge had demonstrated amply that the English weather was only a little more reliable. He was a scientist and yet he had ignored the data, favouring blind faith and a sense of entitlement over empiricism. It had not at any time occurred to him that he should change his plans, make one of the five fine mornings his rest day and save his work for the rain; he had not thought to thoroughly interrogate a weather forecast. He pushed down the suspicion that nature was punishing him for his wilfulness and trudged on through the drizzle.

On sunnier days, the city's fabric shone, etched in honey stone and tawny brick, the filigree of the college facades frozen in halcyon days. The day's damp listlessness had dimmed the modest grandeur of the buildings, but at least it had thinned the tourists from the street and he was grateful to be able to make progress without walking in the road. The net of fine rain wrapped across his face like a spider's web.

The picnic, of course, was no longer an option. His consolation was that he had not been more organised in his preparation: he had bought no hummus, no sliced ham, no baguette, nor any of the small round tomatoes that she liked; nothing that he only ate comfortably in the open air, nothing that would spoil waiting for the return of the sun. They could eat in the pub, then maybe watch a film, whatever Charlotte wanted to do. That he still did not know exactly what she would want to do on a damp Saturday in July troubled him. They had been together for over a year, but he was still not so familiar with her complexities that he did not have to ask; he could still not intuit her wants as easily as his own, as surely he should in a relationship such as this. It would come, he did not doubt, but for now he would have to rely on luck and good will. At least her finals were done with and she would still be in a celebratory, carefree, careless mood. Maybe she would be happy after all, simply to stay in the pub.

The door clanked shut behind him and he paused for a moment, watching the rainwater drip onto the mat; from his overcoat pocket, he retrieved a handkerchief and wiped the rest from his face. The disturbance of his movement released from the gabardine a musty dampness, the taint of the charity shop and the coat's previous owner. Árni frowned, wondered if the smell was as apparent to the others in the bar as it was to him, if they would know it was his coat, him, that had brought the mildly unpleasant aroma into their refuge. He decided to hang it from one of the hooks by the door, stuffing his keys and wallet into his jeans pocket.

'Hi Árni! You made it – filthy out isn't it? You know Jenn? And do you remember Laura? I think you met her at that thing at Jesus last Christmas.'

Charlotte was out of her seat, her arm around his neck, her mouth and nose tucked in close to his ear. Árni pulled her closer, such that he could almost hear her body, its voice muffled by the few millimetres of cotton and acrylic that stood between them but audible all the same; he felt her warm breath against his cheek, her lips shape a silent '*Love you*', and he relaxed a little. The embrace broke and Árni raised a vague wave to each of the others at the table. He had no recollection of Laura but told her in any case that it was good to see her again.

It was clear to Árni that he had some catching up to do. The babble of voices, its sudden excitements and crescendos, betrayed as much as did the empty glasses, the cigarette stubs in the ashtray. Jeremy, a gangly red-head with too prominent an Adams apple, placed a pint in front of Árni. He was pleasant enough, another English undergrad along with Charlotte and Jennifer, the product of one of those middling private schools that manage to inculcate both the correct accent and the particular kind of social rigidity without eradicating the self-doubt that seemed to be the main advantage of the grander schools. Árni suspected his main preoccupation was in trying to make Jennifer notice him, although he appeared to lack any idea of how he might achieve that, much less that he never would.

'Another toast. To Lottie!'

Laura was the first to raise her glass, a broad grin revealing a pronounced incisor among straight white teeth, a relic of something in her DNA. Only slowly did Árni realise that all the while she was watching him across the table, even as she led the others in an only slightly tempered cheer, and a haphazard clashing of drinks. Árni joined in tentatively, bemused. Charlotte squeezed his hand and leant it to whisper into his ear. *'I've got a job. Please don't be angry, I wanted to tell you first but I couldn't contain myself and you know Jenn, she can wheedle anything out of anyone so I didn't have a choice really, especially since you were late.'*

Árni was not angry, only a little baffled. He had not known that she had even applied for a job, but now it appeared that she had also had an interview and an offer and had accepted it. He had only been shut away for five days. Maybe it was more, but in any case, surely all that could not have happened in so short a time. '*Congratulations. When did all this happen?*'

Jennifer heard his question and bustled into Charlotte's embarrassed hesitation. '*Isn't it marvellous? She kept it a secret from us, too. Didn't want to jinx anything, apparently. And now, here she is, at the first time of asking: Editorial Assistant at the CUP, no less. First one of the gang to get a job and it's a peach!*'

Despite himself, Árni felt a turn of irritation, felt it rousing itself into the beginnings of anger after all, but he smothered it with the broadest smile he possessed, flashed first to Jennifer, then to Charlotte, then to his pint, half of which he poured wantonly into his throat.

'*I am really excited Árni –never thought I'd land on my feet so soon. And, since I don't have to start for another six weeks, I still get to hang out with these slackers for the summer. And with you.*'

Charlotte submerged herself in the conviviality of her friends. It was not surprising, in the circumstances, but no-one asked him about his thesis, how the final drafting was going, when he thought he might be ready to submit, if it was all in hand. No-one bothered to find out how he felt about it ending, about the imminent loss of this thing that had filled his mind, sleeping and awake, for the last three years; longer, consuming him through much of his time at the university in Reykjavik as well as here. He had been dedicated and diligent, to the exclusion of much he might have wanted, and now it was nearing its termination. The aloneness closed around him, locked him in with the silence of his confinement. And no-one, not even Charlotte, stepped inside to coax him out into the world.

He recognised her this time. She sat at a table in the corner, head in a book, hair falling across her face, yet she was unmistakably Laura; her legs wrapped around themselves awkwardly, a plait of red tights concluded in thick-soled, black leather work shoes. He had not seen her since that drunken afternoon in the Litten Tree, but it was unmistakably Laura.

'Hi. Remember me?'

With a smile, she pushed her empty coffee cup out of the way to make space for her book. It was a novel he did not recognise, one that did not exist in the boxes that Charlotte had decanted from her father's car into the flat that they had rented together at the start of September. Árni felt Laura's quizzical gaze and he remembered himself. He offered her a fresh coffee, asked if she minded if he joined her; she did not, as she still had some time to kill before her shift at the bookshop started. The unrecognised novel was heavy-going: she would welcome the distraction. When he returned with two cups and an oversized biscuit, she pushed out a chair with her untangled foot.

'Cheers. And thanks: I just needed to talk to a human being. To get out of the flat. I've been locked away for days now. It's nearly done. Nearly. But it's driving me mad. I want it finished, over. And yet...'

He did not know what he would do when it was over. His supervisor had begun to talk about postdoctoral research, but nothing was concrete. Everything was fluid, rising and falling with the pull of gravity, of continents, and of Charlotte. Yet the uncertainty was more comfortable than its premature resolution. Ambiguity was infinitely preferable. Even before the PhD was ended, its ghost was preparing to haunt him.

'Hmm. Must be great to have something that you feel that committed to, can invest yourself in. Believe me, working in a bookshop is not why I went to university. Actually, I worked in a bookshop before I went to university. A gap year thing. Funny that nothing much has changed, despite all the effort. Actually, not funny at all. God I envy you. And Lottie. How's that going, by the way? At CUP?'*

Charlotte had been in her job less than two months and the shine had already begun to tarnish a little. She did not say this, but he could see the beginnings of frustration in her eyes, hear the relief of Friday evenings. And because she did not say this, he did not say this, even though the saying of it might help Laura to feel better about her bookshop job. The integrity of Charlotte's choice must matter more to him than the compensation of Laura's: that was the consequence of his own choice.

'Well, I think. I mean, it's a bit frustrating, a little bit routine, you know? I think she already wants to run the place; certainly thinks she could do her boss's job much better. She probably could.'

Laura laughed and her laugh reminded him of the sound of water skittering over stones in a shallow brook. It was a sound without consequences, and its lightness buoyed him unexpectedly. He looked up to find Laura studying his face, her eyes betraying a curious intent. It unnerved Árni a little, something he could not place, name, or control. She did not let her eyes slip from his face, even as she picked up her cup and drained the tepid coffee.

'Look, I need to go. Got to go sell some copies of Diana: Her True Story. But I'm usually in here on a weekday, about this time, if you ever feel the need for some company. Maybe you can tell me about your thesis. Or about what it's like to grow up somewhere it never gets dark.'

Árni watched her disappear, then watched the space around the door that she had vacated for a short while. It was some moments before he noticed that she had left her book. He thought about chasing after her, then decided that he would simply bring it to her tomorrow. He turned it to face him, read the back cover as he sipped the last of his coffee. The important and memorable work of a Czech writer whose name he vaguely recognised. He wondered why he had stopped reading fiction. As a child he had read as much as any of his friends and neighbours. He had imbibed stories from whatever source he could: books, television too, but especially his grandmother, who would sit with him for hours and take him into endless other worlds. It was only once he was a little older, already at school, that he realised she did not read from the book in her hand, but from her memory. Stories flowed through her, brightening and blurring the realities of days beside the unchanging fjord. Once he had settled into his new life in the university, however, the stories left him, lost in the rigour of the laboratory, in the swirl of lights and distraction afforded by the city. Holding Laura's book, feeling the softness of the page edges against his thumb, he tried to recall the last novel he had read. Unable to, he tried instead to release one of the stories told to him by his grandmother, shaking loose ghosts tethered to his home.

The front door rattled shut in the hall and the key scratched at the escutcheon on the door at the bottom of the stairs. Then the steady, certain rhythm of footsteps on the thin carpet clinging to the steps; a breezy '*Hi!*' and the thud of a handbag on the floor next to the kitchen. She ignored the silence that replied. The sound of the tap squeezing the walls dampened the sloshing of water into the sink, a glass, the sink.

As always, the kitchen was clean and tidy, almost puritanical. There was none of the exuberance signified by mess and clutter, no sign that life was lived there. At home with her parents, the pan left cock-eyed in the sink was a frozen moment of the dynamism of the family, a still memento of a meal, a conversation, of laughter. She was pleased that Árni did not entertain the dirt and chaos of the shared houses of her student days, but even so she missed the informality of a plate out of place, or a coffee cup unwashed. She refilled her glass and drank down the chill water, leaving what was left, uncurated, by the sink.

There was no sign of Árni in the spare room either. His computer was lifeless, his books neatly stacked on the desk. Beside the keyboard, a copy of Milan Kundera's *Immortality*. She frowned. It was the only thing on the desk that could be described as out of place, even though its spine was perfectly aligned with the keyboard's edge. Nothing else gave any clues. She was sure that he had said nothing about being out and in any case he was always in when she got home from work, usually here, at his desk. A shrug. Probably he needed to check something at the lab. She went back to the kitchen to check again, but there was no note. Picking up her glass once more, disappointed that no-one would witness her rebellion after all, she padded down the hall to the living room.

Árni was in the armchair, staring into nothing. His eyes were ringed red, his face still swollen although the tears had dried. His fist was wrapped around a glass of clear liquid, the fingers dead like plastic. Her presence filtered into his consciousness and he recovered enough presence to offer a weak smile, then a broader one until only the pink rims of his eyes betrayed the desolation of moments before. He reached out a hand towards her and she was released from her stasis, grateful that he was once more reliably concrete.

Accepting his invitation, she took his hand and settled on the arm of the chair, as close to him as the furniture permitted. Charlotte kissed the top of his head briefly then reached over to take the vodka from his hand. Sliding onto his lap, she asked what this was all about. The smile playing behind her seriousness melted as soon as Árni, crying once more, stumbled through an account of a phone call, of the news of his grandmother's death, sudden, unexpected; of the disarray in his parents' house, of his father's desperate voice, his mother's concern for her husband.

'When my grandfather died, she just turned all of her love onto us: she never complained, never stood on my mum's toes. She just looked after us. Dad, especially, is going to be devastated.' Charlotte stroked his wet cheek but let him continue. *'When I said I was going to study in Reykjavík, she encouraged me, helped me sort things out, while my mum and dad just fussed, tried to discuss the pros and cons with me, fretted – is that the word? When I said I had a place at Cambridge, they went into meltdown. But grandma, she just smiled, told me how proud she was.'*

She knew how proud her own grandparents had been when she had broken the news about Cambridge. But she had lived all her life in Surrey, forty minutes from London, not some village on the edge of the Arctic; her dad had been to Cambridge before her, had beaten the path. Árni was not just the first to have got to Cambridge, he was the first to have completed school, to have left the West Fjords. She could only imagine the pride that that woman had felt. Árni did not often cry, but even these tears seemed restrained in the circumstances.

'When is the funeral? We need to book some flights – I can come with you, can't I? I'd like to. Really.'

■

The sound of the motorbike dissipated, fraying into the street, lost among the burble and gurgle of the city air. It did not intrude, despite its angry, rasping proximity. Nothing intruded: not the faces passing across the street, not the rising pressure of York stone beneath his feet, not the sting of wind-buffeted drizzle. There was only a numbness, an overwhelming relief, the giddying rush of euphoria, and a sudden listless tiredness. This was how submission felt.

Árni looked at his feet. Tired suede soaked up the day's moisture, and a film of water slicked the kerb stone, the tarmac beyond. He realised he was standing at the pavement's edge, as if about to cross, or to jump. He intended to do neither and so he turned away from the faculty office and began to walk into the city centre. It was too early for a beer, and Charlotte was at work in any case. Yet he wanted to mark the occasion, to share it, so that it would not slip past unnoticed. He reached the café before he had acknowledged that this was in fact his destination.

'Hello you. Bit wet?'

She wore her favourite jumper: a thick mossy knit, flecked with shades of green and brown, a fuzzy warmth against the November air. A book rested on her thigh, its pages fanning from her thumb, half way through. It was a new book, different to the one she had been reading four days before. Once again Árni was startled by Laura's capacity for fiction.

'A bit. Anyway, it is done – thesis submitted. Celebratory coffee?'

He was startled by the squeal as much as by the embrace, but both unbalanced him. He felt the strap of his bag slide from his shoulder, catch at his elbow with a jolt, felt it bounce against his calf as Laura swung him with her infectious excitement; he returned the embrace, allowed in her happiness for him, felt the squirming joy at his accomplishment wash over him for the first time. In this moment, there were no longer things to consider, reasons to temper his relief, his pride. There was just the simple, fleeting thing itself: three years' work, built on twenty years before, had come to its point. Whatever revisions would come, whatever dilemmas about what came next dissolved in a rain-damp embrace with a friend.

'That's great! Really. Congratulations. You must be ever so pleased. Especially with... well, with what happened, with your grandmother...'

She had run out of words and so let the sentence dissipate, tightening her embrace instead. Eventually she released him, allowed him to sit, although she kept his left hand cupped between her own. Her look of concern struck him as overwrought, the face someone felt they should make to convey sympathy in these circumstances. Its lifeless composition irked him. But he was pleased that she did not ask the expected question about the funeral. The need to complete his thesis had meant that he had not been able to return home. Had his parents lived in Reykjavík, then it would have been possible, but buses to the West Fjords were extremely unreliable this late in the year. It made perfect sense. It was the rational decision. And yet still the idea haunted him that others would see him as heartless, callous. Even Charlotte had taken some time to accept his reasoning. He did not want that same look of disappointment from Laura and, after accepting her awkward commiserations, he changed the topic so that the focus returned to the here and the now.

'I think we'll go to the pub this evening. To celebrate. You'll come?' Laura paid no regard to the shift in tone and was beaming again, untroubled by her sadness of moments before. *'Of course. But fuck waiting. They're open now – let me buy you some fizz.'* Árni laughed, pleased to see this Laura returned, but his frown soon

reformed. *'What about work? Don't you have to go sell some books?'* Laura watched her empty coffee cup turn in its saucer, with an unconvincing nonchalance. *'I don't work Tuesdays. I was just here, you know, to read and, well, in case you stopped by.'*

He smiled at this. Its implications, whatever way he chose to interpret them, were thrilling. The smiled broadened and he let her lead him out into the drizzle once more, through the slick grey streets and into a pub he had barely noticed before. The grey light of the afternoon seeped in through smeared windows, struggling against the smoke hanging in the air. While Laura went to the bar, Árni scanned the room, searching the few occupied tables for the smokers, before choosing a corner furthest from them. He had always hated the smell of tobacco, even that smoked by his father, even before he was old enough to know of its dangers; the sour smell it left was enough.

Laura returned with a tray. There was no champagne, but two pints of lager and four shot glasses of clear liquid quivered between her hands; the pale skin seemed more fragile than any adult skin should be; almost translucent, smooth and powder soft. They drank down the first, then the second vodka theatrically, each accompanied by an elaborate toast to Árni's triumph. The other customers' good-natured curiosity inspired rather than inhibited them, and after the second drink, Árni bowed low in his seat, his right hand trilling through curlicues made of air. It was three o'clock in the afternoon, a Tuesday, and he was at the centre of a ball of happiness.

As the second pint emptied and the third vodka nibbled at her equilibrium, Laura shifted from the low stool to the banquette, sliding in beside Árni. For a time, they sat, side by side, silently staring out to the darkening street, both forgetting the conversation that had been broken by her move. Something trembled, maybe her, maybe him: Árni could not be sure through the haze of alcohol. To steady things, he suggested another round, but where there should have been an answer, he felt the touch of Laura's soft hand.

'You've got lovely hair, you know? I really like it. Makes you look like a Viking.'

He wanted to explain that his hair had more to do with the fashions of the west coast of the States than the heritage of the West Fjords, more to do with Nirvana than Norsemen, but he didn't want to break her thought, interrupt the intimacy it implied. He enjoyed the sensation of her fingers. It was giddying in its delicacy and he did not want it to stop just yet. He said nothing, but instead turned a quizzical face to hers.

He did not remember her moving towards him, the narrowing of the space between them; even the first pressure of her lips on his could not be recalled. Only her tongue registered, its cool sleekness sending a wave of sensation racing through him, a fizzing surge. And then, as soon as it had become recognisable, he felt the pull of it rushing back to where it had arisen. The duration of the kiss was as indeterminate as its formation. Árni knew it needed to end, that this could not happen, that it was a mistake, but he wanted to cling to its luxuriant sweetness for as long as he could, for as long as was consistent with his resolve, as long as could be excused, if it could be excused at all.

As soon as the kiss ended, as soon as even a pause was reached, there would be a moment of decision: harsh, unavoidable decision. The transgression would be recognised, made concrete, and he would have either to renounce it or to enter fully, consciously into it. He would no longer be able to tell himself, to tell Laura, that this was just a drunken mistake. While he clung to this beautiful, hanging moment, he allowed his hand to fall to her hip, to where her body bent towards him.

And then it was over. Just an inch. But the space between their mouths allowed in more than enough light. He unpeeled himself from her, even as she tried to pull him back. She watched him, eyes flickering across his face, as her confusion faded through embarrassment, then hopefulness, into anger and then hurt. She was shrinking and hardening before him, but did not retreat, her lips still tantalisingly close to his. She would not save him from his decision.

'Wow. That was... unexpected. Really lovely, but unexpected. And I'm sorry. However much I want to, I just can't. Charlotte. You know? I'm really sorry.'

She looked down to where his hand still rested on her hip, then back up, a questioning smile playing about her lips. She picked up her beer and took a gulp of the sour yellow liquid while he considered his hand and her hip. When nothing moved, she anchored her eyes somewhere across the room and breathed short shallow breaths through her nose. The air hung still for uncountable moments. Pursing her lips, she turned sharply to him. Her mouth opened a fraction, then quivered momentarily as if interrupted by her editing of her thoughts.

'Of course. Sorry. Don't know what happened there. Just thought you felt... Don't you? Feel anything for me, I mean? I thought...'

He did not need to examine too closely their meetings over the past few weeks to realise that such an impression was unsurprising, although he was unwilling to accept as easily the suspicion that he had been an active participant in the creation of that impression. It struck him that they had almost never talked about Charlotte over all of those hours, even though she was the link between the two of them. He became conscious again that his hand still cupped her hip, and he removed it quickly, returned it to his own thigh, clenching it into a ball against itself.

She was watching his face. Her eyes held his for a moment, and he was gripped by a desire to kiss her again. The damage, in so far as there was damage, had already been done; he thought about the righteousness of enjoying his indiscretion while it lasted, whether that would necessarily deepen his guilt. Laura had kissed him, and undoubtedly wanted to kiss him again. She was the author of this betrayal and if he allowed himself to be a passive party to the treachery for a little while longer, it would change little.

'Laura. Of course I feel something for you. If things were different, well, it would be different. But things aren't different. I'm with Charlotte. Your friend. I've made my choice. It wouldn't be fair. To either of you.'

His hand was on her shoulder again, but this time there was no firmness, no pressure to keep her away. And yet she stood to leave anyway. *"I should go."* She picked up her bag and coat demonstratively. Árni looked at her unfinished pint, at the lipstick mark at its rim, and unconsciously wiped at his mouth with the back of his hand.

＊

White and grey and black slipped past in the close darkness; smears of snow muddled the already obscure view from the bus window. When he had described his home, Árni had spoken of its greenness, yet there was nothing green beyond the glass. And while she had known that it would be dark, almost completely, the oppressiveness of the darkness had surprised her. Maybe it was just the length of the journey. It seemed like weeks since they had landed at Keflavík, and days since they had boarded the Ísafjörður bus. She missed the city already: Reykjavík too had been covered in snow, and it had been dark, but there were people, bars, shops, energy. It had been an exciting opening to her Christmas trip to the exotic north.

But now the strangeness of the place was simply jarring. She could not remember the last building she had seen. Árni said that they were there, farms and houses, towns even, but to her there was simply a limitless expanse of white, rising to the distant mountains, pocked with indistinct black. And there was the sea: angry, black, hostile. When the bus stopped to take on passengers at a place that Árni described as a town, she stared from the window to discover only a clutch of snow draped houses set around an icy harbour.

'Hólmavík. It's the last proper town until we get to Ísafjörður. It gets quite remote from here. You might see the Lights.'

Árni returned to his stack of papers, leaving Charlotte to stare in awful anticipation into the darkness beyond. She was pleased that he had decided to take the post-doctoral position with his supervisor. He was not yet ready to let go of discovery and there was a line to be drawn from this work into a proper job, when he was ready. She allowed herself to play with the possibilities of a future and the strangeness of the present became a little more wondrous.

White moonscape dropped back to the sea, and the road clung to the coast as it twisted in endless coils around fjords and headlands with a reassuring rhythm. Snow cloaked mountains fell into the inky water and, sometimes, lights flashed on land and on sea. The first glimpse of the lights of Ísafjörður, blazing across the bay around a last headland, startled her, even though the town was little bigger than a village. They seemed to stretch out into the water of the bay, staining the surface with yellow smears. Only as they passed on the far side of the fjord did it become apparent that the town was built on a spur of land that formed a hook reaching most of the way across the fjord.

By the time the bus pulled into the tarmacked rectangle of the bus station, it was 9pm. Through the darkness, the mountain walls of the fjord loomed and glowed, reflecting both the street light and the stars crowding the sky above. Charlotte let Árni pull the hood of her coat over her head, let him kiss her nose, then her lips, let him pull her to him. They stood a while, wrapped in each other's warmth and lamb's wool, swaying under the imperious sky, gloriously alone, despite the milling passengers gathering their bags just a few metres away.

He had booked a room in a guest house just across the street; the young woman behind the desk recognised Árni from school and greeted him with an open smile, a trill of excitement conveyed in a few lilting, rasping sentences Charlotte did not understand. But she remembered how much she liked to hear him speak his native tongue, how much she loved his strangeness. In the morning, such as it would be, they would take another bus around the next headland to Bolungarvík, to his unknown parents, to the place where he grew up. The day after that, the days would start to get lighter, imperceptibly but undeniably, and then it would be Christmas Eve and she would know.

1969

A few days before Árni Eiríksson was christened, his grandfather had watched Neil Armstrong take his small step on a neighbour's television set. The slow grainy shapes flickered and blurred and the unfamiliar words crackled like static, yet Einar felt the potency of the moment, heard the echoes of his ancestors in the hiss and fizz of history. He had hoped that the baptism would take place on that day, would even have missed witnessing the distant landing in his neighbour's parlour if that had been possible. His own son, Árni's father, had been born on the day that Icelanders had made a country for themselves and it had seemed fitting that his grandson should therefore be similarly marked by history. He had watched his wife hopefully when he had suggested it. But Jóna had sighed and shaken her head, rejecting the idea in an instant, just as she had made sure that Eiríkur had not named the baby Ólafur, after his dead brother. She wanted, she had said, that her grandson did not live under any shadows, neither of history nor of sadness.

Einar watched Jóna's eyes sparkle as the pastor read the blessing. It was a different pastor to the one that had christened Eiríkur, of course; it was a different place and a different time. Yet it was the same church, and this was the same font in which the sins of both his sons had been washed away. From where he stood, he could see clearly the seat from which he had raised his lonely hand on the night of the vote that had cast him out of his home. He sighed, feeling a little of the old anger rising in him. The Bishop, seeing no point in letting a good church waste away under the winter storms, had ignored the protests of the families that had built it and had ripped the red-roofed building from Hesteyri and dropped it by the shore at Súðavík. By the time that Eiríkur and Hrefna had been married, the anger had dissipated somewhat but a bittersweet melancholy remained. It was good that his family's rites of passage could be celebrated between these familiar timbers, but still he hoped that, when his time came, his body would be lain in the hard ground where his father and his son still rested.

'Dad, come on. Gylfi is going to take some pictures outside. Come on.'

Eiríkur held his father's elbow lightly in his hand. The fine wool of the jacket felt strangely yielding to his touch and he faltered for a moment. Many men seemed larger, more distinct, in a suit, but his father was not one of them; Einar appeared to have receded into the gentle fabric, barely present. Recovering, Eiríkur guided his father away from the font and towards the doors. Behind him, he could hear his wife talking with one of her sisters, following, lost in shared histories and remembrances. Freyja said something unheard and Hrefna struggled to dampen her sniggering.

It had been her laughter that had caught him first, not the smile nor the sparkle of her eyes. It had cut through the dull babble of the coffee house, like a stream dancing over stones in the spring sunlight, and it had stolen him away from Gylfi's dull discourse. Weightless and entranced, he had turned in his seat to watch her laugh with her friends.

He had known other women of course. Girls willing to share his irresistible excitement at the world of sensation and longing that dawned in his fifteenth year. Under the summer nights, above the village, he had felt the rush of adolescence run between his body and another, each chest trembling under sweaters. When he had been sixteen, one of the village girls, the daughter of his neighbour, had been bolder still and he had traded his innocence for a few moments of sweaty confusion.

But in the eight years that had passed between that summer's night and the spring morning when he had first heard her laughter, Eiríkur had known only three other women, none of whom had merited mention to his mother. Jóna had watched him with growing unease as the years passed. Two days after his 21st birthday, as they had walked back from the harbour, carrying between them a basket of fish for drying, she had wondered aloud when he might give her a grandchild and, before Eiríkur had had a chance to recover from his embarrassment, she had continued to ask whether he wanted her to help him find a wife.

He had not. In his heart, he had kept a clear and precise picture of his future wife and he had decided that he would not settle for a convenient village girl, especially one imposed upon him. So he had withstood his mother's hurt eyes and, later, the embarrassment of his father at the whispered voices that had stilled as he had passed. He watched his friends marry, even Gylfi, confident that one day the woman who was to be his wife would announce herself to him.

He had not expected that announcement to have been borne upon gentle laughter rising above the bustle of the bakery in Ísafjörður on market day. But he had been sure then that the moment had arrived. He had felt his friend's hand on his arm, heard his curt query, but he would not allow his eyes to leave her face. Even when she had noticed his stare, began blushing, her eyes dropping to the cup in front of her, even then, he had not been able to release her, nor to release himself.

Gylfi had stopped tugging at his arm, his eyes following Eiríkur's to the young woman at the table by the window, among a small group of other women, none of whom he recognised. The town was not so large that he did not know the face of every young woman in it, in the villages around as well, and these three had been unknown to him.

Eiríkur had felt Gylfi's breath hot in his ear, urging him to action, the smell of stale coffee and caraway heavy on the air. He had shrugged coyly, twisting an awkward smile from his mouth; yet he had not entirely let his eyes loose from the woman across the room. She had been about twenty years of age then. Like her two companions, she had been dressed in her best clothes, which were nevertheless a little worn around the hem; her chocolate hair had been braided into pigtails and she had worn a bright red ribbon to keep her fringe from her face. She shot a glance directly at Eiríkur, but where there might have been indignation or shyness, there had been instead a look of calm curiosity, a little smile, before her eyes had dropped once more.

Then there had been a commotion as the three young women began to gather their things. Chair legs had whined on the boarded floor and the little party had busied themselves in their leaving. One drained the last of her coffee before hurrying to catch the others as they had passed through the door and out into the street.

'Watch my things, Gylfi. I'll be back.'

With unanticipated boldness, Eiríkur had risen, brushing crumbs from his sweater, from his trousers. He had reached the door in two strides and had paused only fleetingly, his hand hovering by the handle, before passing through it. Some of the customers had watched his progress with the interest of those leading their lives in a small town, but Eiríkur had been oblivious to their curiosity. On the street, the three young women were some metres off, walking slowly towards where the emptying market stalls clattered with the imminence of evening.

Only as he had drawn level with them had he realised that he had no plan for what to do next, and so he had simply carried on, walking as if on an errand. His eyes had looked rigidly ahead, never straying to catch a glimpse of her, despite the temptation to turn and stare. In no time, he had found himself among the depleted market stalls. Some fish remained, a little meat, a handful of potatoes, but there was little diversion to be had and Eiríkur had found himself drifting among the ironmongery and leather wares, the packaged foods and fancy goods. On the last table beside the road to the harbour, his eye had been caught by the sheen of a roll of Royal Blue ribbon. Its bright lustre whispered to him and he had decided that this colour would better suit her complexion and eyes than the red she wore. Calmness restored, he had asked the woman to cut him a length and, at her request, he searched his pockets for the few coins required.

The ribbon was rolled into a tight spool, fastened with a pearl-headed pin: Eiríkur's fingertip had been fascinated by the soft roundness of the head as he had held the precious roll carefully in his palm. Later, she would take this hand in her own and she would giggle. Even then, the fingers had seemed already to presage the blunt solidity of his father's hands; deep creases, deeper now, grew into his thickening knuckles, knotting the supple willow of his youth. The thumb nail had still flexed easily against his index finger, was still not gnarled and yellowed like his fathers, but there was a faint reeding etched into its surface; salt-soaked lines had already scored ridges into his skin. What his life would be was already written in this hand.

Before that story was played out, she would hold this shifting hand and sit beside him on the quayside, legs dangling above the placid water, and watch the sun fall into its shallow descent behind the snow-flecked fells that ringed the bay. She would lean her head into his shoulder and he would feel the soft satin of the bright blue ribbon against his cheek. They would have talked enough by then, told each other enough, made clear enough their feelings, and they would sink into the warm comfort of contented silence. They would listen to each other's breathing, feel its rise and fall, and they would smile, this time to themselves.

Then, at the sound of the seventh strike of the church bell, Hrefna would shake herself from her contentment and explain hurriedly that she had to rejoin her sisters, her father, before they set off for Suðureyri and home. The ironwork would have been loaded onto the truck and the day's takings counted and apportioned; only her absence would delay their departure. She would leave a brief kiss on his cheek and promise to be at the dance at the end of the month, and then she would scurry away and he would watch her vanishing form, keep watching until long after she had disappeared between the buildings. Then Eiríkur would go in search of Gylfi, hoping that his friend had not already left, eager to share his excitement, to parcel it up and disperse it, so that his chest should not burst.

'Hey, Eiríkur! I need you to look into the camera this time.'

Gylfi grinned from behind his Instamatic, the breeze catching his jacket, turning his fringe into an awkward curl. Behind him, Eiríkur heard a few groans of feigned exasperation; Hrefna squeezed his arm with her free hand while Árni wriggled in her other. Eiríkur looked from his son, to his wife, and to her family beyond them. Hrefna's older sister smiled back at him, wrinkling her nose mischievously: Freyja had made it back from the city the night before, eager to meet her first nephew. Despite the arduous bus journey, her face sparkled, igniting a broad smile that Eiríkur maintained long enough for Gylfi to capture with a click.

The sound released the frozen subjects from the spell and the portraits came alive once more, relaxing into an easy buzz. Hands were shaken, embraces exchanged and backs slapped. Eiríkur recognised the powerful clap on his shoulder without turning. He had met Skúli Hilmarsson a few weeks after he had met his daughter. Skúli had been returning hinges and bolts, cleats and oarlocks to their respective baskets at the end of the market day. A big man, but with a friendly smile, he had brushed his palms along the length of his sweater before shaking Eiríkur's hand warmly with a respectful nod, and then had returned to his work. The following month was much the same, but Skúli paused a little longer, asking a few questions of Eiríkur himself and of his family. The smile had grown more mischievous and Skúli had winked at his daughter's blushing. When it was time to head off back across the fells, Skúli had clasped his shoulder and shook his hand again. The next month, the two men had stood for a time, smoking each other's tobacco, discussing business and football, the endless light of July relieving the pressure to be underway. Over the summer, Eiríkur had visited Suðureyri himself, had been welcomed into the Hilmarsson family, had become familiar with them and with the little house above the harbour.

It was not a grand house, but it was larger than Eiríkur's home. The bustle of the three young women filled it completely, however, and when Hrefna visited Bolungarvík, he felt that his parent's modest clapboard house must have felt empty and desolate, despite the fuss made of her by his mother. Jóna had quivered with excitement for several days before and after that first visit; with each successive meeting, her excitement ripened into contented expectation, such that by the end of summer she had watched her son carefully and silently for any signs that a decision had been made. She had asked no questions, nor offered any advice, for fear that her interference might sour the match.

It had been left to Einar to break the silence, out on the waves towards the end of September. Snow laced the distant hills and the spray had hardened into icy pearls on his beard. They were unhooking the catch from the last of the day's lines. He had spoken with a quiet and faltering voice, so unlike the clear booming that even in the highest winds carried from one end of *Tófa* to the other. Startled, Eiríkur had listened, the fish still flapping in his hand, wrestling against the hook. He had said nothing, as his father had offered hesitant advice and his blessing to a marriage, but before Einar had finished his careful speech, Eiríkur had felt the joy of release course through him and he had tipped his head back, raising his face to the sky to laugh out his happiness.

Two days later and the joy still swirled about him as he had approached Hrefna's home. He had kicked the snow from his boots and waited for the door to open. The low sun had been pale in the sky and the wind had blown from the north east, bringing with it a chill foreboding of the winter to come: summer had slipped too easily by and the bite of autumn had surprised him as it always did. Yet the cold walk into Suðureyri from the junction where the bus had dropped him had not dampened his mood.

He had watched the blank windows for any sign that his knock had stirred the house. Across the yard, the quiet forge had glowed rich red beyond the half open door. He had expected to find Hrefna's father busy in his workshop and, while the silence had surprised him, he had been pleased that he would not have to talk with him among the hammers and tongs. There had been some commotion within the house, some laughter and the clatter of shoes on boards; a hush, then the judder of the door opening. Skúli had regarded Eiríkur's stiff collar, the mean knot of his tie, with an amused, enquiring expression. In the gloom behind him, Hrefna and her sisters had craned their necks to watch but their father had placed his broad shoulders between them and his visitor in a small act of mercy.

'Eiríkur. Welcome. Hrefna mentioned that you might be visiting with us this afternoon. Would you like to step inside for a cup of coffee?'

The blacksmith had shot a glance back toward the young women, sending them scurrying to the four corners of the house, leaving only laughter behind them. A little later, seated by the fire in the sitting room, Eiríkur had recovered enough of his happiness to speak calmly of his intentions. Skúli had listened carefully, seriously, his index fingers joined to a point beneath his lip, had not interrupted him, neither to challenge nor to assist. He had agreed to the match, of course, had welcomed it. He had shouted for Hrefna, who appeared almost immediately with her sister Freyja from just beyond the sitting room door. Shaking his head at their eavesdropping, Skúli had called to Fríða, his middle daughter, to bring coffee and some schnapps, and then he had clasped his shovel-hand to Eiríkur's back, and its solid warmth had suffused him, much as it did now in the summer sunshine.

'He's a fine boy. Do you think he will follow you to the sea?'

Eiríkur looked at his son and marvelled at what might lie before him. Endless possibility stretched out across the years and the desire to keep the boy close wrestled with the hope that he might become all that he could. Hrefna completed his thoughts before they formed.

'Who knows, dad? Maybe he'll follow his auntie's lead and get a job behind a desk in the city. Or maybe he'll want to follow you into the forge. Whichever it is, he's time enough to make up his mind. I just want him to be happy.'

While Skúli Hilmarsson nodded his vigorous approval for the sentiment, Einar felt Jóna's gentle hand on his arm. Neither needed to articulate their own hope, simply that the boy should have the chance to become a man.

The track rose steeply from the town, but their pace did not drop. The basket on the younger man's back creaked in time with his steps, his cloudy breath its only accompaniment, but it was a light load. The bulk of the fish had been dropped at the processing plant by the quayside, and there were only a few dozen left to carry, some for that evening's supper, but most to dry for the hastening winter. Above them, the grey sky was darkening and they were eager for the comfort of home. Eiríkur wanted most of all to see his son.

He looked over to his father, who paused his whistling but did not slacken his stride. He cocked his head in query, to which Eiríkur simply shrugged and offered a gentle smile. They had not spoken since they had collected their payment from the office at the processing plant, folding and unfolding the scant notes they had received, dividing the money into three unequal portions. Eiríkur's was the smallest, but only a little less than that pocketed by his father; the greater part was reserved for Jóna and the house.

The sea was still fecund and the catch had been easily made; the waves untroubling and the cold bearable. There was work still to be done of course, but the long hours passed more slowly for Eiríkur now that the days took him from not only a wife but also a child. He looked along the track and into the gathering gloom. The lights at Siggi Baldursson's house were already ablaze, a beacon by which to steer.

'Smoke with me a while.'

Einar had already come to a halt, unnoticed. Despite his urge to be home, Eiríkur himself stopped and turned back to the spot where his father stood, fumbling with his tobacco pouch, pulling a mossy clump from it and pressing it into the bowl of his briarwood pipe, a relic of the days of Danish rule. Eiríkur watched the busy fingers and waited. A match flared, the flame dipped, tugged down into the pipe, and then the thick aroma of the smoke wove a sweet blanket around them both. He breathed in deeply, absorbing the rich air, before in turn rolling a cigarette from his own tin. Both men became lost for a few minutes, and nicotine and tar blunted the aches in their joints. Einar leant against the post of a long-abandoned fence and sighed out a stream of smoke.

'When winter comes, I want you to stay around the house this year. In case the bairn needs anything. If there is a chance of some fishing, I'll go out myself, or see if one of the lads fancies a bit of time on the water and a few char for their trouble.'

In most years, they would take *Tófa* out a few times over the winter, if the weather was clear enough. The bigger boats worked through the season, but in a craft like theirs, a winter squall would be fatal. They were careful but took the opportunity when the chance arose. Other days, they would hunt ptarmigan or busy themselves about the place, making repairs to house or lines or tools. On bad days they would simply close themselves up with coffee and books and wait for the wind to stop its screaming. But in any case, they would do those things together, as they always had. His father's decree was therefore unexpected, and Eiríkur could find no adequate response, other than to watch the pipe glow red. He pulled at his cigarette, holding the smoke tight within his chest until the ache in his lungs grew too great to bear.

'I don't understand. Why shouldn't I go out with you?'

And then he did understand, before he had finished his question, before his father had straightened himself to reply. Because of Ólafur. Because life was too precious to treat it carelessly, and because the boy needed his father as much as the father needed the boy. If he were near, during those hard dark months, maybe both would emerge into the spring unscathed.

'It'll be harder for the women this year, with the baby on top of everything. You might be more useful at home than on the sea.'

Einar grinned at this, watched his son for signs that he had taken affront at this gentle gibe; that would be better than bringing out into the cold air the fears that stalked him still. The grin held for some moments, until Eiríkur joined him and laughed as well.

'Well I won't complain if I get to stay in by the fire, instead of freezing my nose off, listening to your tuneless whistling all day.'

Eiríkur threw the stub of his cigarette into the night and a trail of orange sparks cascaded briefly, like the tail of a comet. A cold breeze snagged across the dark hillside, driving his hands deep into his pockets. The dark hulk of Ernir hung above him, its outline unreliable, mutable against the dead black sky. There would be no stars, and the moon, when it rose, would be little more than a pale smudge. The prospect of the warmth of the kitchen, of coffee, maybe a little schnapps, suddenly snapped back to the front of his mind. Eiríkur tugged at his father's sleeve and turned for home. From behind him, he heard the sound of whistling. With a smile, Eiríkur joined in, and the familiar tune carried out over the hillside on the cold night air.

1998

The breeze rattled the trees, whirred about their branches, but it did not extinguish the warmth that clung to the world like a lover. He liked the trees. Even after seven years, they were still a welcome novelty. The landscape too. He had traded the stark falling fells for this flattest of flat lands. The countryside around the city was featureless, at least to Charlotte's eyes; she missed the fat-backed hills of her home much more than Árni missed the skeletal ridges and steep-cut fjords of his youth. He had grown up bored by the fells, frustrated at their intransigence; the land's bleakness was dismal in its ordinariness and the sea's sparkle was too often shrouded to excite, too linked to work and then to tragedy to be beautiful.

The orderliness of the England that surrounded him, its domesticity, was a thing of wonder. Ditches and furrows cut rhythmically across the land; everywhere were straight lines, the hedgerows and the horizon, punctuated in turn by the perpendicularity of poplars, clustered in rows or in tight copses. Where his ancestors had simply stripped that land of its trees, laying bare its ugly bones, the people of this place had raised gentle fertility from the swamp. The fens were still a water landscape, although their fluidity had created the land's shallowness, not its depth.

His homeland was more clearly shaped by the movement of water, of course. There were the countless waterfalls, each of which in England would be equipped with a carpark and a visitor centre, but that back home did not warrant even a name; the drama of water was everywhere. But even here, on a low chalk ridge that rose above the land that stretched east all the way to Norfolk, he had the sense that water surrounded him, despite the distance to the coast.

The sun shook free of the clustered clouds and the greenery of early summer shone, the trees shimmering in their gloss. So many trees. This decision, the leaving behind of his homeland, once again felt like a good one, the first of a series of good decisions. He breathed deeply and felt his wife's head rise on his chest. As if summoned by his contentment or by the sunshine, the baby moved, struggling to muster up a cry, half awake and half asleep, surprised by both. Charlotte rolled across the picnic blanket to peer into the carry cot.

'On my god, she is so cute. She's blowing little bubbles in her sleep.'

Árni shuffled in behind Charlotte and rested his chin on her shoulder to watch his daughter. For the past ten weeks, he had wanted little more than that she slept, but now he wanted to wake her, to show her the bright trees, name them for her. He felt his arm loop around Charlotte's waist, felt her hip under his hand.

'I wish you didn't have to go to work tomorrow. The weather is supposed to be even nicer. And it would be great to hang out. Just the three of us.'

It was like this every Sunday, whether there was rain or fair skies. He had learned not to explain, not to set out the reasons why he could not take another day's holiday, would not. It made him sound uncommitted, too focussed on his work, not sufficiently in love with them, and that was not true. The job was simply another of the good decisions he had made since leaving Bolungarvík. As well as the money, his work had put him at the heart of some of the most exciting research imaginable.

He had first encountered the discoveries of the British-American scientist among the rambling entrails of one of his lectures in neuroscience at Reykjavík. It had been early in the second year of his degree, in the drab, bitter autumn after the Englishwoman had returned home to Cambridge. Professor O'Keefe was in London, not Cambridge, but from that distance the distinction barely registered. Only a fragment of the lecture had lodged in his mind as he drifted in and out of other thoughts, but the notion of 'place cells', buried in the brain, providing the context for memories by creating a neural representation of the environment in which events occurred, had resonated with something he had forgotten and it had fired his imagination. He had left the lecture hall and gone straight to the library, searching out the dusty copy of *The Hippocampus as a Cognitive Map* from the shelves. Walking from the stack, he had flipped open the cover and scanned the opening page. By the time he had reached the counter and the librarian had stamped the empty date sheet, he knew that this was the work he wanted to pursue.

So Monday mornings did not dent his mood as they had done for Charlotte, before the baby had built a new routine for her. But he knew not to say that anymore, and instead he nodded and sighed, agreed that it would be great, then reached out behind him for one of those little tomatoes that she liked so much and popped it into her mouth. Her kiss burst with the fruit's sweet aromatics.

'Do you remember that old guy? We met him at the fete? At St Joseph's?'

Earlier, before Freyja had been born, they had attended a small fundraising event for a local community group, the endeavour of one of Charlotte's colleagues, someone who even then was moving from acquaintanceship to friendship, someone who would later become a confidante before work took her to London and she became merely a friend again, in a theoretical way, receding into ever less frequent visits and emails and Christmas cards. But then, the friendship was blooming and Charlotte, eager not to be alone with her baby, had been anxious to nurture it, had accepted the invitation enthusiastically, without hesitation, without consultation. Árni had accompanied his pregnant wife wearily, reconciling himself to the idea that this would come to be an exciting diversion in his future life.

There had been a tombola, stalls selling little cakes and jars of preserve, and there had been hoopla. What seemed like several hundred children too; they scurried about between the adults who, somehow, managed not to trip or to send the youngsters tumbling to the coarse tarmac of the playground. Árni had found the tea stall and, wishing there had been beer, he had wondered how long it would be before he could leave. The squeal of a microphone signalled that there would first be announcements, if only to offer the thanks of the committee and to draw the raffle. Something like expectation had settled over the children and adults alike. The man holding the microphone was already old, but not yet frail; not even close to frail. He had stood, tall and luminous, next to the head teacher. It was only after he was introduced that Charlotte's memory connected forgotten Saturday evening television with her mother's rememberings: decades, lived and unlived, reconnected decades later.

He was an actor and Charlotte nodded in recognition of his elusive familiarity. Árni had not heard of him or of any of the parts he had played, beyond the canonical stalwarts - Shakespeare and the Broadway hits. The TV series that had made him famous was lost to him in a time long before he had even thought about England. Yet he had been transfixed by the modest fame of the old man, strangely thrilled by the presence of celebrity, related to him in excited whispers by Charlotte. He had an aura, there was no other word for it, no other explanation for the compulsion with which he gripped his audience. '*A real professional*', Charlotte had said, naming it instantly.

The actor had beamed his smile across their faces as he pulled numbered tickets from the brightly lacquered tombola. He had held each at arm's length, better to focus on the number. Looking up, his quick smile evoking a confident vulnerability, he seemed to make eye contact with each and every spectator, leaving with them a memento of his specialness. As he announced each number with clipped precision, he looked around with theatrical exaggeration in search of the lucky winner, leading the applause as each came forward to claim their prize, selecting from the table top array of bottles and books and boxes of biscuits. After all the prizes had all been won, Victor Hartness appeared at the tea stall and asked, more politely than Árni had thought it possible, for a cup of tea.

'*I do love these things, don't you? A real sense of community.*'

Victor swept an arm across the playground, a precarious polystyrene cup in his hand. Árni had turned to face him and had been struck by the energy in his eyes. There was a keenness, a vital inquisitiveness in his face. This was not a doddery old man, not some bit-part dolt. His eyebrow raised in challenge.

'*Of course, I know no-one here knows who I am – not even you. Everyone is just too young to remember. I'm simply some old actor. It's nice to be asked, to be remembered, even by those who don't remember you, even when you're asked at the last minute, to fill a gap because your niece is on the committee. That's her, Mary.*'

Victor had pointed across the playground to a middle-aged woman in a tweed skirt, but Árni simply watched his hand: the fine skin, the precise angle of the knuckle, the way that he looped his thumb. He had introduced himself and Charlotte, had taken his hand to shake, had been surprised by the perfectly balanced firmness of his grip. And then Victor Hartness had made his apologies and disappeared into the street beyond the school gate with his niece.

Later, at home, Árni had read up on him online, and realised that he had been in the company of one of the finest film actors of his generation. During the eighties he had returned to the stage, initially in the West End, and then further and further afield as his stardom faded. He'd been on a few TV shows since, including a run on a soap opera Árni didn't watch. Then his career disappeared: nothing had been listed for the previous five years. Charlotte had wandered over to his desk, looked at the screen as instructed, and shaken her head absently before suggesting that he make some pasta for dinner. It was inevitable, she had said later, that careers like that faded, that people became something else; you couldn't go on forever, and people wanted to see new people on their screens anyway. Think of footballers, she had said, they can't all present *Match of the Day* when they get too old to play, and they can't all coach little clubs either, not for a living; they go on and do different things, out of the public eye; it was healthy, she had said, and shrugged. They had not spoken about it again.

'I ran into him again. We had a chat. Last week. In the park.'

It had been an indecisive day. Patches of bright blue had squeezed between with thick fists of dark grey cloud, nudged by a fitful wind. His meeting had finished early and he had decided to take the long way back to the car, looping around the park to stretch his legs and fill his lungs. Some spots of rain had begun to fall and Árni had watched the mothers pause and pull plastic covers over their prams and then remove them moments later when the shower had passed. There were only the mothers and Árni in the park, everyone else was either at work or had been discouraged by the very weather that had persuaded him to linger. Above an empty bench, a plume of midges bided their time, their dance catching in the lemonade light.

Had there been more people about, he might not have noticed him, might not have paid attention, but he was the only occupant of any of the park's benches. As it was, Árni was almost past him when he realised how he recognised the old man. He slowed his pace into a stop and twisted to face him. He'd said his name, twice, before Victor Hartness looked up.

'I'm sorry. I'm afraid you have the advantage of me. I don't think I...'

The uncertainty had made him think that he was mistaken, that this was not the razor sharp actor he had met only a few weeks before. There was something fearful behind the eyes and Árni thought that it would be kinder simply to apologise for his mistake and to walk on, to find his car and put the encounter behind him. But the fear slipped away, or was buried once more, and Victor summoned up some of his former jauntiness.

'You'll have to forgive me, young man. Memory's not what it was. Perhaps a tiny clue?'

Árni had smiled his reassurance and explained where they had met, that he was the Icelander at the fete, the formerly expectant father, the man who'd rather have had a beer than a tea. When it came, he had accepted the invitation to take a seat on the bench and began to ask Victor Hartness about himself. His subject was co-operative, fluent and engaging. Only when he had asked about the present, and the route to it, did the conversation become stilted. It was Victor who had steered things towards Árni and his life. He had seemed animated beyond courtesy about Árni's work. Normally, people would glaze over or construct jokes into questions, hoping that Árni would provide the punchlines;

seldom were people both serious and engaged, let alone informed. But Victor Hartness had seemed as excited as Árni was by the idea that the hippocampus held a cognitive map of familiar environments, that it could identify place, direction, and distance from landmarks, that it provided the basis for episodic memory, that it may hold the key to understanding dementia. When Árni had looked at his watch, not slyly enough, Victor had asked if they might resume the conversation in a week or two.

'What? I don't understand. You mean you're actually meeting him again? Why on earth...?'

Charlotte had thought that the encounter in the park had been another of her husband's eccentricities, or maybe a strange riposte to her chiding him that he should make more of an effort with people. On realising that Árni intended to find time for this stranger, most probably at the expense of time he could spend with his family, she hardened. The cracker she had been contemplating was returned to its packet.

'Well, we'll see. Maybe it's something to do with a part he's after. He said something about a TV series, a drama. Or maybe he's just lonely. But we'll see. He might never call.'

He smiled hopefully and took Charlotte's hand in his, like a bird. She studied the cupped hands with something like a frown, but it soon faded. There was something about him that made holding onto anger or irritation difficult, more trouble than it was worth. It was partly why she had said yes without hesitation, three years before, when he had curled her into him on a black, balmy night, heady with wine, and asked her to marry him. It didn't matter, she decided. If not this, it would be some other novelty that absorbed his curiosity. His restlessness was in itself charming, even if it was sometimes unsettling.

The irises on the kitchen counter retained a striking vibrancy, their vase already lost in the encroaching gloom. In only a few weeks, it would be dark before he got home from work, but for now he removed his shoes without turning on the lamp, savouring what was left of the summer's light. From the living room, he could hear men's voices, knew that they were trapped in the radio, country folk living their everyday lives. Freyja would be napping, and Charlotte would be claiming whatever she could of life beyond her daughter. He imagined the pair of them, harmonious, one sitting on the sofa, the other asleep in her arms. The cooling cup of tea would be just out of reach, but the tungsten glow of the little table lamp, rescued from her mother's house, would seep its comfort into everything. He paused by the door: a strip of yellow light below marked the threshold between that welcoming world beyond and this greyness. Árni decided to let the programme finish before disturbing them.

He poured a small measure of whisky into a tumbler. He had started to drink out of her sight early in the pregnancy, not that he did so often. He put the glass on the table and carefully pulled out a chair. Beside the grey shape of the local paper, he noticed a few envelopes. He flicked through them, but none of the letters looked either important or interesting, so he turned his attention to the newspaper. Shaking it from its fold, he saw a face he thought he recognised on the front page, halfway down. The face was younger, but even in the half-light it was unmistakably his eyes that stared back from the newsprint, even in his unfamiliar youth. Árni felt a momentary quaver of hopeful confusion, but it quickly stilled into a slow sadness as his eyes drifted across to the headline.

Holding up the page to catch the dying day, he read the short story beneath the picture. Local celebrity Victor Hartness had been found dead at his home by his daughter, who had become alarmed after her father had not answered the phone for several days. She had driven up from London to find him sitting in his armchair, facing the half-opened curtains, wearing his customary suit. The cause of death was still being investigated, although foul play had been ruled out; the police estimated that he had been dead for about a week when he was discovered. The paper listed the actor's achievements, highlighting the TV series that had made him a household name in the 1970s. The report ended with a note that Victor had recently been cast to play a supporting role in a new television series. The production company had issued a statement. He had got the part without Árni's help after all. Not that it mattered much anymore.

From the living room, he heard the jaunty theme tune, signalling that the radio programme had ended, but he did not move. He wondered about the daughter, about why she had told the reporter what her father had been wearing, how he had been sitting; he wondered about her mother, about where she was, how Victor had lost her and when; and he wondered how Victor had faced his dying, whether it had been with fear or resignation, with sadness or contentment, whether the news about the new series would have made his passing easier or harder. He played with the variables in his mind, tried to determine how he would feel in those circumstances. Victor's buoyancy had only faltered when Árni had asked him about the fading of the limelight. Regardless of its inevitability, he had to assume that not everyone was content to slip into the shadows.

Charlotte's voice now, bubbling with exaggerated vowels. They had agreed that they would not fall into the habit of talking to Freyja with nonsense words, but both had found themselves reneging on the commitment within a few days of their daughter filling their house with her tiny self. He put down the newspaper and rose from the table. He wanted to be amid the life beyond the yellow threshold. Only later would he tell Charlotte about Victor, assuming she did not already know; once Freyja had been bathed and put to bed, when the TV news had finished. An image of his own father, seated by the window, lifeless, flashed through his mind, and he thought again about the daughter, about the week that had elapsed between their last conversation and the moment when she had walked into her childhood home, into the silence.

■

The line felt slacker than he had hoped. His fingers traced its twist a little before he decided to leave it trailing a while longer. He sat across the thwart to roll a cigarette, his back against the gunwale, one leg stretched out almost to the far oar lock, and he let the wallowing sea rock him. He still had light for a few hours, even though the summer had gone. There was no rush. Better to wait, let the fish come to him and make the trip worthwhile. His lighter battled the coursing wind but after 40 years he was adept at coaxing life into a cigarette in all weathers.

He was used to his own company now, too. Most often, Eiríkur fished alone. Gylfi still came out with him when he could, but he had his own work, his own concerns, and as the years passed their voyages together had become simply an opportunity for old friends to talk, not the workaday hunting of fish. In the spaces between, Eiríkur had grown accustomed to the sound of his own breathing blurring into the swell.

He looked at the scorched fringe of the paper near the cigarette's tip. The wind had dragged the burning to one side and an island of paper, cut off from the mainland by ash, drifted off into the swirling air, carried across the rolling world. He tracked its progress until it was lost between the grey below and the grey above. The sun, hidden behind the thick bank of cloud that draped low across the sky, would be beginning its descent. The coming of darkness surprised him every year, and these days it drained him of energy in a way that he did not remember happening to his younger self. The lethargy would hang about him over the winter until it became unnoticed, and only the lengthening of the days would remind him that it was there at all. Under the midnight sun he would rediscover his true self, then watch it ebb from him again with each passing day. He rose and fell with the seasons, with the tide.

Eiríkur smelled the air, sensed the ocean's turn: he had given the fish long enough. He clicked the winch into life, the engine coughing then purring, the line resisting its pull. It was easier now, of course. The winch had been at Árni's insistence; the new, more reliable outboard motor too. At first Eiríkur had resisted, said that he was not so old that he couldn't handle a boat, but Hrefna and Árni had conspired, had argued for the logic of the solution. It was a simple matter of productivity: with only one man, fishing without motors was inefficient. It meant that he now had to find money for diesel, of course, and so he let Árni send a cheque each month, folded into a short scribbled note of news from there. It was not much, and Hrefna would rather the boy called more often, but at least he knew his son was healthy and content. And now he had a granddaughter. Eiríkur smiled and watched the first of the fish flapping in the air.

An hour later, *Tófa* cut smoothly into the harbour and Eiríkur slowed the motor. He would be done by dark; there would be time enough to drink a coffee before he met Hrefna after her shift at the plant. Once the fish were weighed and sorted, and his chitty had been paid by the clerk, he slipped along the street towards the café at the petrol station. He paused to roll a cigarette, but before he could light it, he heard his name. The young man leaning from the post office door waved to him.

'Well, you've saved me a walk. If you're not too busy.' The clerk waved a package in his left hand.

'What is it?'

'It's a package, Mr Einarsson.' The clerk stepped back a little, into the too slight protection of the door frame.

'I can see that. Where is it from?' Impatience fused with suspicion; Eiríkur turned fully to face the post office but did not take a step towards it.

'I don't know, sir. I, I think, yes, it's from England.' The clerk peered first at the back of the padded manila envelope, then at the post mark, before he spoke. Holding the package as a shield, he searched Eiríkur's face for a hint to his reaction and was pleased to see the nervous smile break under his beard. Eiríkur stepped briskly toward the clerk and signed the receipt, slowly shaping the letters with childlike clarity. He thanked the clerk and resumed his course towards the café. As he walked on, the clerk lingered by the door to watch the old man disappear along the street and was surprised to see him raise the package to his face, as if to smell it.

Eiríkur waited until he had found a seat in the corner, had taken a long gulp from his coffee. The chrome edge of the table glinted in the strip lighting; he sat with his hands rested lightly on his thighs and inspected the package laid out before him. The size of a paperback book, the thick spongey envelope had sustained some damage, was worn and supple but appeared unbreached; it was undoubtedly Árni's handwriting. Eiríkur ran through all the bad news that the package could contain, but was sure that if anything had happened to Árni, or to the baby, he would already have known. Neither man enjoyed idle talk, but when there was news or need, Árni was straight on the telephone. Three months ago, Árni had called, to tell them about the baby, the little girl that had joined their family. Hrefna had been beside herself with joy already, but when she had heard that the child was to be named for her sister, she had wept and her tears had run over his hand holding the receiver to their ears.

His aunt had welcomed Árni to Reykjavík when he had gone there to study. He had lived in her apartment for the first two years, and had eaten there every Sunday for the next. Eiríkur often wondered if it had been her example that had first planted the seed of his leaving, if the possibility of being elsewhere had been a stronger draw than the idea of studying. If he had been asked, Eiríkur would have said that he was pleased that his son had left, had made something of himself, had left the miseries of the sea, the bitterness of the fjords. It was the right thing and the best thing that could have happened. But nobody did ask, too afraid of his response, and so in the absence of articulation he had simply the visceral sense of loss, lumpen in its wordlessness. Even if his son had been one to call frequently or had visited every holiday, that loss would still have been there in the everyday, in his morning walk to the harbour, in the belly of *Tófa* on a bright, chill day. He had lost first his brother, then his father and, in a way, his son.

He turned the package slowly on the table, so that the sealed end faced him. The flap was closed with tape, shiny and uncooperative. Eiríkur took out his pocket knife to gently coax the envelope open. He peered inside: a letter and a handful of photographs. He slid one out and saw, for the first time, his granddaughter.

1988

The smell of soup filled the hallway and his stomach twisted in an exquisite knot. His aunt must have bought haddock on the way home from work. Pulling his slab-cold boots from his feet, Árni was pleased that he had resisted the temptation to stay at the cafe with Gefn and the English girl, despite wanting to know why she had chosen to spend the winter term in Reykjavík. These were the cruellest months, even in the city, and she could have chosen warmer, lighter days, or even not to come at all. Her name had sounded like a breath, and her voice crisp like rime, and he had wanted to know more about how she had found her way to here. He would ask Gefn over lunch the following day. She was sure to have found out the story; her English was better than his in any case.

His aunt called from the kitchen. A cheery, aimless greeting that neither sought nor conveyed information, a simple offering of humanity. He felt the warmth creep into his toes and he moved towards the yellow light at the end of the hall.

'Hello there. Something smells great. I hope some of it is for me.'

Freyja looked up from the pan and grinned a wide grin. Despite the heat of the stove, her cardigan was buttoned to her neck and the blue apron covered a thick woollen skirt that dropped as far as her knitted slippers.

'Cut some bread for us will you, sweetie?'

She pointed to the board on the table, beside the small vase of dried flowers that his aunt kept from summer until spring when it could be replaced by fresh blooms. While Árni sawed at the loaf, Freyja ladled the soup into two large bowls. Soon seated, she poured out coffee for each of them and they set about their dinner with purpose. For a little while they exchanged only shapeless sounds, noises of enjoyment and gratitude, but gradually their soup spoons settled into a less urgent rhythm and Árni told his aunt about his day, about classes and classmates, while she echoed his news with her own.

She worked for the same firm that she had joined 20 years before, when she had left her family and the northern wilds. She still had little interest in aggregates, in the grinding of stone, in its transportation and ultimate pouring into holes that would become buildings and roads. But the people there made her uprooting bearable, and the independence afforded by her own income was something she cherished, even while she had been married. Over the years, responsibility had accreted to her. She began every working day wrapped in the knowledge that she was specifically, personally valued. Were sickness or indifference to keep her from her work, then the books would be unkept, the orders would be unprocessed, and tens of thousands of kronur would be unmoved. The enterprise itself, sustaining some 80 people and their families, would have no purpose. Perhaps because of this, Freyja was never sick.

Since her divorce, she had walked to her office, which had moved inconveniently to one of the steel and glass buildings that had sprouted along the ring road. Her husband had taken the car, in exchange for the tenancy on the apartment and its contents; she did not drive in any case, so it had made good sense to divide the only assets of the marriage in that way. Even the inconvenience of her firm's relocation, from the harbour to the ring road, had not convinced her that mastering the motor car would add greatly to her happiness. There were other things to learn.

'I bought a book today: Teach Yourself Russian. I thought it was time I improved myself. Do they do classes in Russian at the university? It looks very hard, learning it just from a book. They have a different alphabet. Did you know that?'

Árni wanted to say that everyone had a different alphabet, even the Danes. But more than that he wanted to ask why she had decided to learn Russian, when she had only just given up learning Spanish, or when she had stopped learning the guitar after barely mastering the three chords with which she could strum out her favourite folk song. But he said none of this, asked nothing, just smiled and nodded, told her that he was sure that they did, that he would ask, would find a leaflet or something, some information about adult education classes. Freyja smiled and then returned to her soup, tearing a piece from the last cut slice of bread to run around the inside of her nearly empty bowl. She pushed the remainder towards Árni, encouraging him to eat.

'There's an English girl at the university. Sarah. She's only here for a term, on Gefn's course.'

Gefn was not quite Árni's girlfriend. Both they and everyone else assumed that that was what they were, or would soon become, once one of them found the moment or the courage to actually ask the other. They had certainly never kissed; every touch they had ever exchanged could have been exchanged by friends or siblings. Yet they spent most of their lunchtimes together and several evenings would see them in a cafe, lost in one-sided discussions. She was in the school of modern languages, read novels written in languages unknown to him; she invested words in the description of themselves. Many times, the conversation would begin on common ground only for it to drift off on the instigation of one or the other, with the discourse sustained only by willingness and enthusiasm.

'Oh, maybe she could teach me English, while she's here. Do you think she'd be willing? I could pay her a little, if that would help. But only if she is patient. Do you think she is patient?'

He did not know if she was patient, or if she would teach his aunt to speak English, whether a few hundred kronur would convince her. He had only met her that evening, and then for less than an hour. He wondered if she had looked as though she might be patient, which made him think about how she looked, and he realised that the reason he had been tempted to stay in the cafe had been because of the English girl.

There were no clouds. The wind from the north had brought the kind of cold crisp weather that made spring beautiful. The low sun was still bright, catching the buildings along the lake, setting their colourful roofs ablaze. Ducks and geese squabbled for space on the thawing surface, bobbing in the newly open water. Around him the city hummed its lazy tune, almost unnoticed.

His lecture had been his last class of the day and, since there was still some daylight left, Árni had decided to walk into the city, to find distraction until Sarah too was released into the day. Soon term itself would end and there would only be revision wrapped around a return to Bolungarvík. He had made his case to his aunt: that he was likely to do better in his exams if he remained in the city, did not waste days on a bus, nor in explaining to his father what it was he was reading. But she was his landlady and so controlled his access to bed and board. She had said no.

Undeterred he had suggested to Sarah that he stay at the hostel, sharing her room, but she had looked horrified and had dismissed the idea for its impracticality. In any case, he should go home to see his parents. When this failed to assuage him, she had promised that she would still be in the city when he returned from the north. She didn't have to be back in England until the week after his summer term started, so there would be time yet for a proper goodbye, if it had to be goodbye.

Árni sat on a bench beside the lake and rolled the word Cambridge around his mouth to keep the thought of Bolungarvík at bay. If he could not stay in this city, he would dream of another. Behind him a middle-aged couple passed by, talking in hushed and resentful tones about the intransigence of an unknown neighbour. The specifics of the offence remained opaque, but the apparent injustice of the situation added fuel to the fire of his own maltreatment.

And yet, however unfair the imposition, Bolungarvík would not be denied. He would have to return, if only for a week or two. He had no other options. Certainly, he could no longer ask Gefn, and none of his other friends had their own place in the city: only she had been brought up there, was a native of the city. Everyone else would return, like him, to their villages and farms.

The stone skittered across the ice and, at the end of its final low arc, dropped into the flat black water. He selected another piece of spongey grey lava from the ground between his feet and tossed it towards the centre of the lake. This time, the stone cleared the ice and was swallowed in one gulp. The cleanness of the throw pleased him more than it should, and he recovered some of his self-assurance. This wasn't so bad. Bolungarvík would not be so bad. If he and Sarah meant anything at all, then her return to England would not be the end of them. Maybe in the summer, he could visit, see something of another country.

The wind rose, ruffling the surface of the lake and carrying the chill of the remaining ice through Árni's coat and into his bones; the wind drove him from the bench and into the streets behind the parliament. The buildings still crowded around him exuberantly, just as they had the few months before, when he had arrived dripping as much with trepidation as with excitement. The trepidation was gone now, and the buildings and streets were familiar, known. They still lacked the quiver of memory, the animation of a shared history, but even though the few streets of Bolungarvík or Ísafjörður could shake out old friends and lost laughter in a way that the corners of the city could not, such resonances were still a weight to be shrugged off, not a welcome embrace. That embrace was something his father valued, whereas the city offered the newness Árni craved. Years later, he would return to these streets and regret the passing of this coffee shop. For now, however, it offered only a welcome shelter from the wind, strong sweet coffee, and the sense that he was part of something brighter than himself.

The clatter of cups and the hiss of steam chopped into jigsaw pieces the conversation behind the counter. He gave up his attempt to follow the two women as they coursed from joke to joke, and focused instead on the blank page of his notebook. He traced the perforation that ran down the left hand edge and imagined tearing the sheet from the book once he had filled it with ink and intention. The thought of writing a letter to Sarah had bubbled up, slowly at first, then with relentless force, as he had crossed the square and turned onto Austurstræti. He would write it in English, as much as he could. While he had improved since the beginning of the year, he still found difficulty constructing sentences in the language, and his vocabulary lacked the depth required to carry breezy informality convincingly; idiom remained a mystery to him. Yet it was not linguistic constraint that made the task so difficult to commence. There was nothing to say that could not risk breaking everything, or at the very least confusing their situation. To write the word would be easy, but just as he did not know if it was a word that would drive her from him in terror or laughter, he did not know if it was a true statement of himself. Accuracy was important and should not be treated lightly, especially if loose language undermined something solid and real. Even if this was not love, they both seemed to value whatever nameless thing it was. Certainly he did.

If only they had more time. If she could stay until the end of summer, then at least they would have a chance to edge towards the right word, to name it accurately. She would know the right word, of course, and probably in more than one language. Maybe his letter should ask her; maybe he should ask her? He flipped the notebook shut and tried to resolve the matter in his own terms. He had begun his studies convinced that his passion was for chemistry, but as the course had proceeded, he had discovered a deepening fascination with biology. This shift from the inanimate to the animate had not helped him in reasoning people, who remained resolutely undetermined. An element's reaction could be predicted, reliably, without nuance. So it seemed would an organism. And yet the collection of elements and organisms that formed a consciousness remained impervious to such prediction. He had made no promises to Gefn, and yet she had taken his betrayal as a devastating blow. Betrayal. She had accused him with that precise word when he had been discovered with Sarah, mouth on mouth, limbs entwined. And it had felt accurate, had stripped away his accommodations and denial in an instant, exposed his selfish thoughtlessness, his entitlement. If, in the end, he had broken their friendship for something so transient, his betrayal would become yet more profligate. Perhaps it was this thought, buried deep down, that led him to want the relationship with

Sarah to last, to have the summer at least. Perhaps it was guilt that animated him, not love.

The bright ringing of the strings hung on the air, unimpeded. She waited until the last trace of the struck chord had dissipated, then exhaled. It had been such a long time since she had picked up the guitar and she had forgotten much of the little she had learned, but she retained the shapes of C major and A minor in her fingers, as well as something that she thought might be E minor; she could hold a steady rhythm in her right hand, even if the arpeggios had gone. But mostly she spent what little time she had with her guitar trying to remember how to tune the instrument.

When her husband had taken the last of his things from the apartment, she had bought the guitar and had practised daily. She had made her way through half of the book of chords and scales before her attention wandered, led astray by curiosity. It had always been that way. It was the thing she shared most exactly with Jakob, what had attracted him to her and her to him. Perhaps they should have seen that it would lead eventually to their parting, but the realisation came to them only after 11 years. There had been no affair, despite what they told the lawyers, no anger, simply a slow sadness. They had chosen against children, and perhaps in that choice they had unknowingly known that their time together was conditional and limited. They were still in contact. Amicable, the lawyers would call it. Jakob had married again, but Freyja was content to keep herself for other things. And there were so many other things to do.

She dampened the strings with her left hand, listening for sounds on the stairs, and heard her neighbour's door click shut across the landing. Árni would be back soon, but not yet. She had time. The privacy, finally, was one of the reasons why she had waited until after Jakob had left before she had taken up the guitar. Something about the privacy of knowing no-one was listening made the sounds she made more palatable. When her nephew had finally goaded her into playing a few bars of something, her fingers had become more imprecise. That he was around now, she told herself, was probably why she practised so little.

She would not want to be without him however, whatever loss of privacy his presence brought. She regretted few things about her life and the choices she had made, but being so far from her family was one of them, especially that it meant that her nephew had until now been a stranger. She had already been in Reykjavík for a year by the time he was born, so not only had she been absent for his actual life, but also his almost life, within her little sister. When Hrefna had called to say that Árni had a place at the university, Freyja had not been surprised. She had talked with the boy about his hopes over the course of three or four Christmases, and some summer visits. She had been struck by his bright intelligence, his curiosity about the world, especially about its workings, the whys and the whats. She had not needed to be asked, and had suggested that, if he wanted, he could take the spare room in her apartment. She had missed his growing into a man, but at least now she had a chance to reclaim some of what had been lost.

From the sideboard, the clock chimed eight. Freyja looked at her wrist watch, which she set by that same clock, to confirm that it was already past the time she normally ate. Since the summer, Árni was often late back from the university. At first, she had worried that he was neglecting his studies for drinking or for girls. His exam results the previous term had been exemplary. He might, she surmised, have taken the ease with which they were won as a signal that he did not need to try so hard, that he could saunter through the next two years of his studies without effort.

For a few weeks, she had sought the right moment to raise concerns in a way that showed she was sympathetic to his desire to make the most of his life in the city. But no such moment arose before she realised that in fact her nephew had taken his outstanding grades as a spur to greater effort. He was not spending his evenings in the bars of the Laugavegur, but in the laboratory and the library. This worried Freyja more, and she wished that the boy was drunk in the arms of some girl, learning about life. But there was no girl, no friends at all in fact. Even that lovely girl, Gefn, with whom he had spent so many evenings in his first term, had disappeared. The English girl had returned home in the late spring. He had talked about visiting her over the summer but that had come to nothing and he had slipped away to his family, listless.

He had not talked about either girl since he had returned to the city for the new academic year, but he did still talk about visiting England. They had spent several long evenings travelling together through their longings for foreign shores, but while Freyja would slip just as easily to Spain, to the Alhambra, to Las Ramblas, or even to the east, to the Hermitage and to Red Square, her nephew would guide them back eventually to England. No-one in her family had left their parent's hearth so far behind and she delighted in the discovery of a fellow traveller. She slid the guitar into its nook behind the settee and retrieved her Russian phrase book from under a pile of knitting, testing herself against its pages, searching her memory for all the words she had lost.

The sound of the front door, creaking into its frame woke her, but it was only when she felt his hand on her shoulder that she realised that she had been asleep. Even in that half moment between waking and dreams, her sister was still with her, her face expectant and accusing. It was a familiar dream, a reworked memory, turned over and rerun in her mind, whether sleeping or simply idle. The dream-memory always began with Hrefna dressed as she had been that morning twenty years before, although her face had changed with the years. They were sitting in the kitchen at home, paring carrots and slicing potatoes ready for the pot, accompaniments for the leg of smoked lamb that would be their lunch. They could hear the clang of their father's hammer from the forge. Hrefna hummed a tune still playing on the radio, the unfamiliar words of the American song, simply melody without meaning. At least not the meaning intended by the singer.

Freyja had put down her knife, resting her palms flat either side of the bowl on the table. She had watched her baby sister's face for a moment. She loved Hrefna best of her two sisters, although she would sooner die than say so out loud. Her sister's compassion was never an excuse for weakness and her seriousness was never dull; she had a ferocious intelligence that frightened even their father. So it was not simply chance or convenience that led Freyja to choose that moment to share her plans.

'Have you ever wondered what Reykjavík is like?'

The question had stopped Hrefna's hands with its sudden arrival. As was her way, she had taken a moment to frame an appropriate response before saying that she naturally hoped to see the city one day; maybe after she was married, Eiríkur would take her, maybe for their honeymoon; it was not so far, hardly the moon. She had laughed, and Freyja had joined her, laughing at the silliness of distance, at the freedom her sister had allowed her. And she had told her about the job with the aggregates firm, about the guest house that had been found for her until she could make her own arrangements, about the visits they would have together, about the things that they would do, just the two of them, in the city. And Hrefna's face had hardened, had receded, burying laughter in its tomb.

'Leaving? When? When do you go? What about my wedding? Will you be gone before the wedding? What did dad say? I can't believe he's just letting you go, letting you leave us?'

Freyja had not been able to shape answers to any of her questions before her father was there, by the door, face red from the forge. Neither sister had heard the clanging of metal cease, nor the front door crease. He stood there for some time, a startled question hanging over him, but then he told Hrefna to fetch a bottle of schnapps from the parlour, two glasses as well, and he had sat and he had talked with his eldest daughter, without anger or sorrow, and they had drunk one, two, three glasses of schnapps, had hugged each other and promised to keep no secrets from each other in the future. And her youngest sister, the sister she liked the best, even now, had watched from around the door frame, with silent anger and sorrow.

Hrefna had kept her silence until Freyja had put the last of her books into the battered brown suitcase, brought down from the eaves. While their father waited in the van, and Fríða locked the windows around the house, the two sisters had sat on Freyja's bed. The sunlight cut a shaft through slow swirling flecks of dust and made a square on the floorboards. Hrefna had only asked if she was certain that this was what she wanted to do, if she was sure that it would make her happy, that she hoped it would, and yet her voice, her eyes, could not contain her own unhappiness at the parting. Her little sister, who she liked best of all in the world, had told her to enjoy the whirling world until it was time to stop spinning and find her place within it, and all the while her heart had been breaking.

'You can't live every life. You need to choose the one that makes you happiest and let the others go. You understand that, don't you?'

That was the moment at which memory became dream, or waking dream, or a brain idling in the face of the limitlessness of the world. At the time, Freyja had simply smiled and held her sister, glad that the silence between them had been broken, that a blessing of sorts had been given for her new adventure. But since then, and with ever greater intensity, sleeping, dawdling Freyja had struggled to find an answer under her ghost-sister's unblinking stare.

The hand at her shoulder shook again, a little less gently, but still like gossamer. The phrase book that was still wrapped around her thumb leapt from her lap with the snap of her body and went clattering to the floor. The cold slap of paper on tiles chased out the last of her drowsiness, and Hrefna was gone once more, melted into the slow yellow light of her city living room.

'Hm. What time is it, Árni dear?' Her nephew was still bent over her and she felt very old and very small under his shadow. A trace of stale coffee hung in the air between them.

'Just gone half ten. Did you leave me any dinner?' Freyja's sudden hunger reminded her that she had forgotten to cook, had slipped into dreams before she had managed to eat even a piece of bread.

◾

The buildings slipped by in glimpses, their staccato colours jolting into the endless fluidity of the nearer world. She no longer trusted her legs, their reliability suspect in the absence of friction. She could only follow and hope for the best. The wind that ruffled her muffled ears carried Árni's laughter, ceaseless since the three of them had launched themselves onto the frozen lake; Freyja's too.

She felt a prickle of resentment at the intimacy between her son and her sister, the shared fearlessness, their quiet understanding and their raucous joy in life.

Hrefna managed to bring herself to a halt and wavered for a moment, rocking over her feet, seeking out the balance she had known as a girl. It had been years since she had skated, since real life had constructed for her other pastimes. In the cold centre of the lake she tried to remember if she had ever enjoyed this. She thought enviously of Eiríkur, drinking coffee in the warmth of the café on the edge of Austurvöllur square. She could have joined him, left Freyja and Árni to sweep around the ice alone, but she saw her son so infrequently and her sister had him to herself on every other day.

She watched the two of them race across from the far side of the lake, heads down, hands spread, swinging like professionals, only veering to avoid the other Sunday skaters out enjoying the blue sky day. The sun was already low, stretching long-legged across the ice, and the stooped shapes of Árni and Freyja seemed grotesque, at odds with their true elegance. Nearby, others paused to watch, the enthusiasm of strangers sending a trill of excitement through her. Hrefna yelled encouragement to the racers and was delighted when other spectators joined her, clapping their mittened hands into a coalescent rhythm. The tempo increased, the racers becoming more serious with every stroke, until it seemed that they flew above the ice and only the brief shreds rising from their heels betrayed that they were still earthbound.

Árni's stumble, when it came, froze Hrefna to the ice. She waited for the rifle's retort, so completely did he crumple, but no sound came. He slid for only a short while before the ice cracked and ruptured and he half disappeared beneath the surface. She heard a cry and thought that it had come from her mouth, before she saw the man, flailing across the ice without skates, shoes sliding wayward with every frantic step. She recognised her husband as he reached the ice hole, disguised despite the familiar coat by the awkward shape of his running body. She had not noticed him standing on the shore, watching, and she did not known how long he had been there, nor what had brought him out of the warmth of the café to the lake's edge; only that he was there, lying on his chest, arms beneath the surface, pulling his son from the icy darkness.

Others now, strangers, gathered round, offered their coats to the drenched and shivering boy, his father, supporting them as they stumbled to the shore. Freyja was with her, her arm around her shoulder, telling her that it was alright, that Eiríkur had him, that all was well. A siren sounded, summoned from one of the houses overlooking the lake. Her sister guided her through the small crowd that had gathered around her son and her husband, whose face was stretched and damp with the determination that no man should watch both his father and his son disappear beneath the water.

2005

In the instant before she broke the surface, a dome of silvered water gathered about her head. Charlotte watched as it fractured into a thousand fragments of sunlight. Freyja gulped in air and opened her eyes, seemingly startled by the rush and crash that gathered under the high hall of the swimming pool.

Charlotte too began to breathe again and watched the frantic bustle of Freyja's clumsy limbs beneath the water as she struggled towards her mother. She in turn smiled her encouragement, and felt the warmth of pride and nostalgia wrestle against the cold of the pool. Charlotte drifted into her own childhood for an instant and, returning, she looked around her. The pool had changed little, at least in essence. There were newly refurbished changing rooms and a café had been made in the space that had then been occupied only by glass-fronted machines selling crisps and chocolate bars and fizzy drinks. The paintwork on the high arc of the concrete roof was cleaner and brighter, but the space itself, and the chill of the water, were as familiar to her as her parents' home.

She took a small step backwards, widening the gap left for Freyja to cross, just as her own mother had done. It had seemed like a cruelty then, but that had been forgotten somewhere. She willed her daughter to make up the distance, even as she took another step backwards. It was the first time she had seen for herself the product of her daughter's swimming lessons at school; she wished that Árni had been able to be there to witness it too.

The water teemed with other parents and children seeking something to fill the open space of the long weekend. Another step backwards. It had been Freyja's suggestion. A second day at her grandparents' house had brought little inspiration. The pool offered both excitement and a sanctuary.

She looked at her daughter's face, taut with seriousness and maybe a little fear; she tried to summon up in herself the fear that must surely accompany you into the water when you surrender to it, and the memory of another sunlit day flooded in. She had been a girl of maybe eight years old, just like Freyja. They had been on holiday, in Ibiza. She had made friends with the children of another family staying at the hotel. They had been older, already at secondary school, already confident swimmers, and had thought nothing of pulling her further along the pool, into the deepest waters. Had she then felt the terror that should surely have filled her when she had realised that she would no longer be able to reach the safety of the solid tiles beneath her? Charlotte could not recall, only remembered the feeling of being with older girls, of living beyond her limits. Maybe the fear only came later, once you understood a little of death, of consequences.

Another subtle step and Charlotte felt the tiles of the pool's edge against her back. She stretched out her hands to Freyja and guided her into a fleeting embrace, before her daughter wriggled free and paddled off to the fringes of the shallow water. There, she splashed noisily among the seething of other children. Charlotte looked up at the clock that was still pinned to the wall after all these years. Its second hand swooped in its endless circle and she felt a pang of guilt for her brother, who had been left to entertain her young son, Ben, in a soft-play area set up on the other side of the leisure centre especially for the Easter holidays. That Christopher had been able to take a couple of days off ahead of the Bank Holiday to spend with the family only highlighted Árni's absence. She could only assume that banks were more forgiving employers than pharmaceutical companies. Her guilt solidified into frustration and she shivered. It was time to get out of the pool.

'How's Árni's new job working out? Has he sold his soul yet?' Christopher smiled; his brother-in-law's dedication had always seemed like something of a rebuke to his own unrefined capitalism, and he had been pleased when he had traded purity for the rewards of Big Pharma. *'And what about you? Mum says you've had yet another promotion at work. I don't know how you do it. I'm run ragged after a couple of hours with just the one of these little darlings.'* Christopher nodded at Ben who was squeezing the flesh of a banana between his fingers; his mother hissed a rebuke in the boy's direction. She had expended all of her patience on coaxing a complaining Freyja from the water and into dry clothes, and a burst of ineffectual chiding was all that she could manage.

'They have their moments.' She leant across to wipe as much of the stickiness as she could from Ben's clenched hand. *'To be honest, work is a bit of a relief. Freyja, darling, be careful with that.'* She reached over to nudge the glass of apple juice back towards the centre of the table. *'But yes, they've given me the geography list as well. Not sure I'd call it a promotion. I think it was just easier to explain it that way to mum. But it certainly is more responsibility. Things are going well, I think. For all of us.'*

She smiled as she turned her coffee cup in its saucer, delighting in its frictive complaint, lost in its simplicity. Christopher watched her, wondered where the thoughts of work had taken her. His sister had always been the one to disappear into herself. For him, life was quite straightforward: things were what they were and, while they could of course be otherwise, they could only be changed through action. Charlotte, on the other hand, could become lost in her thoughts for hours. As a child he had envied her that, resented how he had been shut out so often, unable to follow her into her unseen world. Maybe that was why she had found in Árni such a soul mate. It had taken him a while to understand that his sister's husband was neither rude nor playing a role, a pretence of silent strength: simply, he didn't talk so much.

'Pass that clamp, can you mate?'

Sam looked up from the carcass and extended his hand towards his friend. A shadow of confusion passed over Árni's face like a cloud over a summer sea, but was gone just as quickly. The bent and clanking metal felt cold, despite the warmth of the day. He weighed its unaccustomed solidity with satisfaction as he passed it to the waiting hand. The nimbleness of the fingers that twisted shut the jaws onto the joint astounded him, as it always did. He looked at his own hands, ashamed.

A final squeak and the pieces were set in place. Sam crouched slightly to look along the lines of the cabinet, ran a light finger across the two pieces, as if not trusting his eyes over the perception of his hands. Straightening, he exhaled a long stream of spent breath through his nose, twisting his clamped mouth into an expression of casual pride. Without a glance, his hand found the mug on the work bench behind him; he took a long swallow of tepid coffee.

Saturdays often passed through his friend's workshop, once Árni had performed the rituals of family. It was a ritual in itself, one that had begun before he had known Charlotte, when he had first arrived in this city. Through the University, he had found a room in a house next door to this house. It had been smaller then, less well-maintained; the brick-built out building containing the workshop had not existed and instead there had been a small patch of thinning grass, littered with the yellow plastic of scattered toys. And yet Sam's garden had seemed pristine compared with the twisted thicket of the space behind Árni's shared house.

It had been on the autumn afternoons of his first term, when Árni had hacked back the green malevolence with what rusted tools he could find, that Sam and he had first talked. His neighbour had watched for a time, amused by the inexpert diligence of the tall young man, before he'd leant over the fence to offer to lend him a strimmer. Two days later, the garden denuded under a low sun, Árni had knocked at his neighbour's door, a carrier bag of Czech lagers swinging expectantly. The next time Árni had taken beer to Sam's door, he had been invited in and the two men had drunk them together in the kitchen while Sam's wife had watched television and listened for prohibited sounds from upstairs.

Sam was a few years older, had foregone university to train as a joiner and had been busy earning money from fitting kitchens and making bookcases for Cambridge professors. While Árni had been studying in Reykjavík, Sam had bought this house and had married. His son had been born a few months later. By the time Árni had graduated and put in place his plan to fly to England, a baby daughter had arrived.

The friendship had evolved slowly and only blossomed once Árni had ceased to be a neighbour. Every few weeks, he would watch Sam work, first in a large wooden shed, and latterly in the workshop. Often they would simply drink coffee and share a few thoughts about the lives they led between times. It had been in these hours that Árni had learned about Sam's occasional infidelities, committed lightly, seemingly joyfully. That his friend was able to enjoy both a family and the infinite pleasures of other women, without apparent guilt, seemed both thrilling and unfair. Árni had never been able even to verbalise the attraction he felt for one of his colleagues, the fantasies he had woven of sudden seclusion and intimacy in unexpected places, in the fear that he might make them real, or at least make real the guilt he felt for them. So instead of guilt, he felt the shame of his timidity.

The last of the coffee gurgled through the filter, gasping and hissing into the glass jug. There would be time yet to tell Sam about his own work, although he would much rather simply watch his friend's busy hands. In recent months, the tangibility of the work, now that it had left the realm of academic purity, had made more sense to his practical friend, as it should. As it did to him. His worries about making a false step, a bad choice, had receded. He had become comfortable with the work itself. It had not simply been because of the salary and the job title after all. He was still being useful; more useful. Memory, attachment, associations long lost, were useful things after all. He sucked at the scolding coffee and heard the sound of his father echo in the cup. At home, his mother would refill an empty cup before it could reach the table; he peered into the mug willing for it to be both full and empty at the same time, and wrapped himself in the inevitable disappointment.

The ragged crows rose above the copse, carried on the restless air, their caws fracturing the steady whisper of the birches. Árni shifted his weight from one leg to the other and the desiccated leaves beneath his feet crackled. He brought his body once more to stillness and let the soft waves of the world wash into him. It would cleanse him, if only he would let it.

He had seen no-one since he had left the car parked at the side of the road: the ruler-straight path alongside the bare field had been empty, as it often was. The woodland seldom saw human visitors in any season, especially so early on a Thursday morning. There were more enticing places in this part of the county: dog-walkers and strollers and runners all tended to overlook this lonely corner, leaving it forlorn. It was why he chose to come here.

The rusted spears of dying dock pierced the ground; a fallen tree some little way off scored a silver line across the golden detritus of the ground. Near its toppled roots, the trunk stood a metre from the floor, a perfect place to sit. If he did not mind dirtying his coat, he would be able to lean against the flat perpendicularity of what had been the ground between the tree's roots. And he did not mind dirtying his coat: its cleanliness was of no interest to him. He wanted only to sit and let the silence of himself and the rustle of the world blur.

She had still been asleep when he'd slipped from bed. Ben had started to make the sounds that signalled he would soon be up, but Freyja's room was silent. The sky beyond the bathroom window had been a pinkish grey, the sun not yet risen. He'd murmured an explanation into the warmth of Charlotte's cheek once he had pulled on yesterday's clothes and she had mumbled something in return before sliding back into her dreams. The house would by now be full of sounds and movement. Full of life. He thought about his phone, decided once more not to switch it on.

He was still off work, even though he had been back in England for a couple of days. Usually he would have resented the imposition. He knew without regret that he had become one of those men for whom work was everything. His work. It was important. It could change things. Everything? He thought again about his children, about his wife, and he was unable to stop himself from thinking about his father and from thinking about his mother. No, not everything.

Compassionate leave they had called it. When his manager had told him that he should take as much time as he needed, that he should under no circumstances return to work before two weeks had elapsed, he had discounted it, certain that he would in reality be back in the lab as soon as the funeral had been dealt with, once his mother had been buried and his father set up with the support and resources he needed to continue. He had not expected to collapse like this.

In the first moments after the phone call, he had thought only of his father. Eiríkur had been absent from the call, the news conveyed by his friend, but he had heard his father's silence behind Gylfi's careful words, his absence betraying their enormity, the devastation of their meaning. Árni had been at work and the sterility of his surroundings and the focus he had been able to give to the practicalities of things had been helpful.

His first thought, after the wind had returned to him, had been to think that his father would be helpless to deal with the practicalities that flowed from death. In normal circumstances, such things would be dealt with by his mother. Another reminder, if one should be needed, that these were not normal circumstances.

Gylfi's voice had sounded attenuated, alien, desolate as he explained that Hrefna had been found just beyond the kitchen door, laundry half hung on the line. The doctor had named that catastrophe as a stroke, yet even to Árni this seemed too small a word to carry the weight of what had occurred: he could not imagine how insufficient it would seem to his father.

He had not realised that he had been crying. Weeping. There had been no sobbing, no convulsions: the tears simply ran clear as melt water over basalt. He had not noticed either the attention of his colleague. The softness of her hand seemed to rest on someone else's arm; her searching eyes as flat and distant as an image projected onto a cinema screen. He had swallowed, hoping to be able to say something reassuring, but had found no words amid the heaviness in his throat.

It had taken him three hours to realise that he should be affronted at having been sent home. Only slowly did he remember that his colleague had driven him there, that his own car was still parked outside the lab building. He had become suddenly anxious about it, worried that he should somehow retrieve the vehicle before it became an inconvenience to someone. To him. He would need it to get to work in the morning. She had stroked his arm to calm him, to guide him to a chair, knelt on the floor beside him while she took his phone and found Charlotte's number.

When she had gone, leaving him with a glass half-filled with Scotch, he had called his father, told him that he would be with him as soon as he could, told him not to worry about arrangements, told him to take care of himself, told him everything that he himself wanted to be told. His father had grunted short responses, stopping each clipped sentence before his voice could catch on the raggedness of his throat. In the end there was only the question *'When can you come?'*

Charlotte had booked him onto a flight the next day. Because of work and the children, she had not been able to travel with him, but had followed on, once work had been informed, once Freyja and Ben had been safely deposited into the care of their still living grandmother. By the time she arrived, the arrangements for the funeral had been made, by Gylfi rather than Árni, and the father and the son had become locked in a broken silence that filled the house.

A thick flat sky had hung above the red-roofed church, barely clearing the stony greyness of the ridge across the fjord, such that the burial itself seemed entombed, sealed up in a cement box. The cloud sucked up the sound of the sea lapping at the graveyard's edge; the mourners themselves brought their own silence, a clutch of black figures among the white crosses. Árni had watched his mother's coffin disappear into the soil among relatives and family friends he had not seen for years; some cousins he had never seen before; his Aunt Fríða, now the last of Skúli Hilmarsson's daughters, had embraced him with taut and trembling arms. And his father had wept uncontrollably.

They'd stayed on over the weekend, watching Eiríkur, waiting for him to return. On the Sunday, he had gripped Árni's arm, suddenly overwhelmed by the thought that his son would leave too. He had asked, politely, calmly, if he would change his mind, if he would abandon England and return to his home. With as much politeness and as much calm as he could find, Árni had explained that his children were in England, his work too, that his wife also lived in England and that he needed to return for them. At this, Eiríkur had looked towards where Charlotte stood, making coffee in the kitchen, with what Árni would later describe as defeated resentment, and slowly nodded. His hand had loosened its grip and dropped from Árni's arm. The silence and distance had filled the sitting room once more.

Before they left, Árni had taken Gylfi aside and made him promise to contact him straight away if he ever had reason to think something was amiss with his father. He had pressed a note of his full contact details into the gnarled hand and asked if there was anything more he could do to help. Gylfi had replied with his usual quiet generosity, *'Come to see him, as often as you can'*, before a stream of apologies cascaded through his beard; there had been no reproach intended, Árni knew that, but Gylfi's simple request cut him deeply. They had embraced and Árni had made a promise he knew he would not keep despite his best intentions.

He was walking again, although he had no recollection of leaving the broken tree and did not recognise this part of the wood, nor how he had arrived within it. Leaves and twigs snapped with each step masking the other sounds, so he paused, held his breath. Somewhere was the sound of running water, clear and resonant. His eyes alighted on the thin strip of the stream some little distance away. He had never noticed it before, even though on other days, free of the litter of the sleeping trees, it would be more easily seen. He listened to its babble, watched the quick-silver snake through a nest of wet stones. Another stream, wider, came to mind and he chased the memory until it was pinned to the hillside above Bolungarvík. Every thought led him back to his mother.

He had seen so little of her in her last years. A handful of grudging visits, clipped as close as could be; her older sister's funeral; her father's; no slack into which confidences could slip. He had not known that she had been ill, did not know if she had been happy. She had simply been there, unchanging, something to which he would be able to return, pick up when he was ready, when he was needful. It had been an unthinking negligence.

His father had said none of this, but Árni had felt it snaking through the silences. He had made only that one attempt to assert his rights over his son, to beg for his attendance, his presence. His demand was too late for Hrefna, of course, and was instead driven by his own desperation in the face of lonely mortality. What had felt like the pain of loss had been simply his resentment towards his father.

A pigeon crashed through the trees above him, startled by something unseen stalking the copse. Árni looked up to catch a flash of pink and teal plumage against the universal grey. It was not grief, but guilt. This hopelessness, he decided, welled up from the guilt he felt, the guilt his father had stirred in him for his absence. It was all of a piece, had always been so, since he had grown from object to subject, from child into manhood. A family, above all other things, is a conspiracy of guilt. Yet he could not deny that his father had grounds for his needfulness, especially now that he was completely alone, in a place that was not quite home.

1950

The north wind snagged the sea and drove the low surf up the sheen of shallow sand. It surged and slipped with the breathing of the ocean, and Eiríkur stood at its fringe, watching it wrestle gravity, unaware of the forces at work but no less cowed by them. Were it not for his brother standing at his shoulder, he might have been afraid. They were, of course, very far from home. Only six kilometres, but he was only small, despite his birthday.

Four days before, the whole of Hesteyri had gathered in the church, dressed in their best clothes despite the weather, to mark the day with singing and talking, prayers too. Even Eiríkur knew that the land was older than he was, and yet he had grown used to the way that the whole world celebrated the birth of Iceland at the same time that they celebrated his own arrival in the world. In years to come he would tire of the coincidence, resent the intrusion of national celebration into his own day and sense that it made him less, not more, special. For now, it simply amused him.

Eiríkur turned to face his brother, losing his question in the turning. Ólafur was staring off to the horizon, but soon dropped his gaze to meet that of his younger brother. One eye was as blue as Eiríkur's, but the other was a vivid green. The village children and their parents alike regarded the abnormality as a sign of his brother's own specialness, a portent of something unknown, the meaning of which would only become apparent when whatever it was came to pass. His few years had given no clue as to what that might be, but even he seemed to believe that he was destined for something for which he should be ready. Often this weighed upon him, lent a solemnness ill-suited to a boy of ten, but for now his mismatched eyes softened, then creased into mischief.

'Race you to the river!'

Before Eiríkur could object, on behalf of his mother as much as himself, Ólafur kicked against the sand and sped off along the beach. The younger boy gave a fleeting glance to where his parents sat on a rug with the remains of a picnic, then followed, his heart beating behind his eyes, the crystal air raking his lungs. The pinched surface cracked with every beat, ruptured and creased, flecks following his heels. He moved further below the tide line where the sand was firmer, like setting concrete, and he pushed his legs to move faster, his lungs to swallow greater gulps of air. But the space between he and his brother only widened. Later in his life, he would wonder why a gap of four years had seemed so unbridgeable, but there on the beach, the capability of his ten year old brother seemed super-human, almost like a grown-up.

Ólafur waited by the stream that cut across the beach, carrying water from the mountains to the sea. It was only five metres across, but it was deep and fast flowing, even this close to the surf, and he knew better than to try to cross it, even if the broad arc of sand beyond was enticing in its scale and emptiness. Around the bay, a few small buildings stood on the distant shore, and he could make out the movements of people as they went about their business. What must have been a dog skittered between them and their houses, chasing unseen quarry. The thumping of feet behind him made him turn. Eiríkur was there, red-faced and heaving for breath.

'I wonder what it's like there, at Látrar, so far from everyone. Do you think there are children?'

Eiríkur could not find words for a moment and laboured at the air, refilling his aching lungs. He felt ashamed of his puniness. He did not care about the children of Látrar, if in fact any were there.

'I want to go back. I'm cold.'

The wind continued to slice through the bay, trailing ghostly trickles of sand up the beach. Eiríkur watched the fine dust snake its way over shells and into the dimples left by a fox's pad. It had not snowed since May, but the path over from Hesteyri had crunched through fields of ice crystal. It was a cold June and, had it not been his birthday, and had he not insisted, the family might well have spent the day in the shelter of their own fjord.

'Here. Let me show you how to skim a stone.'

Ólafur bent down and retrieved a small, flat pebble. Holding Eiríkur's hand, he led his brother to where the water paused in its endless shuttling, then showed him how he held the stone by its edge in the curve of his index finger, how with a snap of the wrist and a well-timed release the stone could be made to skip three, four, five times over the waves before it finally sank into the water. Eiríkur watched, mesmerised and Ólafur looked about earnestly to find another suitable missile, then another.

'Here, like this.'

But Eiríkur could not snap his wrist, nor let go in quite the right way and soon he simply threw stones, in long looping arcs, into the heart of the swirling sea, content just to watch his brother's magic until they ran out of stones and began instead to zag and zig their way back towards their parents. The return took much longer, with frequent detours to leap between the boulders that backed the beach or to balance along one of the salt-scoured tree trunks left by the winter storms. Every now and then, Ólafur would pause and tell Eiríkur which bird had made which footprint, to sing the song it sang, and the boys would laugh together as the younger tried to replicate the sound tunelessly. They ran down to the surf line where the Harlequin ducks gathered to dance, unperturbed by their boisterous audience, and they watched the low sun clear the headland.

It was getting late and, even though the sun would not set for another week or more, Ólafur suggested that they should probably head back. Eiríkur tried to summon the energy to object but the tiredness in his legs as much as that behind his eyes robbed him of his will to make the day last forever. At the blanket, they dropped to their knees beside their mother and welcomed the warmth of her arms.

◾

The wind rattled the shutters and broke Einar's concentration. He grumbled quietly, then returned his attention to the glass of schnapps that glowed yellow in his hand. The liquor's natural warmth grew more intense in the unreliable lamp light and its glimmer captivated him.

'*The little one is getting a chill, I think.*' Jóna rested the back of her hand on Eiríkur's forehead, studied his flushed cheeks. '*Hard to tell, with him sitting so close by the fire. No idea who he might have caught it from either. He's barely been out these last weeks. Maybe the elves are up to mischief under this storm?*'

Ólafur looked up from his book. He often heard the grown-ups talking about the hidden folk, blaming them for minor misfortunes and thanking them for unexpected luck. On summer nights, he would sit up with his brother, long after both should have been asleep, even after their parents had slipped into slumber and the noises of the village had died for the day, and they would watch for them from the window above their bed. But despite these vigils, he had never seen them. The suggestion that they might be at work now intrigued him.

Later, he would explain his suspicions to his wide-eyed brother and they would search under their beds and out through a chink in the heavy woollen curtains, out into the blackness. Under the deathly starless sky, it was easy to imagine the elves setting about their mischief-making, but they remained hidden from the two boys no matter how hard they scoured the white hillside and the slack spaces between the village houses. Eventually, the sharpening chill closed in around them and pushed them back beneath their blankets. Eiríkur peered nervously about the gloomy attic, unable to sleep for a long time after Ólafur's breathing found its steady, heavy rhythm. He bargained with the unseen elves, pleading with them to end his fever, to release him from its grip, and offered up promises of sweet things and favours in exchange. At last, the night overwhelmed him and he dreamt fitfully of elves tormenting him with furnaces and ice, exacting their price.

The fever did not lift entirely for six days, but it was slight. For two days, Eiríkur was moved simply from bed to fireside and back. In between times, he was filled with fish soup, cosseted by his mother and entertained by his brother. His father had listened to the wind for any sign that the weather might calm. On the fifth day, Eiríkur's cough had slackened into a croak.

The following morning, there was no wind. Einar woke to the welcome silence and cautiously peeled back the curtain to reveal the blinter of starlit snow. Without waking Jóna, despite himself, he slipped from the covers and crept along the passage to stoke the kitchen fire and set about making coffee. In the stillness, he listened to the crinkle of tobacco in his pipe and waited for the pot to boil. To be released from the grip of the blizzard felt like spring itself. The winter would hold more storms, of course, but it was nearly Christmas and the days would soon begin to lighten. With the optimism of a clear morning, Einar whistled an old tune and picked out his favourite cup from the sideboard.

'Let me, Einar, my love.'

Jóna's half-whisper reached him like a dream and he allowed his wife to nudge him gently from her place by the stove. Taking the cup from his hand, she reached up onto her toes and kissed his cheek, above the bristles of his beard. As every morning, he was grateful for his good fortune in marrying her and he would not take the steaming cup from her until he had returned her kiss to her own cheek.

'I think I'll take the rifle out, see if I can't find something for dinner. It can't just be me that's tired of fish, and who knows when we'll get another day as fine as this. You never know, I might bag a bird or two. How do you fancy a ptarmigan for your Christmas pot?'

Jóna laughed and wrapped her arms about her husband. She looked up at him, one eyebrow raised.

'Ha, admit it. You just want to get outside after being cooped up this past week. You'll come back with nothing but an empty tobacco pouch! Make sure you take Helgi Gunnarsson. It'll be treacherous up there after all this snow. Now, clear out of my way while I make some breakfast.'

By the time the sun had shown itself on the mountain's south face, Einar had already been gone for three hours. Jóna looked up towards the pass under Kagrafell, hoping to catch a sight of her husband and his friend. The moor stretched out, buried under crisp snow, wind-whipped into meringue peaks. The weak sunlight bathed the hillside like balm. In the depthless clarity of the air, seabirds soared gratefully, greeting each other much as the villagers called to each other in their happy tasks. All of Hesteyri was outside, prisoners released from a familiar sentence. The storm's snow was piled beside cleared porches, cows looked out blinking from their opened byres; the sound of bleating carried from barn doors. Some of the men had taken axes and saws to a tree trunk that had been dropped by the waves like kindling above the shore.

Eiríkur blossomed into the air, coddled in three sweaters and a thick scarf looped over his head and around his neck. It was two weeks since he had seen the sun as more than a grey smudge in the southern sky and he had to shield his eyes as he emerged into its light. Behind him, his brother stamped his feet against the chill air.

Jóna inspected her children to make sure that they were wrapped tight against the cold, but it was only for show. As much as her husband, she knew that they had spent too long indoors and she sent them willingly into the brief brightness, shouting after them that they were to stay close. The brothers ran heedlessly to the flat ground below the house, before the land sloped away into the sea. Every few metres they plunged deep into thick drifts, disappearing up to their waists, collapsing into laughter. Where the bushes peaked above the white crust, the black twigs were glazed in hoar frost and all across the snow's surface wind-raked crystals pointed the way to where the storm had blown. The world glittered in its streaming light, aflame yet frozen.

The first snowball landed a little way short of its target. Eiríkur giggled regardless and set about forming his next missile. He looked up just as Ólafur's reply arced towards him, turning his back instinctively. The snowball exploded just below his shoulder, scattering powder across his sweater, into the ridges of his mother's knitting. He squealed with delight and raced towards his brother carrying loose handfuls of snow. From the doorway, Jóna watched. Her work could wait a while. The shallow warmth of the sun awoke a yearning for spring within her, and she found herself laughing for no reason. Later she would visit Helgi Gunnarsson's house, she told herself, and would whittle away some of the winter in idle conversation with Fjóla, before their husbands returned with whatever the fells had offered up. Shielding her eyes, she looked out across the bay to where, some thirty kilometres distant, a white strip of land cut between the deep blue of the water and the pale blue of the sky. She fancied that she could make out the smoke of hearth fires, rising straight into the air, from a clutch of houses, probably at Hnífsdalur, or at Bolungarvík perhaps. She wondered if she might persuade Einar to take her across, in the spring, to visit the town, where she might spend a few hours in the shops and coffee houses. She might buy something special for the boys' birthdays in the distant summer, if the early fishing was good.

■

A howl of frozen air broke the tranquillity of the kitchen, announcing Einar's return. Jóna watched the lamplight flicker, then settle once more, slow and yellow in the afternoon's darkness. The flames licking the charred log in the grate guttered too, but soon found their rhythm once the door had been barred against the wind. It had blown without mercy since Christmas Day. It had raged over the pass and screamed down the length of the fjord, pinning the people of Hesteyri inside their houses, tugging at the shutters and the floor boards venomously. Once or twice the alarm had been raised and the men had plunged into the death-black night to help a neighbour to secure the lines that kept roof and wall together. Three winters before, Ragnar Runólfsson's place had been ripped from its moorings and cast into the sea with every stick and bolt while the family watched in despair. The roots of the house remained yet, a ragged reminder tangled in sedge: with the dawning of spring's light, they had left Hesteyri, and were soon followed by one or two other families. It had been the start of the exodus.

Einar stood a moment at the kitchen door, his beard brittle-white with frost. Across his chest, three snow-scoured logs steamed out vapour wisps: they would keep the kitchen warm until morning. But Einar's face reflected none of the comfort of the tight-tied room.

'*Sit. Warm yourself a while.*'

She stepped over Eiríkur, who was reading in the lamplight on the rug beside the hearth, and poured two or three gouts of thick coffee into a little china cup, adding sugar from the pot on the mantelpiece. She knocked back the vent under the grate to feed the flames before turning back to the table where Einar was filling his pipe. A shiver ran though his shoulders.

'*Maybe you should keep the vent closed a little. At least until we have a sense of how long the worst of this weather is going to last. There's wood enough but none to spare, not if this wind keeps up.*'

Jóna watched her husband's hands, busy with tobacco. The weather, always bad at this time, bore down with an unusual malevolence. There was no sign of it lifting. When she struggled to the cowshed, to fetch what little milk was to be had and to make sure that Glæta had sufficient hay and free water to drink, the sharp blackness drove into her bones such that it would take twenty minutes by the fire until her shivering stopped. At the shore, the snow reached down to the tide line and would have stretched further if it were not for the force of the waves racing to the shore. *Tófa* lay upturned, her hull fast tied under tarpaulin, useless. Even in the short day there was scant light, such was the density of snow carried down on the wind. She had not seen the sun for eight days.

'But the boy. He needs to be kept warm.'

Jóna's eyes lifted to where Ólafur slept above. He had shown the first signs of fever in the days before Christmas, and he had eaten only a little of the ptarmigan, and none of the lamb. Since then his fever had hardened and, as the wind whipped the closed-up houses of Hesteyri, he had quaked beneath a mound of blankets in the attic room, rising less frequently each day until the New Year had slid in unnoticed under the blizzard. Eiríkur had been moved to his parents' room, so that at least one of the children might sleep.

'Better, my love, that he has heat next week too. We don't know how long the storms will last. How is he, anyway?' He looked into his empty cup and decided instead to fill his pipe. Jóna was quickly at his side with the coffee pot and a kiss for his forehead.

'He's worse. Maybe we should see what the doctor thinks?'

Einar looked up sharply from his tobacco, his thumb still pressed into the bowl of his pipe. He hung there, motionless, while he gathered the words he needed, conscious of Eiríkur's close and expectant gaze. The boy did not understand exactly what one was, but he knew that doctors brought bad news. Many of the households that the doctor visited were soon dressed in mourning-black. He watched his father's face closely for a flicker of dread. None was forthcoming, just a stern instruction to leave his book and find his way into the folds of blankets huddled in the next room.

Morning came in cold grey light. Eiríkur buried himself deeper under the blankets, shutting out the day's feeble glow. His parents were already up and the sheets to either side were chill. He could hear his mother in the kitchen, the clank and clink of pots worming in under the howl of the wind. Above him, beyond the blankets, beyond the dull dank air, beyond the boards of the ceiling, his brother laboured with his breathing. Eyes screwed tight shut, Eiríkur pleaded with the elves, tried to make another deal with them, offering promises in exchange for Ólafur's release, knowing that he had failed to honour those made for his own.

The sound of the door startled him. He had pictured his father at the kitchen table, lost in tobacco smoke, waiting for the wind to slacken. But even as he adjusted his imagined world to include his father returning from the cow shed, carrying firewood, fish or potatoes, the sound of another voice filled the kitchen, amplified by its strangeness. Eiríkur pulled the covers down to his chin, and listened intently. The low drone of the man's voice remained indecipherable, as did his mother's response; the sound of boots on the attic ladder puzzled him and only once the footsteps crossed the ceiling did Eiríkur remember his mother's question from the night before. Anxious and intrigued, Eiríkur slipped from the bed and pulled on his trousers and a sweater.

He reached the top of the ladder in time to see the doctor press a metal disc against Ólafur's chest. Eiríkur had not seen his brother for a day or so, and was struck by the greyness of his face, the darkness around his eyes: there was no flinch when the cold metal of the stethoscope touched his skin and his chest rose and fell only slightly as the doctor listened. His mother stood beside the doctor, intent. When he had removed the stethoscope, letting the shining disc dangle and dance at the end to its tube, Jóna pressed a cloth to her son's forehead and murmured into his ear. Turning, leading the doctor back to the hatch, she caught sight of Eiríkur, his chin resting on the floor boards. In her unguarded face Eiríkur saw tenderness but also fear, fear too deep and too wide for her to subdue quickly enough. By the time she had constructed her smile, Eiríkur already knew that his worries about the doctor's arrival had been justified. At her request, he climbed up into the attic and shook the doctor's hand. He felt the gentle pressure of his mother's hand on his head, but it did not offer comforting solidity, simply dread weight. He answered the doctor's questions as best he could, explained that he had not felt poorly for weeks now. His eyes were drawn to the sallow shadow of his brother's vivacity, and the thought welled up within him that these were not simple enquires after his well-being, nor even a gentle examination of a potential patient, but rather were a rebuke, an accusation of complicity in his brother's condition. He thought back over the promises he had made to the elves while he was ill, remembering all those he had broken once he had returned to health. A low moan rose from the mound of blankets, which shifted before settling once again into an uneasy peace. His brother's breath rasped gently, barely audible but louder than the howling air outside.

His mother was already at the bottom of the ladder. The doctor had begun his descent, his face level with Eiríkur's, eyes cast down to where his boots sought out the next rung. His hair was a blend of greys and below its indistinct line, furrows scratched across his forehead. Perhaps he felt Eiríkur's eyes upon him, perhaps it was simply chance, but the doctor looked up, straight into the boy's face. Whatever he saw there caused him to stop. His grey eyes, as grey as his hair, softened, the creases around them deepening; white, smooth teeth peeled from between his lips, lips that had not often tasted the lash of the sea.

'Try not to worry, Eiríkur. We will do all we can. Ólafur is a strong boy. It's a bad fever, of course. You're a clever lad, you know that. I won't lie, your brother is very poorly, but by God's grace, and a little science, we might yet see him through it. Now, come down. Your mother tells me you haven't had any breakfast. And Ólafur needs rest as much as anything.'

In the kitchen, Eiríkur's spoon lay idle in its bowl, the oatmeal coagulating around it, while the doctor explained the medicines he took from his brown leather bag and placed on the table. Jóna listened carefully, anxious to capture every detail about their application and effects. Einar had stared through the window into the swirling day, his pipe jutted rigid from his jaw, since the doctor had advised him to be ready with the boat should the wind drop sufficiently to allow for passage across the deep sound, to Ísafjörður. The clinic there could offer better treatments, more thorough care. His voice had been natural, even and matter of fact; a simple observation, something to fill the air while he arranged the jars and bottles hidden in his bag. Jóna had looked on quizzically, but Einar had turned decisively to face the window, his back to the room, and remained there until the doctor offered his hand in parting, promising to return before the day was done. When the family were alone again, he resumed his study of the snow carried on the screaming wind, and did not break it even to relight his now cold pipe.

■

The morning after Epiphany, the wind dropped and stars glinted through a fraying carpet of cloud. Sleepless, Einar had watched the changing sky, counted each light as it had broken through the thinning cobbles above. By the time the sun had begun to skirt the southern horizon, Einar was in the doorway. For a time he simply stood on the threshold, watching the horizon, staring into the unaccustomed light. He made no attempt to clear the snow from the bulge down towards the shore that marked where *Tófa* lay upturned. The time for that had passed. There would be no crossing.

Behind him, young eyes watched. Eiríkur had slipped out from the kitchen, unnoticed by his mother. There he studied his father's framed silhouette, too afraid to approach. The silence that had followed his brother's death had borne down on the house, a leaden wake that followed his father into every room and lingered after his leaving. Only his mother had tried to explain what had happened, tried to comfort him as he longed to comfort his father.

Einar's sudden, slow movement startled Eiríkur and he crept to the door to see where his father had gone. From the step he saw him emerge from the cowshed, his spade grasped mid-shaft in his left hand; he watched him trudge up the hill towards the level ground where some of the other men of the village had gathered, each with their own spade or pick axe or shovel; he watched them raise their hands in greeting, heard their voices over the still air, contained, afraid.

'Eiríkur, come in. It's too cold, without your scarf and jacket.'

Jóna did not say, as she would have only a few weeks before, that he would catch his death of cold. Instead she picked him up and held him close to her as she carried him back into the kitchen. The grate hissed in gratitude for the fresh log she dropped into its flames. On the stove simmered a small pan of fresh milk, taken from Glæta that morning, into which Jóna stirred a scoop of the chocolate powder that the children had coveted, but which now held little interest for Eiríkur. The boy strained to look out of the window, to see where his father and the other men had gone, but he could only see the sky and the sea and the low sun edging over the distant hills.

2010

No, he had no further questions. None that he could ask without creating a scene. And despite the near certainty that he had not got the job, he did not want to do that. It would appear desperate, or graceless, or juvenile. He wanted to be none of those things and, if he had to be them, he did not want others to know. He would keep his humiliation buried in his chest. Instead of asking why it was that this boy felt entitled to patronise someone of his experience, his expertise, Árni just smiled as politely as he could and nodded in time to the explanation of the remaining formalities. The woman from Human Resources ran through the next steps without intonation, told him how many other candidates they had left to see that day, and when they expected to be able to make a decision. They would let him know if he had made it through to the next round by the end of the week at the latest. The young man stood, his right arm extended expectantly, prematurely, while Árni scrambled to return to his bag his CV, his notebook, his pen.

Could he tell? The interviewer's eyes did not display any sign that he had felt the quiver of his hand, or noticed that it had been pulled away a little too fast. Yet he must have known, must have felt its cold dampness. Árni tried not to imagine the awkward silence once he had left the room, the exaggerated sigh, the all too brief attempt to identify his strengths, before his candidacy formally ended and their thoughts turned to the next applicant. Passing through reception, he straightened his shoulders and smeared what felt like confidence across his face; he scanned the expressions of the four people sitting in the orange upholstered bowls that served as chairs. He had recognised none of the other names, names he had seen written upside down on the woman's sheet of paper; he recognised none of these faces, but one of them must be the next candidate. Maybe the young man, legs straggling from the orange bowl, who looked a little too uncomfortable in his fiercely ironed shirt, the pristine knot of his tie shackled about his neck. Árni gave him a little smile, a small nod of the head.

Outside, in the cold air, his embarrassment confronted him, leached across his pinched and burning cheeks. It wasn't the fault of the young man folded uncomfortably into the orange chair. He was just looking for another job, like everyone else. He could not be blamed. In any case, this job was already lost to Árni. All he had left were the shreds of his pride; pettiness would do nothing to sustain that. His notice period would soon expire, and then there would only be his redundancy pay, just three months' salary, and whatever was left of his self-esteem. There was no point in frittering that away. It was as precious as money.

He looked along the unfamiliar street: London remained something of a mystery to him and he did not know how this street connected to the one that led to the tube station. Árni stood for a moment, lost, casting his eyes along the pavement, waiting for the memory of his arrival to emerge from the mist. Despite himself, he had been hopeful, but in his nervousness he had failed to pay attention to the turns he had made to reach this point. Carelessness, Charlotte would call it. It had seemed more like confidence, albeit misplaced, to Árni.

At the end of the street, the roads leading to the left and to the right were as unfamiliar to him as the one behind him. There was no sign of the reassuring broken circle that signalled the safety of a station. A bus rumbled past, heading from who-knows-where to somewhere else. Árni toyed momentarily with the thought of turning back, taking the other route, the one not chosen, but since he had nowhere in particular to be, he instead turned to the left and continued into the unknown city. Fragments of Georgian terraces filled the spaces between broad and busy roads and sedate, newly-built piazzas. These were enclosed by the glass facades of offices much like the one that housed the company that did not want him. He watched his reflection as he passed, tried to recognise in himself the failings that the interviewer had spotted so quickly, but they still eluded him. He had always had the comfort of knowing that he was good at what he did, had let that certainty become the definition of himself, but now it seemed that he had been fooling himself, had been leading his life as a lie.

He paused and waited for the illuminated red figure to extinguish itself, to be replaced by its jollier green companion. Above the roar of traffic, he heard his name. The word snaked past his preoccupations and swelled slowly until it became an insistent presence, dominant and over-riding. He felt a hand on his shoulder. A woman stood behind him, changed but unmistakable.

'I thought it was you. Blimey. It's been years. Almost twenty years. Wow.'

The last time he had seen her had been in the late spring of his first year at the university in Reykjavík. She had been boarding the bus to the airport, had turned to look in his direction, to offer a small wave of her hand. The gesture had seemed so perfunctory, so oblivious to the weight of the moment that her broad smile did little to warm the chill of the day. A wind had whipped across the BSÍ forecourt and Árni had shivered; his hand had shaken as he returned her wave. For an instant, he had held her eyes, thought he saw sadness there, but then she'd turned and climbed aboard. She had disappeared like smoke, her place taken almost immediately by another passenger waving to another abandoned soul. Through the reflection of the bus window, he had watched the shadow of her bright blue coat move towards the back seats and then disappear. She must have sat on the far side of the bus, hidden, gone already. He had stood on the desolate tarmac for ten minutes, until long after the bus had pulled away, until it became clear that there would be no change of heart, that the bus would not return, would not bring Sarah back to him.

'You look well.'

Árni realised that he had yet to say anything and he groped around for safe, expected words. And yet, as soon as the banality had escaped him, he wished he had simply continued to stand silent, dumbfounded, mouth ajar. He struggled to take control of himself but her smile set loose a wave that flooded through him, erasing for a moment the life he had constructed in the intervening years. He feared he might crumple and anchored himself once more on her face. The hair was much shorter, flecked with silver, but her eyes still sparkled. Her smile seemed barely to contain itself. She seemed unencumbered. She did indeed look well.

'You too, Árni.'

Her smile changed, softened, slipped into something that echoed things that had been lost between them years before. Unable to do otherwise, Árni searched out her left hand, scanned for her third finger. There was no ring. It meant nothing, of course. Not every wife wore a ring; not every couple married. But the slender paleness of her finger kept open the question he wanted to ask but knew he would not. The thrill of not knowing, of the past made ambiguous, the present too, coursed through him.

She was asking how he came to be on a street in her city. It was an obvious enquiry, but it had been unanticipated nevertheless. Árni stumbled for a few moments in search of an appropriate response: that he had made the move to England in pursuit of Sarah now seemed as obvious as it was absurd; he knew that it must be unsaid, but it was the explanation that filled his mind, allowing space for no other. Eventually he remembered his research, his work and Cambridge, and offered this instead.

'Cambridge. How funny. You must have arrived the year after I left.'

She trailed off and the silence was filled by the squeal of a truck's brakes on the narrow street. Without thinking, Árni reached out his hand and guided her a little further from the kerb. The warmth of her jacket sleeve suffused his palm and he realised that he was cold again, despite the absence of a breeze. With effort he pulled his hand away, let it drop to his side, as if this were normal.

'Yeah, I suppose so. I hadn't thought about it. I mean, Cambridge was just the obvious place for me to go, with what I wanted to do. It would have been nice though. To have had a friendly face. What about you? What's in London?'

She cantered through her own career, upwards through the tiers of management at some of the biggest telecommunications companies in the world. She apologised for the dullness of her choices, embarrassed by the distance between her work and her youthful ambitions, and Árni remembered the plans of the girl he had known back then, the intensity of the dreams she had shared with him.

'God knows how I ended up doing this. I don't begrudge it, it's been very kind to me. The work's interesting, the rewards are good, and I get to travel. All the same, it's not the mark I thought I'd make on the world. Not like you. You've stuck with it, achieved your dreams. It's so impressive. I'm a little envious, to be honest.'

More than ever, he felt the loss of his old job, and his failure to secure this new one in London. He was adrift. Unneeded. The word hung over him and yet he managed to maintain his smile as he avoided any mention of how his inevitable professional advance had come to an end, how the amazing opportunity that had secured his future only five years before, had led to this precipice. Even at the time of the crash, when the world's optimism clattered into the ditch, he had refused to recognise the ebbing of his own prospects. When his manager had proposed that he take a more junior role, a consequence of something he had described as delayering, Árni had questioned why this proposal had not been made to those younger colleagues, those he had mentored or so recently brought into the company. Even before his manager had begun to explain that every case was different, Árni had known that even acquiescence to his humiliation would not save him.

Had he stayed in his job at the university, he would most probably still be in work. He may even have risen somewhat, modestly perhaps, by increments. There would have been no collapse. But instead he had taken the chance that had been presented to him. He had surged and was now receding. Like waves on a spring tide, he had raced up the beach. Effervescent, he had fizzed, hanging, crinkling over the dry sand for some little time, his advance held; but now he felt all his progress sliding back, slipping into the sucking sea.

'I've just been for a job interview, actually. I'm getting a bit frustrated with where I am and fancied a change. If I get it, we could have lunch. They're just around the corner.'

With a tip of the head, he indicated over his shoulder, back towards the scene of his most recent humiliation. He wanted her to smile, eyes lowered, entertaining thoughts of what might have been, and what might yet be. He imagined her raising her face to him, the hanging pause before she exploded, her regret cascading over the years. He thought about the warmth of her sleeve under his hand. It was inevitable. And then it evaporated, burnt off by her nodding shrug, her *'Yeah, that would be nice.'*

There was silence for a little while, neither sure what next to say, searching for harmless words to bridge 18 years of disconnection. When she eventually asked if he had any children, Árni knew that the question arose from English politeness, not curiosity or hope. What remained of the conversation crystallised around them, made the air brittle. Mercifully, Sarah released them both with a glance at her watch.

'Well, I've got to get back.' She reached into her bag and, too easily, retrieved a business card, which she offered to him at arm's length. *'Good luck with the job. If you get it, let me know and we'll have lunch. Whatever, let's not leave it 20 years this time."*

The whisper of her lips still echoed on his cheek as he waited by the barriers at Kings Cross. There were ten minutes until the next train, forty until the next fast service. The afternoon stretched out like an empty ocean and the slow train would do just as well as the fast. It was only the pointlessness of remaining that pushed him from the city. He had thought about simply finding a pub and losing the remainder of the day in its embrace, but instead he had bought a couple of beers for the journey. If he still felt the pull of inebriation when he reached Cambridge, there were plenty of pubs there, one or two of which might even contain friendly faces. He could text Sam from the train, see if he was about for a quick pint.

The first jolt and pull swayed through him, roused him to remember the lager in his bag, but he waited until the confinement of the station canopy slid back, squeezing the train into the grey light outside, before the snap of the first can startled the still air of the mid-afternoon. Árni tipped the beer into him, felt his disappointments step back into the shadows just beyond himself and he watched the jumbled city blur outside.

He remembered the unread book that he had been carrying around for the past two weeks and pulled it from his bag, let the stiff spine press insistent paper into the skin around his thumb. He tried again to begin, but tiredness turned the page into indecipherability, the words blurring, the characters fusing into an even grey rectangle. Notches cut into the left hand edge, yet all else remained opaque. His eyes slid repeatedly from the book to whatever lay beyond.

He woke as the train shuddered into Royston, the clipped recorded voice shaping the syllables into a gentle rebuke. The intonation was familiar, and he thought of his wife. But also of Sarah. To his ear, they sounded so similar. How had he not recognised the similarities before? He felt the frown harden on his face, as the other parallels occurred to him. A monstrous possibility formed in his mind: that he had built his life in pursuit of a brief infatuation, something so insubstantial that it had not even lasted until the summer. He shook his head, muttered '*Nonsense*', before he noticed the glance of the woman sitting opposite him. He shook the can that still nestled in his hand and took a long drink from the flat and tepid beer. As the train swayed across the flat farmland beyond the window, he named the reasons for still being married to Charlotte, forcing other thoughts from his mind.

Charlotte pulled uncomfortably at the short strands chopped into her hair. The clatter of crockery punctuated the rumble of voices; the hiss of traffic squeezed through the door after each new customer, filling the too small space. For the third time, her shoulder was jarred by a passing bag. She twisted on her stool, turning her back more resolutely against the crowd. The dark brown wood of the table top felt tacky against her skin, and she folded her hands in her lap, almost penitent.

From her new position, she could see Laura at the counter, her hands tumbling over themselves in exuberant cascades. Charlotte could not see her friend's face, but she could feel the urgent enthusiasm, see it reflected in the barista's smiling concentration, the swing of her crisp autumn jacket. Undoubtedly, the time that had elapsed since they had last met had seen Laura become more careful with her clothes. Thirteen years of motherhood had eroded Charlotte's flair for style, such that it now appeared that the two women existed in a state of almost precise symbiotic balance. Single life had been kind to her. Certainly, Charlotte would not now attempt to get away with the jeans Laura wore with such ease.

The idea had been a surprise; an unexpected face on Árni's Facebook feed. She was surprised that her husband had reconnected with her old friend, even after she had faded from Charlotte's life, every invitation met with an apology. She had puzzled briefly over this, but was glad to find she was still in touch with her, if only indirectly. It was nice to find a lost friend, the kind of friend that slips into the cul-de-sacs life leaves behind, one of many that Charlotte seemed to have misplaced in the swirl of living. She had sent the friend request and waited. Only when she had given up the waiting did she receive the notification, and she smiled at the thought of watched kettles, recognising again the truth of her mother's age-old admonishment of her youthful impatience.

The prospect of a day in London, a day for herself, made her fingers fizz across the keyboard in response, sending a message asking if her old friend might like to meet up. She had chosen the Saturday carefully, so as to cause the minimum of inconvenience, but it had been straightforward: the universe had placed no obstructions in the way.

Lunch had passed efficiently. There had been a few silences, but conversation had picked up much where they had left it, before she had married and Laura had moved to London, when the world had seemed infinite. Mostly they had exchanged fragments of their shared history, buried remembrances, and they had conducted a thorough inventory of their former friends, their last known whereabouts. The rest had been paler, a synopsis of the events of the previous ten years. But it had seemed sufficient for Laura; at least, she had not demurred when Charlotte suggested that they carry on their afternoon in some shops. She had wanted to find some new trainers, but after the first attempt, they had left the maelstrom of Oxford Street and found their way into this coffee shop.

A white cup clinked in its saucer in front of her, topped with a dirty streak of foamed milk; another landed across the table, and Laura sat behind it, her face wrung into a quizzical apology.

'I only come here in the week. I'd forgotten how mad the West End is on a weekend. Sorry. The coffee is good though.'

Charlotte accepted this as an indisputable truth, something on which her own preferences were irrelevant. She sipped at the coffee, the scalding bitterness slipping under the foam. She nodded, if only to confirm Laura's assessment, to acknowledge that she did indeed know her coffee.

'This is so nice. I'm so glad you got in touch. Too long. I hate how life does this. Things slip by. People.' Charlotte nodded. Life left holes, gaps where other things might have been. Or else it piled things up, things you might have chosen, but that still crowded out other things you wanted. It seemed unfair.

'Do you still read? I mean, for fun?' Charlotte thought she heard a hint of accusation in Laura's question, a challenge. *'Or is it just work to you now? I find it hard to think of words in the same way.*

The magazine is relentless, I'm just turning out blocks of words. I'm not sure that they're always very good blocks of words either. At least, they're only ever as good as words can be when they're about cushions, or reclaimed teak furniture. Just a carrier for advertising.' She snorted, and the old Laura, the jumper and Doc Martens Laura, was back again, and this was not an overpriced coffee shop in the West End but a bookish café in Cambridge; they were no longer tied into the choices they had made, but free of the weight of themselves, loose among the limitlessness of their future lives. Laura leant forward, confessional: *'It's tragic. I have to separate the writing I'm involved with every day from the other stuff, the stuff that used to be everything to me. I can only read novels on holiday, when I'm not in my day to day.'*

She put her hands to her face, rubbed her eyes with her fingertips. The nails were no longer snagged and jagged, but were tidy, even. Not glamourous, not even any varnish, but healthy, smooth, pink. She'd been a biter, at college, and even after that. It had made her seem damaged, desperate, and maybe a little mad. There was no trace of that Laura any longer; no longer nervous, no longer incomplete. She felt the balance between them shift still further.

'But things sound great. You're the editor of a fucking magazine. And a good one. They have it on the shelves of WH Smith in town. Of course, it's not Wuthering Heights, *none of it is. None of us gets that. I'm not sure I'd want it, even if I could. To be honest, I don't think I could handle the drama.'*

Charlotte paused. She realised that she had wanted this moment to say something about her life, about the absence of drama, or rather its latency, to someone close enough to understand, but distant enough not to judge. Someone who was not Árni, nor her mother. But here, now, Charlotte realised that she did not have the words. She took another sip of coffee. It was getting cold now, its bitterness sharper, crystalline. She knew that they would need to make a decision soon. One of them would have to suggest that they struggle to the counter again, or that they should leave for another place, or that they should simply part. She did not want that, to part so soon after so many missing years, and she grasped for something that might keep her there, to keep her listening.

'But sometimes, I do think things might have been different. You know? Just, different. I don't even know how I'd want it to be, what I should have done or not done. Some of the things I wanted for myself, well, they just didn't happen, and I guess I regret that.' Charlotte's voice trailed off into embarrassment and her eyes swung down to her trembling hands. The chipped varnish on her nails argued eloquently for things to be other than they were. The touch of Laura's hand on hers startled her.

'Do you remember Jenny? From Blandford?' She always said, "You should only regret the things you don't do, not the things you do." Usually right before she did something stupid. It seemed like the wisest, most life-affirming advice at the time. But they're the same thing really, aren't they? I mean, any decisions we make about anything, anything,' Laura shifted a little on her stool, tried to relax her voice so that this did not feel quite so much like a sermon 'well, that precludes something else. There's no point in regretting what we didn't do, any more than what we did. Either choice will change us. We either regret all that we are, or we are happy with it. Content, maybe. We decide what we want for ourselves, but we can't escape the loss of all the other possibilities. Choosing is losing.'

She sat back in herself, stifling a little smile of satisfaction; Charlotte looked across at her, eyebrow raised, and laughed until Laura joined her. 'God, you're right, that was terrible. It's a good job I didn't decide to be a copy-writer. Anyhow, let's go get drunk.

Without any regrets, of course. I know a place that does a lethal mojito.'

Despite Laura's best efforts, Charlotte was no longer drunk by the time she stepped down from the train at Cambridge, but she was surprised by how fast time was moving. Somehow, she found herself outside her house, just as the street lights flickered into sickly life. She stood to watch as the taxi turned out of the Close and out of sight, then allowed herself to sway a little. Tentatively, she approached the front door. The key entered the lock with little complaint and Charlotte swung on it into the hallway.

'I'm home.'

Her voice scraped into the grainy light gathering at the foot of the stairs. There was no immediate response, beyond the faint ripples of noise cascading from the first floor, and a TV muttering behind the living room door. She kicked off her shoes at only the second attempt and headed towards it.

'Hello love. Nice time? Have you eaten?'

Árni looked up from the sofa, his legs stretched out along its full length. The news flickered images of smoke rising from a volcano in a snowy landscape; an English voice wrestled with the bouncing rhythm of Eyjafjallajökull as it explained the full extent of the closure of European airspace caused by the eruption. Before the voice could introduce the thoughts of a series of stranded holiday makers, the sound ended with a click, and then Árni was beside her, his arm around her, his lips resting on her forehead.

'I can make something. Some pasta? You, uh, you seem a bit, well, a bit tipsy.'

She smiled at the way in which he would discover new words and use them relentlessly until they were nearly exhausted, then abandon them, sometimes for years. 'Tipsy' had not been part of his repertoire for ages, not since college, and its reappearance, today, now, warmed her. She leaned her head against his chest, felt its rise and fall, the steady thud, thud, thud of his heart.

'How was it?' He was guiding her to the sofa, steadying her as she dropped into its softness. *'You sure you're OK?'*

'Yeah, fine. I'm not drunk. Laura took me for a drink after lunch, but I'm pretty sober now. Just a bit tired.' This was not entirely a lie. Maybe some food would help.

'And how was Laura? Still the same?' Árni was hovering. Unsure whether to leave for the kitchen or to stay while Charlotte told him about her day, he had opted simply to stand in the middle of the room. He looked awkward, unsure if sitting down again would be interpreted as an unwillingness to make food.

'Yeah, she's good. Different. Really good, I think. Things have worked out for her.' Her frown carried an inflection of surprise, as if the thought had startled her as much as it was bemusing. There was no reason why Laura's life should not have unfurled as it had, nor why her friend's contentment should affect how she felt about her own. They had parted with the warmest of embraces but Charlotte knew even while her hands still rested on her friend's shoulders that their promise not to leave it another decade would fade, and she knew that that hurt her more than it did Laura. She sighed and slumped onto the sofa, lost in what looked like melancholy.

Árni rolled the word around his mouth, unvoiced, grateful for the exemplification of the concept behind it. She had used it to describe him a few weeks before, but it was only now that he fully understood its meaning. He shifted his weight onto his left leg: he was no longer entirely sure why he was standing in the middle of the room, swaying gently, aimless. He spent much of his life now with this sense of aimlessness, hanging between things he should be doing if only he could grasp them with any solidity. He said he was sorry once again, certain that the sadness draped over her was his responsibility. The thought that Laura might have confessed to their ancient indiscretion flickered briefly before he decided that it was unlikely and, in any case, whatever guilt he associated with Laura had been irrelevant for years. Even if it had been revealed, it was surely just another thing that they would choose not to talk about.

Slowly he realised that Charlotte was asking about the children, and he told her all that he could about how they had spent the day. She frowned at the vagueness of his recollection and he felt another shame rising, There was nothing shameful in how he had spent the day, and yet he felt ashamed. In the weeks since his work had ended, and in the absence of new employment, their roles had changed. Symbolically at least. To him, at least. After all, Freyja and Ben required little in the way of looking after, while Charlotte's employers seemed insatiable in their need for her.

With each passing interview, for successively more junior roles, his own necessity had become ever more distant, and only a half-belief in his essential competence remained. The memory of having once been useful, of being in demand, seemed solid enough, but the longer he interrogated it, the more unreliable it became: a sense of déjà vu, or a half-remembered dream. Now, the University had come to his rescue and in a few weeks he would begin a fixed-term contract, working on a research project he had originally set in motion five years before, just as he was leaving for bigger, brighter things. The sense that he would be working for an idea of himself in the past had almost prevented him from taking the job, even more than the relatively low salary and insecurity. But he had been beaten and he had accepted the work meekly. The worst of it was that he knew that, once the job began, he would only be able to think of these wasted days as just that: time lost carelessly.

The clock measured out the day as it measured out every day, paring time, reminding him that things moved forward, even if they appeared to stay the same. Eddies of dust turned slowly in the afternoon sunlight, undisturbed. They kept their own rhythm, separate from the seconds, minutes, hours, and years that described his life, and yet their turning was relentless all the same. Each particle would rise and each would fall, according to patterns already established. Their trajectories could be determined, predicted, even if they were opaque to him.

Those trajectories could be altered, of course. An unexpected event, such as the opening of a door or a sneeze, would utterly alter the course of things. A gust of wind was capable of overturning the most perfect equilibrium, sending a stable particle into free fall, or pushing a rising mote out of the shaft of light altogether. These things, at least, he understood and so he kept as still as a corpse and simply watched the dance, learning the steps from his chair.

He woke again, slowly. The room was in shadows, the last of the day's light long gone, and he blinked into the gloom. Tentative movement caused his shoulders to crack like dry timber on a fire; he winced at the pain in his back, tested his limbs cautiously. He did not know how long he had been asleep. The tick, tick, tick of the clock on the shelf offered no clue, and he saw little point in straining his eyes to make out its face. Instead he reached for his tobacco tin and began to assemble a cigarette. He had no saliva for the gum when he came to seal it, and swallowed hard three times to summon moisture to his mouth. He was filled with a metallic taste, the residue of coffee and smoke and too little food.

The orange light of the match flooded the room with colour for an instant, before the monochrome moonlight reasserted its dominance. His smoke curled on the flat air, lingered around his fingers, lazy, uncertain. The chair's creak echoed the complaints of his bones as he reached to the ashtray. The morning's exertions had taken their toll. With Gylfi's help, he had begun the familiar rituals of preparing *Tófa* for the winter: repairs and checks; smoothing, sealing and caulking. Then they had turned her to rest on the timber sleepers beside the house, and spread the old tarpaulin across her boards, tying it off against the nagging wind. Tomorrow, Eiríkur would check the motor and winch, before packing them away in the outhouse, wrapped in oilcloth. All would be settled for another year.

'I know love, truly. My bones tell me loudly enough that I am getting too old for this. But what am I to do? No-one else will care for her.'

The moonlight cast a shadow across the empty armchair on the other side of the room. There was no sound but Eiríkur listened anyway, as he did most evenings when there was only him and his memories of his wife. They would talk about the past, the times that they had spent together, or they would talk about the boy, their pride in how well he was doing overseas; about the grandchildren, how they were growing. They spent evenings together like this, because there was no other way that they could spend evenings now. Eventually, Eiríkur would light the lamp and he would be alone again, but for these few hours, he chose to sit in the shadows, where he could find his Hrefna once more.

Lately, the others had begun to join them in their hidden time. At first his mother had sat quietly on the settee, knitting socks for the little ones; sometimes his father would join her, and the smell of his pipe would fill the room. Eiríkur would join him in humming an old tune, something carried on the salt air. Only Ólafur refused to come to him. Sometimes he thought he saw his shadow in the corner, but he would not answer and Eiríkur knew that there was no one there.

That his brother should hide from him, should shun him in this way, troubled Eiríkur. At first it had seemed simply that he was lost still, out in the snowy wastes above the village, unable to find his way across the great fjord. But then an older thought resurfaced, nagged at him. He had become convinced that his brother blamed him for what had happened. He knew about the deal Eiríkur had struck with the elves, how his little brother had betrayed him, had condemned him. His mother told him to stop his nonsense, that Ólafur's death was not his fault; even his father, who had forgiven him for his own death, reassured him, told him that he had been a child, not culpable. But the conviction would not leave him, had begun to seep into the sun-lit world, and into the lamp-lit hours.

His stomach clenched and a sound like bubbling mud spiralled up through him. He should eat. He clicked on the lamp beside his chair and the room emptied. Yellow light chased out the thickest of the shadows, and the bulb's hum drowned out the whispers of the past. There was fish stew in a plastic box in the little freezer. It would take twenty minutes to defrost and cook through in the microwave. He decided he would start the dish spinning, then make another cigarette and some coffee. Maybe put some schnapps in it, to help pass the time.

1982

The smell of fish bubbled through the empty house. Only the clink of bowls and spoons in the kitchen betrayed the presence of living things. The two women did not speak, did not need to, occupied as they were with familiar tasks. While Jóna set three places at the table, Hrefna tended to the pot on the stove and sawed slices of dark bread from the cloth-covered loaf. She looked up, twisting to see the clock turning above the door. It was seven thirty already. Outside the window, a fine summer evening slipped by, nudged by a lazy breeze. Beyond the village, beyond the shore, a dazzling sea flared under the bright sun.

'He went to visit Haraldur Jónsson's boy, you say?'

Without turning, Hrefna nodded in response to Jóna's question. A's usual, Eiríkur had been waiting for her at the gates of the processing plant. Only his smile had been different. His mouth rigid, his eyes strained. At first, she had feared that some tragedy had occurred, that one of the fishermen, Gylfi even, had drowned, or worse that word had come down from the fells about her son. She had gripped his hand, afraid to ask, and waited for the blow.

But Árni, Gylfi and the others were safe and well. Eiríkur's strangeness had been nothing more than his embarrassment at asking if he might spend an hour or so taking a few drinks with some friends. She'd had no objection, had paid little attention to the explanation that he had offered up, and had walked up the hill alone, content to have so considerate a husband. Only now, under the questioning of her mother-in-law, did it strike her as odd. She pushed the thoughts away and picked up the bread knife once more.

Behind her, Jóna pulled out a chair and sat; a sigh. Hrefna listened. She was unused to the almost-emptiness of the house this evening. With her husband drinking with Gylfi and with her boy away tending to Siggi Baldursson's sheep, there was only quietness, the sound of labour and little more. But the soup was done now and there was not much left to cut from the loaf, and only the timbers of the house spoke for a time.

'Can I pour you some coffee, Jóna?'

Hrefna turned with her question to find Jóna lost in her thoughts, her hands spread palm-down in her lap, the sags of paper skin sliding slowly with the passing years. But her eyes were sharp as knives as they wandered across the horizon that was scratched onto the window pane. The sun was already in the north-western quarter of the sky, and the thin green strip of Hornstrandir hummed with golden light. Hrefna repeated her offer of coffee, gently so as not to break the spell too abruptly. Jóna inhaled deeply through her nose, then expelled the breath slowly, a tiny whistle spiralling above the hiss.

'That would be lovely, dear. Maybe some of that schnapps in it, too?'

Jóna nodded towards the cupboard in which Eiríkur kept a bottle of Brennivín. Amused, Hrefna took down the bottle and placed it on the table, then arranged the sugar bowl, two cups, and two empty glasses around it. Without asking, she poured out two generous measures and sat down across the table from her mother-in-law.

'To what shall we raise our glasses?' A glint of mischief in her eyes, Hrefna picked up her glass between thumb and forefinger and, her elbow on the table, waited for Jóna's toast.

'*To the men and women of Hesteyri, of course.*' A moment of confusion passed through Hrefna like a cloud before she remembered that it had been thirty years since the village had been abandoned, since Einar and Jóna, and Eiríkur too, had left their home. Hrefna knew the story well, had heard how they had packed everything, house and cow and all, onto a boat and had sailed away from all that they knew to find a different kind of life. Each year, Jóna became wistful at this time, and each year it surprised her. But now, Eiríkur's absence made some sort of sense, even if she was not sure if it was the desire to be with his friends, to deepen his remembrance, or to avoid his mother, to lessen it.

'*Do you miss it?*' The question was unnecessary, simply an invitation to talk. Hrefna finished her schnapps and stirred a sugar cube into her cooling coffee, waited.

'*Of course. I think about Hesteyri often. How can I not? At times, it was the most unpleasant place, but it was ours. In a way that Bolungarvík cannot be, even though I've spent more of my life here than I ever did there. A place like that, it leaves its mark on you.*'

Hrefna found her thoughts racing over the mountains and fjords to Suðureyri and the home she had left on account of Eiríkur Einarsson. Yet, she found no mark left upon her by that place, save for that left by her family. The rise and fall of Súgandafjörður were simply an outline cut by sea and sky. The view down from her father's forge at the back of the village revealed the shape of the hooked spit on which most of the houses stood, but there had been no elegance in its sweep as far as she could recall. Places were places: you could build a house upon them, raise children there, make a life. But, so long as the ground was solid and the climate kind, they were much the same. Embarrassed, Hrefna refilled their glasses.

'Would you like to visit? It's a nature reserve now. Boats go across from Ísafjörður, I think.'

Jóna's laugh was sharp, derisive. 'I went back once. With Einar, and Eiríkur. Just a few years after we left. The cow. She wouldn't milk and Einar thought that it was because she missed the grass of Hesteyri. So we went back. The four of us, Einar rowing Tófa all that way. We stayed for the summer. And you know? Glæta started milking almost as soon as we were on the turf.'

A smile, such as Hrefna had never seen, spread across Jóna's face, easing from her face every last crease and wrinkle, as if the years between had been erased by this simple recollection. Hrefna counted three of her breaths before the smile snapped from Jóna's face, and time returned. Jóna emptied her glass in a swift and brutal movement.

'I can't go back. Not now. How can I go back? Everything has changed. It is not the same place, and I am not the same woman.'

There was no bitterness in her voice, nor resignation. The words were simply a statement of fact, free of regret. Jóna turned her cup between her fingers, then laughed with the lightness of a girl still to face disappointment.

'I'll tell you where I'd much rather go. To Copenhagen. Or even to New York. Maybe to an island where the sun shines all year round and the sea is warm enough to dip your feet into without worrying if all your toes will come back out!'

She was laughing uncontrollably now, tears wetting the corners of her eyes. She reached over and poured two more measures of schnapps. Her smile was all mischief.

'Don't tell your husband I said that. He'd see it as a betrayal of the homeland. Especially Copenhagen. What about you? Where would you go, if my son would ever allow it?'

She felt uncomfortable, as if she was being invited to plot against

Eiríkur, but the sparkle of Jóna's eyes was infectious. The names of places tumbled through her mind, but none seemed to hold any greater allure than the others. She wanted to say Reykjavík, but knew that it would sound so dull that it would kill the joyfulness of the moment. Her sister, Freyja, would have a thousand ideas of places to visit, of course, but she could not call upon her for inspiration.

'I don't know really. But somewhere with forests. Thousands of trees. Tall trees rising like columns into the blackness above. Maybe Russia. If they can spare all the driftwood that comes ashore here, just think how many more trees they must have.' Hrefna looked wide-eyed at Jóna, thrilled by the possibility of being elsewhere, of being a different version of herself. *'No, not Russia. Too cold. What about a jungle? Africa? Or South America. Yes, Brazil. Then I'll have my trees, but also lots of sunshine, and lots of coffee too!'*

Jóna slapped the table, then filled the glasses to the brink.

'To sunshine and coffee!'

❖

He watched the blank windows for any sign that his knock had stirred the house. Across the yard, the quiet forge glowed rich red beyond the half open door of the workshop, mocking the apparent absence of both his grandfather and his aunt. He peered into the empty kitchen through its crystal clear window. A coffee pot stood lonely on the stove; only the faintest glow suggested that the fire held any sort of life. There were no cups on the table, no crockery by the sink.

He imagined the calm coolness of the air inside. Envied it. For two weeks now he had been buffeted endlessly by the wind, whether tramping over the fells by day or seeking sleep under a pale night sky, curled within the rude turf shelter. Mr Baldursson had not built a chimney, and the guttering fire filled the cramped space with swirls of choking smoke, so Árni had preferred to seek comfort instead only in his mother's blankets. Fortunately, the summer had thus far brought neither real cold nor wet, but the wind snagged at him incessantly and he hated it almost as much as he hated sheep.

He understood his father's reasons for sending him to tend Siggi Baldursson's flock. Even on calm and warm days, he had been grudging in taking Árni out onto the shallow waters, teaching him the basics of his trade but no more, as if he had known even then that he would be too afraid to take him further out to chase fish when the time came. Since his grandfather had been lost beneath the waves, Árni had felt his father pushing him inland, away from the sea, away from his life aboard *Tófa*.

So, it had not been a surprise when the decision had been made, but it had been a disappointment. Árni had no love of fish, but he would rather have spent his summer in Bolungarvík, with his books and with his friends and with his family. The drab landscape of the fells was no more diverting than the sea: simply greys and greens and dirty whites that blurred into featureless slabs without punctuation. There was nothing to break the monotony except the sheep, and to Árni they were just more ugliness in a realm of ugliness. The prospect of a glimpse of a fox, flashing blue on the hillside, was the only excitement and yet, despite his purpose there, he had seen none to threaten the lambs.

That morning he had followed the flock south across the wasteland, as it skirted the shoulder of a grey, flat-topped fell, indistinguishable from any other fell. The sun held some warmth and the wind had dropped a little. The land had fallen away to reveal the glistening blue of Súgandafjörður curving to the west.

And there, where the confinement of the bay opened into the breadth of the ocean, he saw the tangle of houses and streets that combined to be Suðureyri.

He had visited his maternal grandfather only a few times, despite the short distance between his forge and his daughter's hearth in Bolungarvík. Each of those visits however clung happily in his memory. There was the forge itself: a terrifying, exhilarating kingdom, filled with sights and sounds and smells quite unknown to him. And his Aunt Fríða always seemed to have just baked a cake and its scent would curl around the door before he had even crossed the threshold.

But it was his grandfather himself that had left the deepest mark upon him. His one remaining afi was a mountain of a man, a tower of iron; his solidity and permanence had reassured him in the tumult that followed the death of Einar. All the boyish affection reserved for grandfathers had been piled onto the one that remained, one who fortunately could bear the weight of it. After his lonely days on the fells, the prospect of even a moment of comfort at the fireside of Skúli Hilmarsson was irresistible. He had abandoned his woolly charges with only a moment's thought and begun a loping descent to the water's edge. In one hour, he had rounded the head of the fjord; another hour brought him to the outskirts of the village. The bustle of the little harbour did not distract him, and he continued on and up, beyond the clutch of white boarded houses, until he had reached the forge that stood on a rise above Suðureyri.

The whisper of the sea was carried on a gust of wind, sending a shiver through him. Instinctively, he twisted to face it, but there was nothing to see except the empty workshop. Within, the glow of the forge rose and fell like the steady breath of comfort, and Árni trudged across the yard to feel its warmth, convinced that there was no-one inside the house and that repeated knocking at the door would serve no purpose. The absence of Skúli Hilmarsson and his aunt still troubled him, but the breeze had risen and he could just as well worry about it in the warmth as on the doorstep.

Fríða was the only one of his aunts yet to leave the tidy house in which she and her sisters had been born and raised. In counterpoint to his father's parents, it had been Árni's grandmother who had died prematurely, long before the boy had been born, before even his father and mother had met. Her passing had left Skúli with the care of three young girls and no other adult relatives on whom to call. It was a responsibility to which he had risen with robust tenderness, despite his grief. Only his failure to successfully set Fríða on a happy course out into the world gave him any cause to reproach himself.

Despite his love for his Aunt Fríða, Árni had a secret admiration for his other aunt, the one in distant Reykjavík, the one who had found her husband after she had left; the one who had left not simply her village behind her, but the whole of the West Fjords. To Árni, his Aunt Freyja might as well have left for the moon or for New York, such were the limits of his world. And he already knew that he wanted nothing more than to follow her example. Life did not need to be a choice between fish or sheep.

Absently Árni leant upon the arm of the bellows, pushing a fierce light into the coals. The heat crackled across his face, stinging his eyes. Retreating to the anvil, he felt the heft of his grandfather's hammer in his hand. The smooth surface of the shaft betrayed the decades of wear it had endured, beating locks and brackets and sparks from the slow-moving glow of steel. In its curve, he felt the presence of his grandfather, the craft and the calluses gained over years. It would be a shame to miss him. Mr Baldursson would be on the fells tomorrow, to check on the sheep and to bring fresh supplies for Árni; he would need to be there to receive them, and to reassure his neighbour that the sheep were well protected. He began to wonder if his excursion had been a mistake, but the warmth of the forge overwhelmed the idea of heading back out onto the chill slopes across the fjord just yet.

Perhaps it was the roar of the forge, or simply it was his daydreaming, but he did not hear the footsteps behind him and he was startled by the sudden and considerable weight of Skúli Hilmarsson's hand on his shoulder.

'Got you, you little thief!'

Before he could turn, Árni was swept from his feet and spun into his grandfather's embrace, legs flailing at the empty air. There was a warmth about the man, a tangibility to his whole-hearted love of his grandson, that thrilled Árni, intoxicated him, and once his surprise had passed he tugged tightly at Skúli's neck and revelled in the whirling spin of the embrace.

'Afi! I thought I'd missed you. I can't stay long, but I wanted to come down to say hello.'

Setting the boy on the dusty ground, Skúli studied him suspiciously. *'Come down? Where have you been? And why, for heaven's sake, can't you stay? Surely you'll stay long enough for your Aunty Fríða to make you something tasty to eat.'*

Árni explained through breathless gulps that he had been tending to Mr Baldursson's sheep, that he had seen the village in the fjord below his perch and, craving warmth and company, he had been inspired to abandon his duties, to spend a few hours before he had to return. In the telling, Mr Baldursson's arrival the following day took on a more menacing air than it deserved, and Árni blushed at his embellishment. But Skúli Hilmarsson maintained his broad grin even as he admonished his grandson for leaving the sheep without protection. He did not see the boy often enough to waste time in reprimand. Sweeping him up under his arm, the blacksmith carried the giggling Árni out into the yard and shouted to his daughter to set another place for dinner, since they had a special guest.

'Now, lad, you go in to say hello to your Aunt Fríða while I finish a few things in the workshop. She might have been baking this morning, and there might be something to tempt you in the kitchen.'

The quiet air of the empty house, as seen so recently through the kitchen window, was now orange and soft with lamp light and the smell of cinnamon. The fire in the stove had been revived and it crackled with gentle excitement. His aunt ceased her trilling song at his arrival, replacing it with a smile and a babble of welcomes as she ushered Árni to a seat at the table. By the time Skúli Hilmarsson stooped beneath his door frame, the biscuits had been eaten and Fríða's questions about her sister had been answered.

He could hear laughter even before he slipped the latch loose. Eiríkur allowed himself a slanted smile before the full strangeness of the sound solidified and his expression twisted into a frown. Laughter like this was more at home in the parlour he had left only ten minutes before than in his own kitchen, and he wondered if he had taken a wrong turn in his slack-headedness, ending up where he had begun. And yet, those were the voices of his wife and his mother. He had heard each of them laugh many times before of course, but not together, not only them.

His stumble over the step brought the laughter to an abrupt halt, but it erupted again before being drowned in shushes. A chair scraped across the floor beyond the kitchen door, under which a low murmur of yellow light leaked into the greyness of the hallway. The sun would soon dip briefly below the horizon; the grainy dusk barely penetrated beyond the threshold, and the half-light told him that he had stayed longer than he had realised. He shook his head to clear his thoughts.

If only Siggi Baldursson had not insisted on another drink out on the step, after Gylfi and the others had left. But Eiríkur had had too much talk of Hesteyri and the leaving. The prospect of some words with a man who had never crossed the great ice fjord, had never felt the turf of Hornstrandir beneath his boots, was too appealing. Not only that, but Siggi was off in the morning to take provisions for the boy. It was the best he could do, in the circumstances. With his son so far away, his emissary neighbour would have to suffice.

'Hello, my love. Let me fetch you some supper.'

Hrefna's smile greeted him as he stepped into the kitchen. She was already at the stove, turning soup in the pot, the steam wisping into the air. His mother sat at the table, on which stood a bottle of Brennivín and two glasses. His resolve evaporated and he reached into the cupboard to retrieve a glass for himself.

'Would you not rather have some coffee, son? I can make a fresh pot for you.' Across the table, Jóna watched Eiríkur pour out a measure from the nearly empty bottle.

'I thought I should claim a little for myself, before you drain every drop.' He nodded at the bottle with a good-natured laugh, then tipped the glass's contents into himself, felt its burn spread across his chest. He refilled his glass and waited for Hrefna to bring his bowl. The aroma hanging in the air snaked its way in through his nose and his hunger erupted, unexpected but inevitable. When the soup arrived, he sucked down the chunks of fish and chewed impatiently at the crust of rye bread soaking in the bowl.

'Sorry I'm so late. I had to hang around to walk Siggi back up the hill. He'd drunk far too much. And he's got to be up early.' Eiríkur paused to push more food into his mouth, to chew it sufficiently to make space for more words. 'He's off out onto the fells in the morning, to take some things for Árni, to make sure he's OK. If you have any biscuits ready by ten, he said he'd carry them up for you.'

Hrefna sat back down, and poured the last of the schnapps into the three glasses. Silently, she added its replacement to the list of things she would have to do in the morning, after she had made a tray of cinnamon biscuits. Idly, she picked at one of the remaining slices of bread lying on the board at the centre of the table. The sticky blackness clung to her teeth, releasing its sour tang into the Brennivín as she sipped it.

'Of course. But why not take them yourself? You could go with Siggi. It would be good for you, a day off in the hills with your friend. And Árni would be so pleased to see you. I mean, Siggi Baldursson is good company, for sure. But the boy would rather see his father, don't you think?'

There was a short silence, filled only by the sounds of Eiríkur's chewing and the creak of Jóna's chair. The sky beyond the kitchen window bled into a grey pinkness signalling that the sun had made its way beneath the horizon for an hour or so. The clock chimed a single note. Eiríkur swallowed the last of the crust and let out a long sigh.

'I'd like to, of course. It would be good to see the boy. I miss him. But, you know, someone has to put fish in the pot, bread on the table. And Gylfi too, don't forget about him. He'll be expecting me. Much as I'd like go for a hike on the fells, work is work.'

He took a sharp sip from his glass, confident that the matter had been settled. His wife's persistence irritated him and his eyebrows clenched above his spoon.

'But it's just one day. And Gylfi can take Tófa out himself, or perhaps have a day off. It wouldn't hurt him either.'

Eiríkur tore a piece of bread into two then three pieces, before setting it to rest among its crumbs. He pressed his knuckles lightly together. 'There's not the time for that. Remember, it's only one of me working, and the summer doesn't last long.' He watched his wife, daring her to go on through narrowed eyes, unaware of his mother's rising anxiety.

'Well, there's only one of you because you won't fish with your son...'

Jóna's short breath did not, could not deter the coming collision, and when Eiríkur replied his eyes were fixed upon his hands, rather than on either of the women. 'The boy is safer on the fells. You know that. You know why. I shouldn't have to say this. You know it.'

'It's the sea that is a danger to him, not you. It seems sometimes that you have no interest in spending time with him. A son should not be kept from his father, no matter what has passed before.' Her cheeks reddened at the last of this, and Hrefna emptied her glass to stop herself from speaking further; the liquor's warmth only added to her blushing. She looked to Jóna for some support, but she had closed herself away once more, their evening's intimacy lost.

'To hell with you, Hrefna Birgitta Skúladóttir.'

She did not see him stand and turn, only heard the squeal of the chair, the heavy step upon the boards. When the kitchen air had settled itself, she unclenched her eyes to the sparkle of lamp light. Jóna stared at her glass in her hands, at the trembling surface within it, before she emptied its contents into herself and bade her goodnights. Hrefna followed her tread on the stairs, all the way into her room in the eaves.

He had already rounded the head of the fjord and begun the long ascent by the time the sun tore free of the land, casting a pinkish glow across the low sky, streaking bright peach accents on the thin cloud. The early pace he had set slackened now and his breathing became heavier as he pulled against the drag of the world. The rough path snaked up the flank of the valley, curling through impatient greenery that soon gave way to grasses, then mosses and lichens, to the hardness of stone. Stones scattered from under his feet, skittering away towards the bay below, such little regard did he give to his footing. The wind whipped off the ridge, where patches of snow clung on, waiting for winter to return.

The morning air stung his face after his night beside the fire in his grandfather's house. His aunt's porridge and pancakes still warmed him, but the company of both had warmed him more and had been harder to leave. Fragments of thoughts leapt between the rhythm of his steps: his grandfather's laughter at the stupidity of sheep; his aunt's wincing at his description of the hut in which he stayed; their attentiveness to the detail of his books and studies, to the names of his friends, the futures he shared with them. But always his mind turned to the news that he was carrying.

In the warm light, he had chewed at the roasted lamb his aunt had placed on the table in front of him, certain only that, while there was little to choose between sheep and fish, the one tasted better than the other. Its flavour had obscured much of his grandfather's explanation of his earlier absence, and he had listened only loosely to how the two of them had walked down to a neighbour's house, after the arrival of the second post, so that they might find a telephone. Only at the mention of his Aunt Freyja did he pause in his chewing.

A letter had arrived, small and unremarkable; the shape of Freyja's hand had been immediately recognisable. It was not unusual: Skúli Hilmarsson neither trusted nor could afford a telephone to be connected in his house, and so the post was the only way that his distant daughter could traverse the space between them. There had been news within the envelope, words that even now, on the hillside, did not entirely make sense to Árni. But they contained sufficient power to pull the fastidious Fríða from her work, and then to cause Skúli to leave the forge burning unattended. In shared silence they had scurried to their neighbour, the wife of a trawler-man, to ask if they might use her telephone to call Reykjavík, where their daughter and sister was on the brink of divorcing her husband.

Freyja had been resolute. There was no convincing her, even though there had been no betrayal and no violence. Simply an ending. A parting. That was how she had described the seismic split that had occurred between them. Despite her family's pleading, she maintained that she had seen sense already, that an amicable divorce was best for everyone. Things could change, people could change: a path did not need to be followed, simply because it had been begun.

The path crested the ridge and led on across a crystalline snowfield for some thirty metres. Beyond, the land sloped gently down, a smear of grey debris pocked with dirty white patches, a shallow bowl that swooped through the heart of the high fells; the solid green of turf nestled in its cup. Árni frowned at the desolate emptiness, the ugly monotony, then strode on, anxious that the sun was rising too fast. Mr Baldursson would be at the hut sometime around noon, and Árni had only four hours to account for the sheep and set a fire, to have coffee bubbling in anticipation.

As well as inspection and resupply, Mr Baldursson's visit had additional importance now. Árni had promised to relay the news of Aunt Freyja to his mother via their neighbour. His grandfather had not said so, but Árni knew that he hoped his daughter, always close with her sister, might be better placed to persuade to her to change once more, to commit herself to her husband and the life she had chosen in the city.

And yet he felt uneasy about sharing the details of his family with Mr Baldursson. It seemed a betrayal, not only of his aunt but of his mother, even of his father. That their neighbour should know more about the life of his aunt than his parents did troubled him, and he thought through the consequences of neglecting his grandfather's instruction. Surely, his aunt would have sent a similar letter to Bolungarvík, perhaps containing greater detail than that shared with her family in Suðureyri. Perhaps it had arrived some days ago and his mother had known before his grandfather. Maybe, she had already decided that her sister was right, or that while she was mistaken, there was nothing that could be done about it. The divorce would simply need to be accepted. There would then be no need for their neighbour to become involved.

His boots were still wet from the grainy snow when his first foot sank into the peaty turf. He had lost track of himself, had wandered from the relative certainty of the path and out onto the sodden moor. Cold black water poured under the leather tongue, seeping into his socks. His foot hanging limp, he shook his leg impotently.

'*Fuck.*'

The expletive surprised him, even more so that it had hissed from his own mouth. It also disturbed the fox about thirty metres down wind. The blue-brown face rose from the tufts of sedge and turned abruptly to face Árni, ears alert to further sounds, limbs poised to dart for higher ground. The boy and the animal held each other's gaze for some moments before the fox turned and trotted off in a wide arc, maintaining its distance with cautious nonchalance, casting glances back towards Árni with decreasing frequency until it settled in the cover of a large rock. From there it stared at the boy with what seemed like curiosity.

Árni looked back, just as curious. It was the first fox he had seen in nearly two weeks on the fells, and he was struck by its lack of fear, its apparent communion with him. His satisfaction faded as he realised that it was also the first night he had spent away from Mr Baldursson's sheep. In a panic, he set off across the spongy ground to the grassy hummock where the fox had been.

One of the lambs. Baldursson's mark on its bloodied and twisted back. Its glassy eyes and lolling tongue frozen in terror, as if its body had just this minute been struck down. Only the progress made by the fox through the beast's entrails revealed the hours that had elapsed since the blow had been struck. Árni stared down at the corpse, struggling to connect its lifelessness to the bleating and bucking of its cousins only the day before. Something like compassion rose in him and he felt tears pricking his wind-taut cheeks as they slipped down.

There was no time of course. The other sheep, he hoped, still lived and he would need to account for each of them before their owner appeared. He noted the location of the dead lamb so that he might bring Mr Baldursson to see it, and set off across the wide moor, calling pointlessly into the wind for the others.

2012

The sea slapped against the breakwater, its echo carrying on the still air. He strained to hear the lost voices, as he did each time he returned, like the tide, to this shore. As ever, the voices stayed in the past, refused to speak to him as he was sure they someday must. On the bay, a vast white vessel lay at anchor, quiet now, its tenders tied to its flanks, its passengers secured aboard for the night. The mountains' slopes were scratched by the late sunlight; the last of the snow, still clinging in rills and gullies despite the summer's warmth, was washed golden and the basalt blushed roses. There was no sound, but the slap, slap, slap of the languid sea.

Árni had sat on this rock often as a boy, hidden from the town by the little houses of Fjarðarstræti. He had talked with school friends late into many summer's nights, before the return to the confinement of home became unavoidable. Back then, Ísafjörður had seemed extravagant, a city of infinite possibility, and the village boys had clung to it. It was here that shops stocked more than the staples of life, where it was possible to buy clothes that were no use on the fells or on the sea. And it was here that the bus began its journey to the world beyond the West Fjords. Many of his friends had, like him, taken the bus and escaped, but many others remained and, as he sat staring at the liner and the mountains beyond, Árni wondered if they were sleeping in beds behind him, unacknowledged and oblivious. Was his leaving a kind of death to them, unmourned and unremembered?

The sun dipped below the ridge at the head of the fjord. The town and the spit of gravel on which it stood fell into chill shadow. Even there, on the ragged north edge of the town, the shade slipped over Árni and he shivered. It was half past midnight. He looked into the paper cup cradled in his hands. The service station coffee was cold, but it contained sufficient brandy still to make swallowing the last of it pleasant enough. He pulled his jacket close about his throat.

Off in the distance, the sun still caught the tops of Hornstrandir; Hesteyri itself lay hidden by another headland. He would see it soon enough, carried on the morning boat. See it for the first time. He had never been taken across, even as a child, and yet he felt he was as familiar with the land as he was with his own skin, had read its contours in the depths of his father's absent eyes during the silence of those winter evenings or up on the fells on summer Sundays, when the two of them had paused to rest, the man to smoke and the boy to eat the piece of chocolate given to him by his mother before they set out. Hesteyri had hung about his father like the smoke of his cigarettes, pungent but unspoken.

His grandmother had told him about the view from the house when it had stood above another shore, about the endless skies of summer she had seen from it; the neighbours and the friends they had had there. He had only a slight memory, wafer thin, of his grandfather, and within it lay the old man's pride in the place that had been his, the jealousy with which he clung to the freedom of its slopes. But Árni could not be sure that this memory had not been laid instead by others, since Einar had died too soon for the boy to recall much more than the unfathomable depth of his beard and the steel grey of his eyes. It had been left to his Uncle Gylfi to whisper about the darkness of the place, about the leaving, and about the real uncle he might have had. His father had said little and had always made the crossing, when it was made, alone. Eiríkur had form.

◾

The call had left Árni numb. He had been cooking, had assumed that the ringing phone signalled that Charlotte and the kids had arrived in Surrey. He had cursed her and scuttled across the kitchen flicking anxious glances back towards the steaming pan. The slight pause at the other end of the line had unsettled him even before Gylfi's broken English had hissed into his ear. Gylfi was the only person in Bolungarvík who had his number in Cambridge, other than his father. In the hanging moments before he could speak, could let Gylfi slip once again into the comfort of his own tongue, a thousand possibilities careened through Árni's head, but all of them formed eventually into his father's corpse. Behind him, the pan boiled over, hissing and seething unseen, unnoticed.

'Hello, Gylfi, it's me. Árni. What's up?'

The language felt roomy, supple, even after the months it had lain unused somewhere between calculus and his mother's recipe for fish soup. He had stopped thinking in Icelandic years before, no longer translating his thoughts from one language to the other: ideas and feelings both blossomed unbidden in the shape of English words. Their attempt to raise Freyja as bilingual had already slid into the realm of good intentions by the time that Ben had been born and Árni had no other use for the language except to communicate with his father. He had not spoken to his father for five months.

He held his breath, braced, and waited for Gylfi to deliver the blow.

'Hello, Árni. So good to speak to you. It has been too long...'

The last time Gylfi rang the Cambridge number, it had been to tell Árni that his mother had died. Eiríkur had himself collapsed, stunned, unable to recognise the continued existence of the living, so consumed was he with the enormity of his wife's death. So it had been Gylfi, who had been there at the beginning as at the end, who had brought the news.

'*Look, it's your papa. Nothing to worry about, not yet anyway, but I thought you should know...*'

So not dead then, at least not yet. A serious illness, or an accident perhaps. A hospital bed with all the wires and tubes, and his father's eyes flickering, his face pale, grey skin grainy like a black and white photograph. For some reason, the white walls of the ward had a greenish tinge, as if the windows of the hospital had become overgrown with ferns.

'*...he's taken* Tófa *and, well, gone.*'

Not a hospital. Not an illness even. Instead, his father had pulled the tarpaulin from his great grandfather's upturned boat and set off across the fjord. Gylfi had seen the preparations, had even helped his friend haul *Tófa* to the shore, helped to test her seaworthiness, believing Eiríkur's intention had been simply to do a little fishing under the summer sun, like in the old days. He had been disappointed but not surprised when he had walked past one morning and seen that the boat had gone. But then there had been no sign of Eiríkur the following morning, nor the morning after that. When the house had been shut up for three days, closed like a tomb, he had taken the key Eiríkur had given him years before and entered, cloaked in trepidation.

Inside, everything had been orderly, spotless. The dishes were cleaned and stacked in the kitchen, the cloth folded neatly over the handle to the oven door. Everything was as it should be, but the larder was practically empty: there was no coffee, oats or sugar to be had, and the shelf of tins was bare. Gylfi had checked the cupboard that usually housed the bottles of schnapps they would share of an evening and, seeing that that too was empty, realised that his friend had not merely set out for a day's fishing.

'He'd been talking a lot about Hesteyri, all through the Spring. But it wasn't until I saw the schnapps cupboard that I put two and two together. He didn't mean to go fishing as we had done as young men, but as he had done as a boy. Árni, I believe your papa has gone over to Hesteyri. I asked the lads down at the harbour to keep an eye open for him, but in the meantime, it might be best if you make arrangements to come over. He'll be fine for a couple of weeks with what he's taken, but if the weather turns, or he has an accident... I'd go myself, but I've my Guðrún to look after and, in any case, I've never been able to get him to do what he doesn't want to do. He'll listen to you.'

Árni laughed with relief; Gylfi too, hesitantly at first and then with gusto, once he realised that this meant Árni would come, that he had understood.

Footsteps creaked on the landing and a door clunked closed; in moments, the rushing whine of water crackled through the pipes hidden behind the wall. Árni looked at his phone. Still twenty minutes until his alarm. He rolled onto his back and the little bed quivered beneath him. It took an extravagant sigh to pull his eyes fully open, to reveal the pink light of the room. Sitting up, he pushed the thin curtain aside to look out over the corrugated roofs of Ísafjörður, then back at the stuttering wall. When he had checked in, he had interpreted the vagueness of the girl on reception as meaning that the guesthouse had few if any other guests. The proximity of the bathroom had seemed therefore fortuitous. Now, he remembered that things were seldom wholly one thing or another, that convenience and disturbance were finely divided.

He collapsed back onto the bed, draping a forearm across his eyes. There was no point in getting up, since the shower was occupied. He decided to reclaim the time until his scheduled waking, if not in sleep then in indolence. Since Gylfi's call the previous Friday, he seemed to have been perpetually waiting, either in boredom for taxis, planes and boats or nervously for awkward conversations, such as that to come with his father or that which had passed with his wife.

Charlotte had returned on the Sunday, late afternoon. Árni had not mentioned Gylfi's call that evening when Charlotte had rung to announce her arrival in Surrey, and he had let the sparse and bloodless exchange close without disturbance. His own call, timed to fall before the family sat down to the ritual of Sunday lunch, had not been to discuss his imminent trip, but instead simply to ascertain when she might be back, whether they would have eaten or whether he should put something in the oven; whether Surrey was as warm as Cambridge had been. She in turn had told him about her parents' health and their holiday plans, without him once interjecting to mention his father's own trip.

The children had tumbled out of the car shortly after six, clutching gifts given by their grandparents, still fizzing with the excitement that absolute attention can generate, but it was not until after ten that Árni had presented what he described as his predicament rather than his plans. Whatever resentment she felt for his unexpected absence, and the consequences it held for her responsibilities, she showed no sign of disaffection as he told her the details of what was unavoidable. Two days later, she had offered an awkward doorstep embrace, conscious of the taxi driver's gaze, had kissed his cheek and told him to take as long as was needed. He in turn had kissed Freyja, then Ben, and promised to bring them back something from his trip. As the taxi had pulled away, he had twisted on the back seat to wave a final farewell, but Charlotte had already led the children back into the house.

The rising trill of electronic tones startled him: he had slipped back into sleep. His right arm tingled, cold to the touch, as he wrestled his drowsiness to reach the phone and kill the alarm. With an unexpected act of will, he did not retreat back under the covers but instead pivoted himself out of bed. He had fifty five minutes before the boat sailed; forty five before he needed to have left the little guesthouse. He stood shivering for a moment, surveying the items he had left in piles and heaps across the floor, things that needed to be folded and rolled and stuffed back into his bag. He looked at the bottle of brandy: still four fifths remained. He made some calculations, and decided that while not enough to last indefinitely, it would have to do. The bottle shop would not open until long after the boat had left. He cursed his decision to buy only one bottle when he had arrived at the airport, and to consume so much the evening before. He kicked gently at the one jumper he had managed to pack and wondered how he had forgotten the chill, even of summer. He wanted to start over, to begin this journey once again, to have made different choices.

He looked again at the bottle, thought briefly about the implications of taking a drink, then shuffled to the door. Hand already on the latch, he remembered to pick up the towel slung over the back of the chair by the window. It too was pink, like the curtains. He caught sight of himself in the mirror above the corner sink and was surprised by the pinkness of his skin, unsure if it was real or simply a trick of the light.

A puffin skimmed the low waves, white belly catching the morning sunlight with every turn. Off in the distance others bobbed on the surface, weary of the dance. With every thud of the hull into the cobalt banks, Árni almost lost his footing but his eyes followed the bird's path without interruption. When it crossed the bow, he staggered to the starboard side of the boat to track it anew. A young couple, blonde and earnest, politely moved their backpacks to allow him to pass before returning to their shelter from the spray by the cabin door. Árni did not mind the drenching thrown up by the sea; he wanted only to follow the puffin's course. He missed these improbable birds acutely, and had been upset that Freyja had reacted with indifference when he had first pointed one out to her. The puffin curved off into the broken light reflecting from the mouth of the Drangajökull, the glacier hanging over the bay, all but blocking the land route into the peninsula.

From the other side of the boat, an English voice announced that Hesteyri was in sight. Árni looked over at the three men and followed their arms to their pointing fingers and out across the water to the clutch of white shapes that formed the remnants of the village. Árni tried to make out the house that Gylfi had described, the place he most suspected Eiríkur would be holed up, but could not discern anything, so instead he watched the men. Their excitement shamed Árni, but less so than their ability to recognise the place before he had, a place to which they had no connection. Árni stared again at the scatter of white-washed shacks, willing buried memories from his blood.

Another boat. The white vessel cut across the blue bay leaving a line of spume pointing back to the city. Every day they came, leaving a handful of people, interlopers, dazed at the water's edge. Gradually they would disperse into the emptiness of the moor, over towards Aðalvík or up onto the fells to the East. Some stayed longer, drinking coffee in the sunshine outside the house that had been the home of the doctor, but which had now become some kind of guest house. Every evening, another boat would come to take those left in the village back to the city. All but the couple that ran the guest house. And now Eiríkur.

The thought of coffee stirred him from his place on the step and he hauled himself to his feet and turned inside. He had been in the house for over a week now, but his joints still ached. The journey across had been harder than he had imagined when he had decided to make it, even with the outboard motor, and the mornings passed awkwardly while his body loosened to its tasks.

He had set himself a routine. One day would be spent out on the bay, fishing until he had pulled enough from the water to make a proper dinner and lunch as well, and also to fill what space was left on the makeshift drying rack. He had built this on his first day, hidden behind the house, out of sight of the jetty, using the lengths of wood and cable he had brought with him from Bolungarvík.

On alternate days, he laboured through the morning with the timber washed up on the shore line, collecting smaller pieces where he could and swinging an axe at an old trunk he had chosen some way behind the beach. When he had cut four large pieces for laying down and gathered enough smaller pieces to cook his supper and brew his coffee, the day was his own.

The chair scraped against the dusty boards. From the table, Eiríkur could see a bright splinter of the day beyond the doorframe, but even in the kitchen's gloom the coffee glinted bright, slick like oil, as he stirred in his sugar. Too early yet to add a finger of schnapps; once the wood was cut would be soon enough. Perhaps he would take a walk up onto the fells later, maybe as far as the shallow ridge from where you could see the water on either side of the land, could watch the sunlight stretch off to the north, to where the ice lurked even now, waiting for its time.

Gylfi had said that Eiríkur still had the key to Helgi Gunnarsson's house, even though Helgi himself was dead these past twelve years: the sons had not yet stirred themselves to act upon their inheritance and the house would be empty. He was to look for the house with blue boards, up beyond the church. But the church was gone and Árni did not know which way to begin. He stood, caught between the land and the sea, as aimless as the hikers. The three English men were arguing over their map, while the German couple tightened the straps of their packs and braced themselves for departure. There was no-one else in sight, no-one to ask, and no way back; the boat had already left the jetty behind, headed off further into the bay looking for its next haven.

A building, larger than the others, built over two storeys, stood beside a stream some way back from the shore. Green window frames were set into white, clapboard walls; a t-shirt fluttered from a line strung between two posts. A woman sat at the table beside the open door, a cup in one hand, a cigarette in the other.

'Hi. Can you help? I'm looking for someone.'

The woman looked up for the first time, having ignored Árni's approach across the rough meadow. Like him, she was in her forties. The trace of lines haunted her eyes, but they still sparkled with mischief. Her hair was tied in a red scarf; her grey sweater was decorated in the Icelandic style, a white pattern ringing the neck. Árni caught a glimpse of a pair of wellington boots crossed under her chair.

'Are they staying here? In the guesthouse?'

She indicated behind her with a jerk of her head. While he processed his answer, she drew fiercely on her cigarette and exhaled extravagantly through pursed lips over her right shoulder, almost blowing kisses to the mountain above.

'No, I don't think so. I think he might be staying at Helgi Gunnarsson's place, if you know it.'

Her look suggested that she did indeed know where he might find the house, and indeed his father, but that she had no intention of betraying either as easily as that.

'Sit down. Let me fetch you a coffee.'

Without waiting for an answer, the woman twisted in her seat and shouted for someone called Kjartan to bring another cup and some fresh coffee. Turning back and seeing Árni still standing awkwardly, she gestured impatiently to the space across the table from her. She waited while her visitor complied, compelled. She pushed the packet of cigarettes towards him and, unthinking, Árni took one and lit it before he remembered that he hated smoking, had no idea how to smoke, let alone why anyone would want to. He coughed apologetically and held the cigarette at arm's length, unsure if stubbing it out would appear ruder, more ridiculous, than his awkward inaction. Her question, when it came, was simple enough, but its answer eluded him and its final formulation took longer than it should.

'No, not really. Well, yes, actually, I am from here, but I don't live here anymore. Not for years. I grew up in Bolungarvík.' The hand clutching the cigarette flapped uselessly behind him, pointing roughly towards where he assumed the village to be. *'But my*

father, he was born here. In Hesteyri. I grew up in a house that had stood here. I was christened in Súðavík, in the church that used to be here. So I suppose, yes, I am from here. It's complicated. But my father was one of the last to leave. Back in the fifties. It's him I'm looking for. He went missing.'

He felt strangely childlike and, unable to fathom why, his voice trailed into the tussling breeze. Kjartan brought the coffee with a greeting, to which Árni could only nod a response. Once they were alone again, he busied himself with the hot, sweet drink, wishing that he could reach into his bag for the brandy bottle and not worsen the impression he was making. Running out of places to look, his eyes once more met hers and he was surprised to find that their smile was neither cruel nor mocking but one of welcome.

'So you're Árni.'

From somewhere under the grey sweater, the woman produced a small metal flask. She poured a little of the clear contents into her own cup before offering it to Árni with an encouraging nod. He took the flask with a little too much enthusiasm and, once the schnapps had fused with the coffee and sugar on his tongue, he handed it back, his shoulders slackening gratefully. That his father should be known to the only other residents of this ghost village was, on reflection, unsurprising, but his mention of Árni, by name, to a relative stranger, remained unexpected. It seemed unlikely that, in his distance, the son should loom so large in the father's mind. Árni wondered how long a conversation would have to last before he mentioned Ben, such that she would recall his name later, talking over coffee with another stranger.

Another cigarette lit and a second cup of coffee laced, the woman became Sirrý, no longer a stranger. She has spoken to Eiríkur twice: in simple greeting on his second day in the village and then a few days later when, bored in the absence of guests, she had taken a walk along the strand. From the sand she had seen him in his boat, pulling fish from the water in the old way. Fascinated by this old man and his ghost work, she had sat on one of the Russian logs to watch and when he had returned to the shore, she had tried to help him haul the boat up the beach against his protestations. She had offered a cigarette and they had sat out listening to the waves stroke the shore, talking about the quicksilver sea and the grudging land, the shifting sky and the roots that passed from each of them into the rough turf at their feet.

Árni watched her as she spoke, the delight of the recalling passing across her face like sunshine on a windy day in spring. He had not guessed that his father could elicit such lightness in anyone, much less a strange woman almost half his age. As she went on, he learned that, like Árni, she was the daughter of a son who had left Hesteyri with his own father in that same summer. Eiríkur had known her grandfather, had played sometimes with her father. Of course Árni's name had fallen into that conversation. But while he had run still farther after his studies in the city, Sirrý had returned to Ísafjörður, first as a teacher, then gradually as a guide, then inexorably as the guardian of this guesthouse, where she lived for two months of the year, while the weather allowed for visitors: walkers, birdwatchers and the curious.

'Have you eaten? We could stretch to another plate if you want some lunch.'

He had not noticed the passing of time, the slip of the warm sun to the south, the hunger rising above the sticky intoxication of the coffee, the unfamiliar tang of nicotine. He looked at his watch, needlessly. He should continue, find Gunnarsson's house, see his father; he had already taken too much of their hospitality. And yet his appetite, his hollowness, undermined his protests and he acquiesced quickly, accepting the plate of fish soup with enthusiasm. As Kjartan returned to the shadows of the house, Árni asked Sirrý if her husband would not be joining them.

'My husband? I hope not. He's been dead seven years.' Her shock turned to laughter and her nose wrinkled. *'You mean Kjartan? He's nice enough, but I only met him a month ago. He was a hut warden at Þórsmörk before that and fancied something a bit more… remote.'*

A piece of fish quivered on her spoon, steam rising. She shook her head one more time, then swallowed the morsel with a grin.

There had been no-one home. Had Sirrý not been so clear, he would have doubted that this blue-boarded house belonged to Helgi Gunnarsson, much less that it was now inhabited by his father. Awkwardly, he had peered through the kitchen window. There was nothing to be seen that indisputably belonged to his father, but the room was spotless. There was no dust or any of the signs that would indicate that the house had been abandoned for years. By the sink was an upturned cup and a coffee pot sat quietly on the stove. Only when he skirted around the property, and saw the rack of fish drying on the wind, did he know for sure. He had looked down to the bay, but no vessel could be seen on the water; below, on the beach, secured by a line against unexpected storms, he had made out the familiar shape of *Tófa*.

At a loss, he had found his way to the stone cross marking the site of the rectangle of turf on which the church had stood. It had been taken, plank by plank, to Súðavík in time for his christening, but around the little monument, grave stones recorded what had been. All were in good condition, trim and tended, but only one carried a still-fresh posy of marsh orchids. He did not need to read the inscription to know that it belonged to his uncle, to Ólafur.

A whip of wind snapped across the hills to the north, slanting over the shoulder of the highest crag behind the village. The turf rippled and Árni chased the shiver down his spine. He thought about his jumper, wondered if he should go back up to the house, retrieve it from the bag he had left on the paving beside the door. Instead he found a crease in the sloping ground and curled his back into it, snug against the gusts rolling down from the ridge, so that the sun's weak warmth could soak into his bones unopposed. And he waited beside the long dead brother for the one still living to appear.

A chill finally woke him, and he felt the dampness of the earth that had seeped in through his jeans while he slept. The sun no longer shone directly on him, the shoulder of the land casting him in shadow, but the sea still sparkled and, through its dazzle, his eyes slowly focused on the man sitting on the grass a few metres away.

'You came, then.'

Eiríkur was smoking, half turned towards the horizon, with his profile silhouetted by the shining bay. If there was a smile, it was hidden. Árni struggled with the stiffness in his limbs, the slowness of his waking, but Eiríkur continued his conversation before his son was able to form a response.

'I was over in Aðalvík today. Do you remember that day we were there together, playing on the sand? It was my birthday. You taught me to skip stones on the sea. I wasn't very good at it, but I've been practicing since then. I span one today and it hopped five times.'

Maybe his father was losing his mind. It would explain his decision to abandon his home and to come here, beyond the reach of the support needed by a man of his age. Árni struggled to see if there was another person present, so that the recurrent terror of his father's descent into dementia might be stilled. Only gradually did the fact that he had forgotten his father's birthday establish itself bluntly, brazen, in his mind. It was today.

'Hey Dad? Are you OK? It's me, Árni.'

He emerged fully from his nook, standing unsteady on uncoiling legs. With the changed angle, Eiríkur's face became clearly legible in the evening light. There was no trace of confusion or distress, just the same old solid flatness; alert rather than engaged. At his birthday wishes, Eiríkur's eyes twinkled, but Árni could not tell if this revealed a gladdened heart or the certainty that the greetings were too little, too late. Perhaps there was no glint at all, just the sunlight and the silver sea playing tricks: Árni could not be sure.

'I'm surprised to see you, son.' A pause. 'So that'll be your bag by the door?'

Árni nodded and searched for more words, any of the thousands he knew in several languages, but none came and so he nodded, longer than a man with all his senses should nod. Perhaps it was he who was losing his mind. Only with his father's embrace, the warmth of his words in his ears, did the giddiness leave and his head come to rest. All was right once more.

'Your uncle was just here. We were talking about another birthday of mine. A long time ago. I would have liked for you to have met him. Another time perhaps.'

The sharp eyes misted momentarily, but their sharpness returned before a gust of leaden air, chill like the morgue, slid down the slope to the shore. Árni pulled his jacket closed at the neck, tried to ignore his father's dismissive shake of the head.

'Shall we get you inside? If you're not used to it, that wind can be a little cool, even on a beautiful evening like this.'

They walked together up towards the blue-boarded house,

talking about the grandchildren, about the long departed family of Helgi Gunnarsson, about Bjarki, the best footballer in the village, about Sirrý Guðmundsdóttir, about anything but the things that Árni most wanted to discuss. They could wait until they had eaten and the brandy bottle was on the table. Once the wind was shut out, he could think more clearly, approach things more subtly so as not to put his father on the defensive. No point in backing Eiríkur into a corner, not if you ever wanted him to come out of it.

■

In the grate, the last of the fire fizzed, breaking the silence that had gathered about the table. On it were two empty bowls, two spoons and two glasses, freshly filled with schnapps; otherwise there was only the breathing and thoughts of the two men. The grey light of late evening slunk in through the window glass, barely enough for Árni to be able to tell if his father was angered by his question or merely ignoring it. It did not occur to him that he might not have an answer. Since their meeting among the graves, Eiríkur had displayed no strangeness, had seemed his usual robust, if reticent, self. As the fish soup slipped down, quickened by schnapps, he had felt more reassured, certain that he had simply misunderstood what was being said about his uncle, that there was nothing actually wrong with his father. A misunderstanding on his part, or simply the poetic language favoured by earlier generations; in any case, there would be a simple explanation. By the time the meal was done, he had felt sufficiently confident to ask his father why he had decided to spend the summer, this summer, in Hesteyri. It had seemed an innocuous question, but Eiríkur had said nothing for several minutes. The only sign of life had been the brief moment in which the old man had pushed the spoon with his outstretched thumb around his empty bowl, from 5 o'clock to 2, eating time in a staccato arc.

Árni sipped at his schnapps. It would taste better with a cigarette, he decided, and his eyes, searching for something other than his father's opaque face, fell upon the packet by the bottle. The cigarettes were the same brand that Sirrý smoked. A coincidence, most likely, but he could not resist the idea that maybe something was happening between Eiríkur and the trim, blonde guesthouse keeper. Maybe cigarettes and recipes for fish soup were not all they exchanged; maybe this adventure was a lovers' tryst. The thought lingered until the slow creaking of his father's voice chased out such nonsense.

'It's sixty years since we left, you know? Your grandfather, he tried to argue against it, but everyone else, mama too, had just had enough. I was too young to know much about it, but was happy enough to leave. There was electricity over there, television, motors. Girls. Bolungarvík felt like the future.'

Nostalgia then, and maybe some guilt. An anniversary pilgrimage to something lost. It would explain the conversation with Ólafur, and solitude would explain how that conversation escaped from Eiríkur's imagination and out onto the wind. Árni realised that his concern had not, until that moment, left him and he felt his shoulders drop, an uncoiling of his back. With a swallow, he emptied his glass. Immediately, he refilled both glasses and offered a toast to the Hesteyri that was lost. Eiríkur raised his glass, said the words and drank off the clear spirit. He dragged the bottle back towards him, and filled the glasses once more. He lifted his to about an inch in front of his face, a beacon atop his forearm; his right eye bulged through the viscous curve for a moment, before the glass was lifted higher still.

'To Ólafur, my brother.'

Both men drank and the silence closed in again. Only embers remained of the fire, the ash whiter than white in the grey light. Even though the air was warm within the kitchen, beyond the reach of the searching wind, Árni rose from his chair and laid a new hunk of bleached wood in the grate. He crouched beside it, listened to the hiss of it, watched the tendrils of smoke grow from the deadened log, smiled at the first lick of yellow flame. Behind him, he knew that his father was shaking his head at his son's profligacy. He would collect more wood tomorrow, even though Eiríkur had already stacked enough to last the whole summer.

'You've never talked about him, you know? All I know of my uncle came from grandma, and second hand from Uncle Gylfi. Nothing from you. All my life, even his name has been unmentionable in your hearing. Like a ghost, something taboo.'

The words stumbled from his mouth. When they had stopped, Árni stared at the ever larger flames flickering from the belly of the log, unable to turn to see the anger or hurt he had caused. He heard the scrape of metal on flint, the fizz of gas, the tearing of the flame through paper and leaf; a deep inhalation, followed by a long low breath on which the smoke would be streaming in the half light.

'My brother died, Árni. He died here. In the depths of winter. His passing destroyed my father. I learnt not to talk about Ólafur from my father. He blamed himself for staying too long in Hesteyri, but never wanted to leave, despite what staying had meant. Can you imagine what that would do to a man? Knowing that your choices had killed your son, but knowing that you would repeat those choices if you had to. If you could.'

The voice was level, calm; controlled. Árni listened again as his father drew in the smoke, let it play about his tongue, held it in and pushed it back out through his nose in a slow release; he heard the bottle scrape on the table, the short gulp as the schnapps scuttled into one, two glasses. A gust of wind pushed smoke back down into the stove, sending it billowing into Árni's face, stinging his eyes. He should turn, go back to the table, take up the glass and drink with his father, but the damp redness of his eyes would betray him, without good cause.

'And me. I bargained with the elves, but I did not honour the deal that I made. If I had, maybe Ólafur would have lived. I've carried that shame all these years, and it's time that I made my peace. With Ólafur, with the elves.'

Árni swung on his heel to face Eiríkur, aghast. The remorse of his grandfather he could understand: there were real choices he could have made that might conceivably have altered the outcome. But Eiríkur had been a boy, an infant, with only fantasy bargains to call upon. That he should have borne any guilt for what had happened, much less a lifetime of self-reproach, seemed cruel and unnecessary. He thought of his own son, agonised by the possibility that Ben should carry any such wound into his life.

'What shall we drink to next?'

The smile wrinkled through Eiríkur's beard. The skin had closed once more over the wound and there was only the long grey night and the bottle and the cigarettes left to them, to help them skate over the world until it was time to sleep.

'Do you ever wonder what your life would be like if you'd never gone to Reykjavík, never met your husband?'

They had been talking about this and that, about family, work and the distance life had taken them, only to drop them back where they had begun. Árni had been in Hesteyri for four days and he had chopped as much wood as he could stand to. Sirrý's coffee and conversation consumed more and more of his time, and not only when Eiríkur was out on the water, as he was that morning. *Tófa* bobbed on the low swell some 800 metres off the coast and, occasionally, the stutter of her motor drifted in on the wind, reminding him of his father's presence.

'No, not really. How about you? I mean you still have a wife, still live away. The distance between there and here must be greater for you. More to wonder at.'

She drank her coffee, eyes dropped to the rim of the cup. Árni waited for her to look at him once more, but she did not. Perhaps she too felt that her question contained some kind of accusation. Árni waited a little longer, and listened to the bluster of the motor as Eiríkur turned *Tófa* for another pass along the lines. He did not need to formulate his response: he had carried it with him onto the bus to the city all those years before, had accepted the distance that had already been laid in the years since his grandfather had died, and he had felt no guilt at making concrete the absence that already engulfed him.

"Before, then, it's a question that would never have occurred to me. Life took me where it would. And it worked. I mean I was near the top of my field by the time I'd turned 35. There was no reason to look over my shoulder then. I used to be someone, really. I was someone, but now..."

"Now you're someone else." Sirrý threw the cigarettes onto the table in front of him. As he reached for them, she rested her hand on his like a whisper, but it was gone before he could find her eyes. Instead of talking further, they smoked and drank coffee and listened to the wind raking the scrubby grass, the sound of the water chasing itself down the stream, chuckling and burring over rocks, gurgling to itself in moss-choked pools.

The razor had gone. He had left it on the washstand, he was sure. He scrubbed his palm against the coarse growth. He had not shaved for three days, for reasons he could not remember, had not looked for the razor in that time, but he was sure it had been there. He looked again, as if simply staring would coax it from its hiding place. He shook the uninvited thought of elves from his head.

'Dad, have you seen my shaving things?'

His voice rang around the house, but failed to provoke a response. He listened for Eiríkur's breathing, the creak of his chair, but there was nothing. The air felt thick with absence. His face still dripping, Árni trudged through the rooms in turn, without expectation. It was early still, but his father kept strange hours, and he could no longer be relied upon to be where he was expected to be.

In the kitchen, an empty coffee cup and bowl still sat on the table; a pan was in the sink, filled with water and a few stubborn oats. He felt the cup. It still held a little warmth: Eiríkur hadn't gone far. Árni pulled the curtain to one side and scanned the village. The hikers in the campsite were stirring, stretching the sleepless night out of their bones; smoke rose from the chimney of the doctor's house; between the two, almost hidden among the headstones, Eiríkur was crouched by one of the graves. He appeared to be deep in conversation. There was no-one with him of course. Árni had become used to the hours his father spent talking to his dead brother. He no longer saw it as a sign of encroaching dementia, and instead understood these conversations to be the natural emergence of buried grief. He would allow him this time.

How much time, however, was becoming an ever more pressing question. Already, he had been away from his family, from his work, for over a week and he had yet to broach the subject of when they might return. While his office had been understanding and Charlotte had yet to edge their short, infrequent conversations with the grit of her resentment, the patience of neither would last forever. He felt the coffee pot standing on the stove, swilled its contents, and poured a little into a still-damp cup. Without thinking, he added sugar, took a cigarette from the pack on the table and drew heavily on both once seated. He looked at his hand. The cigarette fitted between his fingers, as comfortable as an old friend. How quickly these things could blur into you. Aside from a few half-hearted attempts at university, he had never smoked; he did not sweeten his coffee, much less drink cup after cup of it from morning to night. He was a scientist. He knew what these chemicals did once inside the body, the reactions they could cause. He took another drag on the cigarette, let its smoke play about his tongue, felt its pressure in his lungs, the long cool release.

The fish. Through the fuzz of nicotine, the thought crystallised and he sat upright, stabbing the cigarette into the ashtray with sudden determination. There were more fish drying on the rack behind the house than Eiríkur could possibly need, more than he would need to trade for as many of Sirrý's cigarettes as he could smoke. And the wood stacked under the eaves. Eiríkur had been laying down four times as much as he had been using. Even if he stopped now, he would have enough of both to last well into autumn.

He says he's not going back. I don't know what to do. He's not even adamant about it, just really calm, decided.

The sound of Charlotte swearing, even hushed and through teeth, usually surprised him but any other reaction would have been more startling. Árni wondered if the curses were directed at him or at his father, then decided it made little difference. In circumstances such as this, and at this distance, both men were effectively the same person.

From the next room he could hear Kjartan talking with a Belgian woman about the route across to Hlöðuvík. Her English was much better than Kjartan's and Árni wanted to put the phone down, so that he might translate for them. It would be more useful, and less awkward, than his conversation with Charlotte. He wondered where Sirrý was. She had not been in her usual seat outside the kitchen door when he had arrived. Her absence unsettled him, so used to her presence had he become. He would have liked to talk to her about his father's obstinacy, about whether she had known of his plans. With an effort, he focused on Charlotte's voice.

'Isn't there some kind of social services you can contact? I mean, if you can't sort things out. It's not ideal you know. You've been gone for almost two weeks now. I've been as supportive as I can, but it's been a real strain with the kids. It's not fair on them. On me. And have you been in touch with work?'

He had not. He had instead decided that he would not return to the University in any case. Something else would turn up, something better. Something different. He would tell them at some moment convenient to him, once the more pressing business of his father's obstinacy had been resolved. It was not too late to change course, he had decided, to become something as yet unimagined, to pick up a current left behind years before, neglected in his rush to become who he had been these last years. Every corner he had passed since leaving Bolungarvík had been crowding him for days, offering glimpses of what he could have been. But he said none of this to Charlotte. There would be time for that conversation, once his father was safe.

'I suppose so. There's someone I can ask about that, but she's not here today. At least I've not seen her. She'll know more about these things.'

He not had mentioned Sirrý before, had only said that there was a small guest house in the village which had a phone line that he could borrow occasionally, there being no other reliable phone signal in Hesteyri. He wondered how Charlotte would react if he were to tell her, already certain that he would not.

·

It was dark outside, and the lamp light sent shadow flares across the kitchen walls. They had settled around the table because the stove still gave off some heat and because there was nowhere else to go, except to bed. And neither man wanted to crawl away to the comfort of sleep. Eiríkur poured out two more measures of schnapps and glowered at his son.

'I don't want to go back to Bolungarvík. It's not my home, no matter what you say. It's just an empty village across the bay.'

Most of the schnapps emptied into him and he snatched at the packet beside the glass and pulled out a cigarette with trembling fingers. In the flare of the match, Eiríkur's face became ghoulish for a second or two, and Árni wondered how he had let this conversation become so destructive. It had been intended as a gentle but firm presentation of the case for ending this summer sojourn and returning to the world. There had been a first flurry of snow already, a dusting that clung on in the shaded hollows of the bay, and he had thought that he would be able to make his father see reason. Instead, his intransigent father sat across the table angrily sucking at a cigarette.

'Those things will kill you. Do you have any idea what's going on in your cell structure right now?'

'What does that matter?' His father's eyes became sharper, but their meaning indistinct: they were laced with reproach, with defiance, but also carried a softness that might have been fear, or simply pleading. He inhaled and his bent shoulders straightened into the shape Árni remembered from when he was a boy, when his father was a vigorous man, honed by the sea and wind, sculpted by the oar and the net. A shiver of regret and fear disturbed the sticky stillness of his schnapps haze.

'Besides, I'll be fine as long as I'm here. This land gives strength to its people, to all living things that are raised here.' Eiríkur stubbed out the cigarette, and held up his other hand to prevent his son from interrupting. He emptied the remains of his glass before continuing. 'We had a cow, you know, when your grandfather was alive? She came with us in the boat when we left Hesteyri, along with everything else. But she never milked over there.' Eiríkur nodded in the direction of the window, which faced north, away from Bolungarvík, but Árni did not correct him. He knew the story of Glæta, had been raised on it. He knew that the cow had miraculously begun to milk within days of finding herself on her home turf once more; how she had in fact leapt from the boat to swim ashore, so keen was she to be home. As a boy this had seemed the most marvellous story and he had believed every word to be true. As he had learned more about the world, about the basic biology of mammals, he had come to doubt that cows would refuse to milk if they were denied the grass of home. But he had never before challenged the story, because it was simply a family myth that could harm no-one. But now it had become a parable that threatened to keep his father tied to Hesteyri through the most vicious of winters, a winter that would most probably kill him. He was half way through his calm explanation of the science when his father exploded.

'*Do you think I'm stupid? I know this, but I also know what I saw. You weren't there to see it, so how can you tell me that it didn't happen?*' It was not a question to which an answer was invited. Eiríkur's eyes flashed and rolled, as he pulled a reluctant cigarette from the packet; two, three strikes of the match and the tip glowed incandescent. '*And I'll tell you something else. I was in the prow of the boat when Glæta leapt over me and into the sea to swim for the shore. A cow willingly throwing herself into deep water. Explain that, mister scientist.*'

Eiríkur poured more schnapps into his glass, then looked over to Árni's, still half full. He topped it to the brim and glared a challenge towards his son. Árni picked up the glass, felt the sticky fluid spill over, running onto his fingers, and was content to subject himself in this way to his father's will.

'*In any case, isn't this exactly what you spend your life working on? The idea that there are parts of our brains, all of us, animals too, that recognise places before we do ourselves? If that's true for your rats, why not for a cow? Why not for a man?*'

Árni's mouth hung open a little, although there were no words to come for some moments. All the while, his father watched him with a mild impatience. He was anxious to put an end to the question of his staying in Hesteyri, to make it clear that he would remain here now until the end of his days, with his father and mother, with his lost brother. There was nothing across the water now, only a son who was almost a ghost himself, who had been lost on the fells among Baldursson's sheep, when he should have been with his father. Eiríkur had lost a father and a brother he had kept close and yet, in trying to protect his son by keeping him away, he had lost him anyway.

'You understand my research? All these years, you've been listening to me?' The flutter of the lamp was all that disturbed the still air of the kitchen. Árni watched his father's beard twitch, saw grey smoke curl up from the stub of the cigarette resting between the fingers of his right hand where the skin was stained to a dirty yellow.

'Of course, Árni. You're my son.' Eiríkur lifted what was left of the cigarette to his mouth and pulled its smoke into himself, the orange intensity piercing the gloom with an unexpected sharpness. The squeal and crunch of the stub twisting into the ashtray mesmerised Árni and he watched the blunt fingers work the remains into the sea of ash. He no longer had the heart to continue their argument. Tomorrow would be soon enough to resolve the question, and he decided he would rather let the lamp's dull yellow light wash through him for the time that remained before tiredness carried them both to their beds.

A breeze raked over the pass and Eiríkur felt the chill nudge into his bones, a reminder that summer would not last forever, would soon in fact be gone. He looked up at the morning sky and even with the light of the low sun washing down the valley, there were already signs that the gloom of winter had started to gather. A shiver ran through him and he dug his hands into his pockets. In his right hand, he felt the course rasp of the match box, the glossy suppleness of his cigarette packet and he sought out a sheltered spot that would allow for the precious indulgence to be enjoyed fully and at leisure.

Taking his seat, he slid one of the cigarettes out of its packet and examined it, the stark white straightness, and he carefully ran his fingers along the length of its supple paper, remembering the sensation from before the calluses and scars had put a wall between him and the world. With a sigh, he placed one end between his lips and fumbled with a match until it burst into a brief and fizzing frenzy. He sucked on the cigarette, listening to the crackling of the paper's consumption. Only once he had released this first gulp, did he look up to take in the view.

The country opened to the north, to where the shore lay at the mercy of the winds that blew in over the Greenland Sea. He could trace the crenulations of the land, each cut against the deep blue of the ocean. Looming over the broad bay of Aðalvík, like a fat finger pointing to the north, was the mass of Straumnesfjall. He searched its broad back until the little smudge of buildings showed where the soldiers had made their base during the dark days of the Cold War. He remembered how he would sometimes see the Americans in Ísafjörður, smiling and relaxed, enjoying the comforts of the town, drinking forbidden beer, glad to be young and at liberty.

The last of his cigarette came too soon, and he shook the stub into the wind. His limbs complained bitterly as he stood once more, the solid air buffeting at his back as he set off. He swallowed down the desire to return to the warmth of his bed, swung his aching legs into a young man's stride, his sixty eight years nagging at his heels.

The path led across the stone field, the imprints of hiking boots left in the few patches of soft ground. Soon tufts of grass and sedge, the clumps of Moss Campion bulging from the grey gravel, filled these spaces, measuring the rate of his slow descent. Where the flat ground dropped away to the coast, the expanse of the valley opened before him. Eiríkur scuffed his boots on the loose earth and rock that fringed the course of the waterfall down to where the meadow was thick with orchids, where the water crashed and gurgled into mossy pools, then snaked off along its course to the sea. In another hour he was at the mouth of the stream, on a beach under the sand-caked bow of Mannfjall. The waves broke in from the open ocean, rolling and ripping across the margin of land and sea. The wind swallowed all sound but that of the water's crash and suck.

Above the elemental roar, Eiríkur heard laughter from another time on this shore. There had been a lighter wind that day, just a breeze tugging at his loose shirt, brushing Ólafur's hair against the grain, into his wide eyes. The surf had been kinder as they had run barefoot though its tingling race. He could recall how the sand above the tide line had been soft and dry between his toes, and he could remember how his brother's hand had felt as he led him back up the beach, towards the path and home. He felt it now, the touch of his brother, heard the sound of his voice clearly. Other memories tumbled into him, easily, comfortably; memories that had been closed to him for as long as he could remember were returned to him, as fresh as the day they had been made. Eiríkur looked about him, certain that hidden eyes were watching him.

It was done; the score had been settled, the debt repaid. His brother was released to him. He had not expected it to come so soon. They would be able to see out the next few weeks in pleasure rather than penance, until the first proper snow fell, and then he would let his son take him home. Next year maybe they could return and Árni could bring his family. They could stay in Helgi Gunnarsson's empty house and he could introduce his grandchildren to this place.

Kicking off his boots, and tugging away his socks, Eiríkur walked slowly towards the surf line. The sand was coarser, colder, and age had produced aches that could not today be denied, but he walked on. The surging waters snaked around his ankles, the sand sucked gently at his feet, and Eiríkur threw wide his arms to embrace the distant horizon.

■

She was still drinking her first coffee when Árni climbed panting onto the wooden terrace, a haunted look in his eyes. She ran a glance across him, frowning at the poorly laced walking boots, and settled finally on the idea that her new neighbour was in a hurry. She stiffened at the thought of what may have provoked such careless haste, at what might have had gone wrong. She thought of Eiríkur's broken body lying prone at the foot of the stairs, or else wheezing weakly in sweat-drenched sheets.

'Hi. Morning. Sirrý. Aðalvík?' Árni breathed a couple of deep breaths, slowed his delivery to be better understood. 'Sorry, bit out of breath.' He shook his head in frustration at his statement of the obvious. Sirrý poured coffee, indicated with her palm that he should sit. He was only anxious, not distraught. The problem was not such that immediate action was needed; she felt her muscles slacken, and realised that her body had set itself to attention.

'What's up? Everything OK with the old man?' She offered a cigarette, as she did every morning, and when he declined, took one for herself with a shrug.

'Do you know how I get to a place called Aðalvík?' Eiríkur had spoken of the place several times, had been there that first day when Árni had arrived. When he had discovered his father's room empty that morning, and when he had seen Tófa still beached below the village, it had been his first thought of where he might have gone. He had mentioned the bay the previous evening, one of the places that made his return here unarguable, as if the simple fact of it made it inconceivable that he should be anywhere else.

Something about the quietness of the house, something that echoed in its timbers, had woken him. It was a strange quietness, deathly, and it had made his father's absence feel unlike those other mornings when Eiríkur had left Árni sleeping to fish or hike or to sit with Sirrý and drink coffee and smoke her cigarettes.

'Did he stop by? Maybe to pick up some more cigarettes?' There had been a great deal of smoking the previous evening. At least one packet had been crumpled and thrown into the bucket by the back door, and another had been stripped almost bare by Eiríkur's angry fingers in the heat of their hushed argument. Sirrý's shake of the head troubled him. It was not like his father to go too far without more than enough cigarettes.

Leaving Sirrý to await the arrival of the 9am boat, he wearied his way up the track rising alongside the stream above Hesteyri. The rush of the waterfall was lost among the sound of the wind, the coarse rasp of his own breath, and the heavy thudding of his heart. Before he had reached the pass, where the rough-made track disappeared in the chaos of the stone field, the wind began to bite at his back. Kagrafell loomed above him, and the mountains and inlets of the great bay stretched back to Ísafjörður, to Bolungarvík. The sun broke free of its cloud-snare and flashed a brilliant light across the world, igniting turquoise pools and electric mosses, turning grey snow fields into brilliant flares. Árni lingered, not simply to catch his breath, but also to absorb the majesty that surrounded him. Nothing was unfamiliar in the shapes and colours: they were the base ingredients of his life, seen every day for his first eighteen years. And yet here, now, everything seemed new, everything seemed remarkable. For the first time since he had found his father missing that morning, he experienced a lightness in his heart.

He tried to remember what it was that had made Aðalvík special to his father, rather than why it should cause him concern. So much of Eiríkur's story ran through this landscape, it was inevitable that he would feel the need for the sustenance it gave. By the time Sirrý and Kjartan shut up the Doctor's House at the end of the season, Eiríkur would be ready to leave too, Árni was sure. It was only his own urgency that had pushed his father into obstinacy. Time moved differently here, for his father especially. Work and family were the drivers of his desire to pull Eiríkur back to Bolungarvík, not concern for the old man's health. He was more robust than he ought to be: he could still pull *Tófa* into the sea, still haul the lines of fish from the water, and Árni was sure now that there was no trace of dementia in his father. He had simply mistaken the sadness of loss for a disease. It would be nice to spend some more time with him here in this vastness. He might even come to understand the things he himself had lost, maybe even begin to recover something that had been misplaced years before. He turned to face the north and let the wind push him across the slab of wet snow that stretched off towards Aðalvík.

The ground changed from grey and white to green and pink. Campions bobbed in the brief summer light. The view to the north opened into a vast scoop of green than ended in the blue bow of the sea. Below him, vibrant meadowland stretched out, scored by streams and rivulets that coiled around themselves, like a twist of sinew and vein. The sound of a waterfall hissed up over the edge, near to where what looked like a path disappeared into air.

He paused at the brink, saw the path bifurcate on its winding descent, then each bifurcation split again, endlessly, until faint lines that might have been paths wove between rocks all across the face of the slope. Despite the dizziness flickering through him, he took a breath and followed the line that shadowed the course of the water crashing down towards the valley floor.

The loose earth slipped beneath him but with each step he gained confidence, remembering how he had skittered across slopes just like this chasing Siggi Baldursson's sheep as a boy. He began to enjoy the looping route, the sudden precipices and the satisfaction at finding the best course around them. All the while, the water raced passed him, headlong, without restraint, without doubts. Soon he was nearing the bottom, and the path flattened slightly. He no longer feared for each step.

Below him, he could see the path veer off to the eastern edge of the valley and he remembered the water that clotted the floors of valleys such as this: the path skirted the marsh to keep walkers' boots out of the worst of it. Árni looked at the cobweb of paths around him, most leading down and away to the west. He would need to ford the river to make it to the drier path, unless he crossed the stream here, above the last step of the waterfall.

The stream ran fast but shallow. A liberal scattering of rocks offered lodging to feet seeking a dry route over. Árni scanned the far bank: there would be a little bit of a scramble, but nothing insurmountable, nothing that he had not undertaken a hundred times before. Gingerly he placed his right foot on a flat stone half a metre into the flow. Shifting his weight, back and forth, it did not budge and since it was wide enough for both feet he swung himself out.

As he progressed, the rocks became smaller, less stable. He moved swiftly, continuously, since none afforded a steady resting place. In mid-stream, where the spray of the falling water rose above the lip, he paused, legs astride between two stones, conscious that eyes were upon him. Above him, some 20 metres from the other bank, a fox stood rigid against the green hillside, her intrigue and mistrust locked in unresolved tension. Árni stared back in a silent communion, both between species, but also between the man as he was and the boy he had been. He smiled, felt the weight of the last weeks, of the last years, fall away. Then she was gone, silent and fleet. He tested the next stepping stone with his left foot. It was damp, but did not move. Picking the next target, a larger, flatter stone, its surface just below the silvered flow, he took a short breath and swung his right leg onto it, feeling its movement too late.

◾

When Eiríkur found it, the body was face down in the pool below the waterfall, near to the shallow ford. The blood had been washed away by then, and only later, once he had pulled his son from the water, would he see the crumpled hole in Árni's skull from which the sticky redness of his life had flowed.

It was mid-morning and only moments before the sun's warmth had brought up the scent of the tiny orchids dotted across the meadow. On his walk back from Aðalvík, he had paused often, kneeling in the sodden turf to count the delicate heads, brushing each fragile mouth with a senseless fingertip, remembering their sensation. He had spent the short hour thinking about his wife, not with the sadness of her loss but with the joy of her existence in his life, even now. He had felt his brother walk with him.

He had smiled at Ólafur's presence, and the smile had stretched his face further than it had stretched for years. Árni had been wrong. This place could make a cow give milk, and make an old man whole once more. He'd looked up at the waterfall and whispered the name he had given it, like a promise to a lover. And then he had seen the grey-blue of Árni's jacket.

He pulled his son from the chill water, but there was no life left this time, no son to save. Just a body, and a confusion of purple and red and white where once the most precious of faces had been. Too late he understood that the land gave nothing freely; all must be earned, every blessing paid for. Eiríkur raised his face to the sky, his throat exposed, and emptied his chest into a howl that carried up onto the wind and out across the meadow, beyond the waves slapping against the distant beach and on across the northern sea.

END

Acknowledgements

I am indebted to a number of people for their help in making this book. For their insightful comments on earlier drafts, I thank Pam Orchard, Tom Bolton, Lawrence Mockett and especially Ásta Björk Jónsdóttir for her guidance on Icelandic social norms and naming conventions. For accompanying me on my various, slightly obsessive trips to Hornstrandir, I thank Theo, Simon, Alex, Adrian, Mark and Katherine. And for telling me a story about a cow, I thank the young Icelander on the boat to Hesteyri that first time.

Special thanks are due as ever to Matthew Smith, the dynamo behind Urbane Publications, for his continuing support and enthusiasm.

"Adrian Harvey writes with a flowing ease that carries the reader off into sprawling, beautiful settings."

Kate Noble, *the Quiet Knitter booksite*

Since escaping the East Midlands to find his fortune in the big city, Adrian Harvey has combined a career in and around government with trying to see as much of the world as he can. He lives in North London, which he believes to be the finest corner of the world's greatest city. *Time's Tide* is his third novel, following *Being Someone* - which was selected for the WHSmith Fresh Talent prize - and the acclaimed *The Cursing Stone*.

Also by Adrian Harvey:

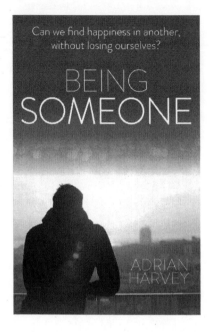

Being Someone is a life story, a love story, a human story. James has fallen through life, plotting a course of least resistance, taking each day as it comes and waiting for that indefinable something to turn up, to give his story meaning. His journey lacks one vital element a fellow traveller. Then he meets Lainey. Confident. Beautiful. Captivating. And James rewrites himself to win her heart. Lainey gives James a reason to grow, paints a bright future, promises the happy ending he has sought so keenly. But when we discover we can live the greatest story of all, are we able to share the pages with someone else?

Being Someone is an emotive tale of love, of self-discovery and adventure a story of the eternal search for happiness in another, without ultimately losing ourselves.

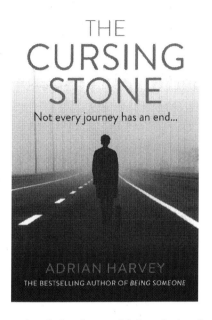

THE
CURSING
STONE
Not every journey has an end...

ADRIAN HARVEY
THE BESTSELLING AUTHOR OF *BEING SOMEONE*

Fergus Buchanan has led a charmed life: a doting family, a loving sweetheart and the respect of his neighbours. All is as it should be and nothing stands between him and the limitless happiness that is his destiny.

But then he is sent from his remote island to retrieve the cursing stone, and his adventures in the wild world beyond cause him to question everything he thought he knew. Succeed or fail, nothing will be the same again.

This is a wonderfully entertaining and emotional contemporary story of courage, duty and revenge, of family ties and loves lost and found, and of finding what matters in the big, wide world. Ultimately, it's the journey we all take to find our true selves...

AVAILABLE NOW ON AMAZON
AND IN ALL GOOD BOOKSHOPS

Urbane Publications is dedicated to
developing new author voices, and publishing
books that challenge, thrill and fascinate.
From page-turning thrillers to literary debuts,
our goal is to publish what
YOU want to read.
Find out more at

urbanepublications.com